Novels by J.L. Weil

Saving Angel (Divisa #1)
Losing Emma (Divisa #.5)
Hunting Angel (Divisa #2)
Breaking Emma (Divisa #2.5)
Chasing Angel (Divisa #3)
Luminescence (Book 1)
Amethyst Tears (Book 2)
Moondust (Book 3)
Starbound

Dedicated to those who are reading this book right now. Without you, I wouldn't have had the courage to write another book. You guys rock my flip-flops (I love 'em).

Hunting Angel

J.L. Weil

Kindle Edition Copyright 2013

by J.L. Weil
http://jlweil.blogspot.com/
All rights reserved.
Second Edition June 2014
ISBN-13: 978-1490962795
ISBN-10: 1490962794

Cover design by Kelly Walker

A DIVISA NOVEL

BOOK 2

Chapter 1

Chase Winters was the bane of my existence.

Some people have death experiences and realize how precious life and love is.

Not me.

Just the opposite.

Oh, I appreciate life. I love feeling the wind in my hair, the taste of dark chocolate on my tongue, and I even came to love the country scent of Spring Valley, Illinois. What I didn't have was an epiphany about my love life.

Instead of falling head over heels in love with Chase Winters, my savior, I actually loathed him more, if that was even possible. Okay, maybe loathe was a strong word. Truthfully, I didn't know how I felt about Chase. Sometimes I saw glimpses of kindness. He could be sweet, considerate, and incredibly protective. But even so, Chase wasn't the kind of guy who was easy to love. Sure, he looked like he was sculpted by the Gods, but the second he opened his mouth the godly illusion evaporated. Mostly all I got was a selfish ass. To make matters worse, we were linked by some Grim Reaper voodoo.

Thank you, Death.

Chase has saved my life not once, not twice...shit, at this point, I've lost count. Maybe I should have shown a little more gratitude. Maybe I should have tried harder to get along with Chase a little better, especially considering that neither of us really understood this connection we have. Or maybe I should have stay as far away as possible.

I might have, if he suddenly hadn't gone from being a douchebag to someone I barely recognized. The arrogant, snarky, asshole was still there, but with me he was different. And I found that even more dangerous. It was throwing me through crazy, messed up loops. That was what he was doing lately—messing me up.

I could handle the sarcasm all day long, but it was the charm that played with my head. Since *that* night everything changed. Or maybe it was just me who changed. Mom had gotten one heck of a surprise when I saw her that night after work. I hugged her like I was afraid to let go. We had spent the rest of that night on the couch together watching our favorite movie until I'd finally fallen asleep. She had sensed how much I needed to just spend a night with her, like we used to. It was the best medicine in the world—a mother's love.

And her special chocolate milkshakes.

There really was no point in dwelling on what I couldn't

change. What was done was done. I should have been focusing on what happened now, like finding out if I was still human or some genetically altered badass. Hey, it was possible. As much as I despised to admit it, Chase was *the badass*. So it was deducible that some of his awesome badass-ness could have rubbed off on me.

Oh who was I kidding? I didn't feel like a badass. It was strange—I felt different, yet I couldn't put my finger on what those changes were. When I looked in the mirror, my face looked exactly the same. Not one blasted freckle out of place. My hair was still as straight as a board and as black as spades. I hadn't gained or lost any weight. I was still only five foot three, and my tongue was just as sharp as ever—maybe sharper.

What I really needed was a distraction from my own rambling thoughts, something to fully occupy my mind. If I kept going at this rate, I would drive myself straight into the loony bin. I knew just what I needed.

No, not Chase.

Tiptoeing down the hall in my striped knee-high socks and white cotton shorts, I skipped down the stairs trying not to disturb my sleeping mother. It had been a long night. Sprawling out on the zebra print sofa, (mom was totally into animal print) I flipped the TV on, finding my favorite YouTube channel. Yes, this probably raised my geekdom levels, but I couldn't help it. I was addicted to YouTube.

I was completely immersed in the repartee between Sips and Sjin when I felt the familiar heat skirt down the back of my neck, and the tattoo now gracing my hip tingled. Every time *he* was near, the same symptoms came over me. It was both disarming and irritating.

"What are you doing?" he asked, making himself at home on the couch beside me. His long legs stretched out in front of him. Letting himself into my house whenever he felt like it, had also become a habit.

My eyes were glued to the screen. I fought the urge to look over at him, finding it more difficult than it should have been. Whenever we were in the same room, I instinctually sought him out. Our eyes would connect, the world would standstill, and then we would go on as if nothing had happened. So recently I began to challenge myself, to see how long it would take me before I caved. "What does it look like? I'm watching TV, genius. Even you should be able to figure that out." I answered, in a droll voice never taking my eyes off the tube. Try as I might to ignore his overbearing presence, I failed. Epically and continuously.

"This is not TV," he argued, remaining as difficult as always.

"It's Sips and Sjin," I added, clenching my fists. My nails dug into my palms. It was all I could do to not look at him.

I felt those silver eyes on me and shifted under his gaze. "Is that supposed to mean something to me?" His voice alone could cut straight to my heart and make it beat a million times faster.

Tossing a handful of green and red skittles into my mouth, I snickered at the banter between my two favorite gamers. "They do a play through of games and post them on YouTube with snarky humor. It's a-ma-zing," I informed, chewing on the wad of rainbow candy.

"Attractive." His weight sunk his side of the couch.

I grinned, finally giving in and meeting those smoky eyes that haunted my dreams, no matter how much I willed otherwise. "It's totally turning you on," I teased, over exaggerating my chomping. I hated that just a peek at him in ripped jeans and a black t-shirt could leave me breathless.

Joke was on me. His silver eyes flickered gold, and he shot me a devilish grin. "You're right."

Shit.

I swallowed. Uh, that totally backfired. My pulse picked up, and I could feel myself pulled toward that god-worthy body. "Whatever," I shot back weakly and returned my attention to the TV, though at this point he'd ruined it for me.

My feet were pressed against his thigh, seared by his incredible heat. He was like an inferno. "Okay. So let me get this straight. Instead of playing video games, you are now watching someone else play video games?"

I kicked him lightly in the thigh. "You got a problem with it

—leave." I put on a much braver front than I felt. Truthfully, if he did leave, I knew that the moment he was gone I would miss him. Pathetic.

"God, you are lame."

That was it. I didn't even think about what I was doing, I just tossed whatever was in my hand directly at Chase's smirking mouth.

It happened to be the remote control.

I watched as his hand snatched it out of the thin air before it connected with his beautiful bad boy face. Damn his demon reflexes. "Nice try, Angel Eyes. I love it when you're feisty."

I scowled at him. "Mom is upstairs, you know."

He lifted that stupid brow with the hoop in it. Envy-worthy long lashes fanned around his twinkling eyes. "That sounds like a challenge."

"God, you are warped."

His wrist snaked out before I even saw it coming and gripped my ankle. With a quick tug he pulled me to him, and I shrieked in surprise. "You like it," he murmured, his breath tickling my skin.

Suddenly I found myself in a very precarious position, straddled over his lap. Being this close to Chase meant trouble—of the good kind. I pushed aside the butterflies of excitement and anticipation. My body knew what was about to follow the kind of look he was giving me, and it was on high alert. "If you came over for a quick tumble you'll be sadly disappointed," I said, trying to sound completely bored and uninterested.

Yet the golden gleam in his eyes said no one was fooled, least of all him. His hands spanned on either side of my hips, burning right through the flimsy white cotton of my shorts. I cursed myself for not wearing more clothes and lots of layers. No, instead I strolled around the house next to naked.

"Nothing I ever do is quick, Angel."

Every time he said my name my pulse decided to race like it was on speed. I bit my lip to keep from sighing. The last thing I needed to do was stroke his already out of control ego.

"Do you need a demonstration?" he whispered, his voice dropping to dangerous octaves.

I swallowed, entranced by his eyes. He tipped his head forward grazing his lips across mine. A blaze of heat tore through my body leaving me achy and wanting more. I knew that I should pull away while I still had opportunity, because the small window was closing quickly.

As if I had a choice.

Wrapping my arms around his neck, I watched as his eyes darken and flicker. He wasn't the only one who could use the element of surprise. I laced my fingers into his hair, loving the way his eyes changed right before me. Never losing contact, I moved in to seal our lips together, needing—

Like I weighed no more than a pound of sugar, he lifted me in the air, and dropped me down on the couch. For a split second I was stunned…then I went up in flames. Roughly pushing the hair out of my face, I glared up at him, seething. "I am going to make you regret that, Chase Winters."

He stood hovering over me with a stupid grin. "I'm looking forward to it."

I jumped off the couch, meeting him head-to-head. Okay, well, in reality it was like head-to-chest. It wasn't my fault he was so damn tall or that I was so short. Cursed genes. "I think you better leave before I give in to the urge to stab you."

He chuckled walking to the door. "There is never a dull moment with you." Pausing in the doorway, he leaned against the frame. "It's why I like you, Angel Eyes." He brushed a piece of loose hair behind my ear.

Without further ado, I slammed the door in his face. As usual, his laughter seeped through from the other side. This seemed to be our signature goodbye more and more lately. I think he liked it in some twisted way. It was as if he lived to get under my skin or under my shirt. Propped against the closed door, I closed my eyes and released a whoosh of breath I'd been holding from his touch.

"Angel," Mom called from upstairs.

Ugh. I had woken up sleeping beauty with my outburst. "Sorry, mom," I hollered back.

Hello Monday morning, you suck. That was my first thought of the day—lovely wasn't it? Lying in my bed, I stared at the ceiling. Today there would be many firsts for me.

First day back to school since my…*accident.* Is that what I should refer to it as? An accident?

First time I would see Brandy since she lured me into a trap. In her defense she had been compelled, so I couldn't really hold it against her. Chase on the other hand, had absolutely no qualms about holding her entirely responsible. Nothing in his thought process made any sense to me. Or maybe that was just guys in general.

First time I would be leaving the confines and security of my house. I would have to be a fool and an idiot after all I went through to not be nervous and cautious about the creepy and scary as shit things that are out there. They weren't just stuff made up in nightmares and horror films.

Rolling out of bed, I stood in front of the mirror and pulled up my t-shirt. There it was—the black swirly design. A constant reminder of *that* night, the night I became something more than human. It had been a week since that hellish night—a week of me skipping school. Mom thought I had come down with some kind of extreme illness. I told her I caught it from Chase, which in a funny way was the truth.

The intricate swirls were no longer red or caused me pain, but the mark did sometimes tingle or get warm. Tracing the tribal lines with my finger, I thought about Chase and what he had done to save me. I still didn't fully understand what he had sacrificed other than tying our souls together forever.

Forever.

It sounded so definite. Forever with Chase. I should have been horrified by the idea not...

Thrilled.

Eager.

Elated.

Huffing at my reflection, I pulled down my shirt and went to my closet. School waited whether I was ready or not. I'll admit there was some apprehension coiling in my belly. Tossing on a pair of jeans and a cardigan, I raced downstairs.

Heading into the kitchen, I went to grab myself a bowl of Lucky Charms. I could use a little luck of the Irish. There was a pink note on the granite counter that captured my attention. A small box sat under the note. It was from Mom.

Angel,

I love you dearly, but I swear if you drop this phone in the toilet, run it over with your car, or any other excuse you can come up with, it will be the last time you use a phone. Got it? I'm pretty sure the guy at the phone company thinks I eat cell phones for dinner. Please be more careful.

Love, Mom

P.S. Speaking of dinner, I made extras tonight for Chase.

Good Lord. Now my mom was cooking him dinner. He even had her wrapped around his finger. I would deal with that later, but right now I grinned as I tore open the box to my new iPhone.

Hell yeah.

The worse part of getting a new phone was that I had to input all my contacts again, which I guess wasn't as bad as it seemed. I mean, I live in Spring Valley. There really weren't that many people to add. Glancing at the clock, I realized my glee was to be short lived. If I didn't hurry my tushie, I was going to be late for school. Slipping my new kickass phone into my backpack, I threw down a bowl of leprechaun cereal just before a car horn beeped outside my house.

Chapter 2

The horn beeped again two seconds later. "Hold your boxers on," I mumbled. He could be so intolerable. Why had I agreed to ride with Chase and Lexi to school this morning?

Oh yeah, that's right. He hadn't given me a choice. Chase had gone all macho and bossy insisting that we ride to and from school together, for my safety of course.

What a bunch of baloney.

Grabbing my bag from the corner, I locked the front door behind me. I don't know why I bothered. There wasn't a lock Chase couldn't get around. It was on his long list of skills. There, in my driveway was a shiny, brand-spanking new, silver Audi. The color reminded me of his eyes. I was starting to think that Chase went through vehicles as much as normal people change their sheets. It was insane—and costly.

Plopping into the passenger seat, I smiled at Lexi in the back. "What happened to the bike? Don't tell me you totaled it already."

He gave me a disarming grin, ignoring my barb. "It's been retired for the season. You like?"

I shrugged. "If you're into flashy. Not my style." I was trying hard not to be impressed. It was a very attractive and sleek car—sort of like its owner.

"I'm flashy, and I'm your style," he said cockily.

Lexi snickered from the backseat.

Laying my head on the back of the seat, I groaned.

"Better buckle up. This baby has quite the pickup."

"Fabulous," I muttered under my breath, clicking the seatbelt securely in place. Just what he needed…another ultra-fast car to kill me in. Given that I could be killed—again.

We arrived at school in record time, which was a good thing, because we were running late. The bell rang just as we were walking through the parking lot. Hall High looked exactly the same as the last time I'd been here. I shuddered, not realizing how being here again was going to affect me. This school was definitely filled with unpleasant memories. Somehow I always ended up fighting for my life.

Chase was immediately at my side. "Hey, you okay? Your face just lost ten shades of color."

I nodded, unable to speak. My throat had closed up on me as I mechanically put one foot in front of the other.

Nodding for Lexi to go on ahead of us, he put a hand on my shoulder, halting my movements, and turned me toward him. "Angel, look at me." With his thumb, he titled my chin up, staring into my face. "Nothing is going to happen to you. Not while I'm here. I promise."

I wasn't convinced. "You can't be sure of that. What about when I'm alone?" Yes, I was totally acting like a frightened, needy baby, but that was exactly how I felt. No matter what I do or where I turn, trouble found me. I was like a heat seeking missile for misfortune. To make matters worse, I was now marked. There wasn't a safe corner for me to hide in.

"You won't be alone."

I gave him a funny look. "What? Are you going to follow me into the girl's bathroom?"

He smirked as if the idea held promise. "If I have to."

The big jerk probably would and enjoy it too. "Be serious, Chase."

His hands ran down my arms leaving behind tendrils of warmth. "I am actually. Look, last week Lexi and I sort of talked with administration. We rearranged our schedules so that one of us will be in your classes."

Oh goodie. I had babysitters.

By talking, he really meant they had used compulsion. I took a deep breath. Looks like I was going to be spending a whole lot more time with Chase than I ever could have imagined. If I thought one class was bad…what were multiple classes going to be like? A part of me knew I should have been outraged, not relieved, yet I couldn't rationalize anything *normal* anymore.

"Come on. We need to get to class before we're late. I wouldn't want us to spend your first day back in detention. I have plans after school."

Plans? I ignored the tiny flutter of panic that sprinted across my heart. If he was going out after school why should I care? It was not like he had to check in with me or anything. He was a free agent and able to come and go as he pleased.

Then why did I feel this irrational beating against my ribs at the thought of being away from him? It made no sense. It was not like we were with each other twenty-four seven. He lived next door for God's sake.

I was shocked how easy it was to get back into the swing of things. It helped that Chase had made sure I didn't have any homework to make-up. I am sure that this applied as cheating, but in this case I was willing to let it slide. Though I think he was using his mind-altering talents a little too freely. I was going to have to have a talk with him before it started to get out of hand.

In-between classes, Lexi (my assigned shadow for the period) and I were at my locker when I heard a voice that made me cringe and stew with distaste. I felt a foul taste in my mouth like coppery blood and battery acid. Yeah, it was that bad.

"Oh. My. God. You've got to be kidding me." Glancing over my shoulder, I found Sierra glaring at me with hate. "It's true."

I scanned the halls looking for the source of Sierra's freak-out, even though I knew she was talking about me. "What the hell is she spazzing about?" I asked Lexi beside me. I figured that the other Divisa had been brought up to speed about what went down that night. Hayden had been there, he must have told them what happened. So what was Sierra's deal? Maybe she had a hard time believing it, or maybe she was just pissed off that I hadn't died so she could have Chase to herself. Sorry to disappoint.

"I can't believe it. I just can't believe it," she went on and on like a broken record. Her screeching voice was making my ears bleed.

So much for lying low and not causing a scene on my first day back, I should have known that it would be Sierra who was the hiccup in my otherwise normal day. "Why's that so hard to believe," I spat, crossing my arms. It was no secret Sierra and I hated each other's guts, though it was probably not the smartest idea to bait her. She was part demon after all, more to the point— she was a bitch.

"I get that he saved you, is *always* saving you," she dragged out overdramatically.

I clenched my jaw.

"But this," she threw her hands in the air making her red locks fly with the exaggerated movements. "This is too far. She reeks of him."

"Sierra," Lexi warned low. "If Chase finds out about this…"

Lexi's words implied that he wouldn't be happy.

She smiled smugly at me. "At least he hasn't completed the bond. One out of three, I guess that's a small consolation."

I wanted to slap that superior grin off her gorgeous face. Forget that I had no idea what she was talking about.

What the hell was going on? What did she mean I reeked of him?

Before I could demand answers, a rush of warmth spread through me, and my tramp stamp started to tingle. I didn't even need to turn around to know who stood behind me. He was like a looming force of steel.

"Is there a problem?" he asked Sierra in a condescending tone.

She glared at him over my head with tiny spears of disgust, and then promptly turned on her Dior heels and stomped gracefully down the hall. I watched in a haze of confusion and animosity as her painted on jeans sauntered away.

Hello Hall High…I'm back for your amusement. Step right up as we watch Sierra make mincemeat out of me. *Ugh*. Sometimes being a teenager sucked. Being an altered teenager bound to a half-demon was proving to be cumbersome.

Chem class proved to be even more entertaining, if that was possible. Chase assumed his bodyguard duty behind me, causing the temperature in the room to rise by about a hundred degrees.

Pulling out my notebook, I heard my name whispered to my right. I glanced sideways to find Brody, the football jock, smiling at me.

His chocolate eyes were bright with excitement. "Hey, I'm glad to see you are back. We really missed you around here."

I blinked. In school this size it was impossible to not be missed. "Thanks, I think."

His boy-next-door-grin widened. "Anytime. This class just isn't the same without your pretty face."

I got the feeling that he was being overly friendly, almost as if he was into me. Not that long ago he sort of asked me to homecoming, and that hadn't ended well. I just assumed that had been the end of it. I must be the most clueless girl in the school. "I'm sure anything beats Mr. Edginton's monotone lectures," I replied, trying to downplay what I thought was a come on.

Chase shifted in seat, leaning forward and making his presence known. I don't know how anyone could forget he was in a room. Try as I might, I never could. Brody's eyes darted to Chase warily and then back to me. He cleared his throat, and I knew from the shuffle of his feet under the desk what he was going to ask before he said it. "Maybe we could, I don't know, hang out sometime."

Oh boy. He was totally nervous. And I was dumbfounded. The day wasn't even half over and this was like the third time a guy had suggested that we *hangout*. For real. The first one I figured no big deal. The second one I thought coincidence, but a third one? This had to be a joke. I most definitely was not that popular, even in a school this small.

It was on the tip of my tongue to tell him to bite me, yet… Chase leaned back into his seat and snickered. Not just any kind of snicker, the kind that made me what to make him crazy, insanely, jealous. Served him right. "Sure," I found myself answering.

Truthfully though, I knew that when the time came, I would find an excuse why I couldn't go. It probably would have been easier had I been up front with him, but I was too nice and afraid to hurt his feelings—again.

Class started shortly after that, and I was listening intently to Mr. Edgington's lecture, hanging on his every word. Okay, that was a total lie. What I was really doing was trying to pretend that Brody wasn't winking and air blowing kisses at me from the next aisle over. Uh, maybe the air-kissing was going too far, but still, what the hell? I was also trying to ignore the rapid tapping of Chase's pencil on the desktop. Apparently, I wasn't the only one who had noticed Brody's cheesy attention.

Boys could be so oblivious.

Did Brody actually think that was the kind of attention I wanted when I'd said yes? He had to be out of his mind, or more likely drunk, to try and hit on me in front of Chase. Everyone knew that we sort of had a thing going on even if *I* didn't know what exactly that thing *was*. I was pretty sure Chase was going to choke-slam him after class if the growl that came from behind was any indictor of what Chase thought of Brody's behavior.

I slumped lower in my seat, trying to make myself as small as possible. I was so ready for this day to end.

After school, Chase dropped Lexi and me at home, and then went off to do something that apparently was none of our business. I huffed and tried to pretend my heart didn't tighten as I watched him drive away. Whatever—it was fine by me, so I stuck out my chin. I had a few questions for Travis and Lexi, plus it would give Travis and me some time to gush over the upcoming release of Black Ops II. Hell yes. The video game of all video games—the newest Call of Duty. I'd been counting down the days since I pre-ordered a copy, seemingly eons ago. Travis was the only one who I could talk to, the only one who really understood.

I walked into their house after Lexi and found Travis already assuming his usual position on the couch. Devin was at work, so it was just us. I sat beside Travis. He grunted an inaudible hello, never losing concentration from the game he was absorbed with. I totally sympathized and just reclined into the couch.

"Travis, you need to get a life," Lexi announced, clearly annoyed with her brother. He ignored her. "You are such a TV hog," she whined, stretching out on the chaise.

"Sshhh. You are going to get me killed," he shot back.

Lexi pouted and grabbed the newest Victoria Secret magazine that had just come in the mail.

I should probably have intervened before things took a turn for the worst. "Have you guys noticed anything different about me? Something a normal person wouldn't pick up on?" The question had been rolling in my head since seeing Sierra.

"Yeah. You stink of Chase," Travis answered without peeling his eyes from the game.

"Funny, but I'm being totally serious here."

"So was I," he answered.

Lexi nodded her head. "No, it's true. You give off this scent that screams you belong to another half-demon."

"What do you mean scent?" I did not like where this was going at all. Not. One. Single. Bit. I didn't want to smell like Chase.

Travis dropped the remote on the table forgetting the game for a moment, a sign that this was going to be a solemn discussion. "I can see the little wheels working in your head. It's not like you think. You don't physically smell like Chase."

"Thank God," I sighed.

"Well, don't be relieved just yet. You do give of this vibe or odor that states you belong to another one of us, a half-demon. It's a way of letting others know not to mess with you—a hands-off kind of policy. Those who know Chase will recognize the signature as his. It also makes you a target for all the nasties."

"And how long have I had this *scent?*"

Lexi pulled her knees up. "Since that night."

Meaning, since the night my life changed forever. Since the night I died and Chase bartered for my soul. Since the night we became linked. "Figures. And before that, I didn't have a *scent?*"

"Nope," Travis grinned wickedly. "You were fair game then."

"And now I'm not fair game?"

"You got it toots. There isn't a Divisa around who would risk Chase's wrath by touching you. They would have to have a death wish."

I looked at Lexi for confirmation that Travis wasn't just pulling my leg. She nodded sending her blonde ponytail swishing with the movement. "Yep. You are like, sprayed with Divisa repellant."

I slumped against the back of the couch. "Great. I stink."

Travis gave me a lopsided grin, throwing an arm around my shoulder. "You might smell like crap, but Lex and I still tolerate you."

Lexi snickered from her chaise lounge.

"Thanks," I mumbled dryly. "You better not get too close, or you might wind up dead," I added snarky. I couldn't help it, I was feeling snarky.

He removed his arm slowly, a playful gleam sparkling in his

turquoise eyes. "You're probably right. This face is just too damn good-looking to withstand a thrashing from Chase."

I snorted. Like that had ever stopped the two of them from going at each other like two cage fighters, if anything, he was probably looking forward to good fight with Chase.

I stayed a little while longer before hiking the short distance to my house. I had most definitely not been waiting around to see if Chase would show up—which he hadn't. Not that I cared.

There I go lying to myself, again. Maybe mentally I didn't give a monkey's butt what Chase was up to, but this link we had…um, it had a mind of its own. And it was growing more anxious by the second.

As I got ready for bed I caught myself several times picking up my new phone to call him. Since I got home, I'd spent the rest of the night messing around with all the options and adding a gazillion apps to my iPhone. It could pretty much do everything except pee for me, and I was sure there would be an app for that soon. I had customized the crap out of it, including programming Chase under Douchebag. I had quite a giggle over my ingenious.

Curled up under the covers, sleep evaded me until the moment I heard the crunching of his tires next door. Then a serene calmness overcame me, and I promptly fell to sleep.

Figures. Stupid bond. I hope he suffered miserably.

Chapter 3

It was the end of October, which in Spring Valley, Illinois meant tumbleweeds, tilling fields, and of course hayrides were a given— Hickville. For me Halloween had a slightly different impact. I just loved the idea of loads of candy corn, insane parties, and sexy costumes. In Arizona we never had to factor in the weather as part of our costume. Here, they dressed in layers or long underwear, which you can be sure I wouldn't ever be caught dead wearing.

Bahahaha.

I loved Halloween. And it just so happened this year I lived in my own personal haunted house. No matter where I walked you could guarantee a floor board will creak, a cobweb will be hanging in a doorway (not a decoration, but the real deal), and sometimes the lights flickered for no apparent reason.

My first week back to school flew by in a whirlwind of chaos. Out of the blue, I had become a hot commodity at Hall High. Guys I had never seen before said hi to me between periods. I even received an anonymous note from a secret admirer. It felt like there was always a small crowd around me, until Chase got there that was. I hated every second of the attention. Chase's presence became my saving grace—the only time I was left alone. One frown from him and they all scrammed. I never thought I would be grateful for the overbearing jerkwad's company.

But I had bigger and better things to think about...

Halloween was right around the corner and it was starting to seep into my pores. I was itching to start my costume shopping.

Shopping.

Once upon a time that word would have elicited excitement, now it made my feet hurt. I swear, I got blisters just thinking about shopping with Lexi. But there was no getting out of it. The commitment had already been made.

Every year there was a Halloween party thrown for the high school kids at a local farm. It was on a pumpkin farm—how original. This town oozed originality. I was told it was a regular hee-haw, complete with obnoxious music, a bonfire, tractor rides, and a costume contest.

And it was unsupervised.

Lexi insisted I couldn't miss it for the world. Truthfully, she just wanted a reason to drag me shopping with her. Lucky for her, Halloween was my holiday. For one day I got to pretend like I was somebody else—anybody else. Lara Croft. Selene from Underworld. Mystique. I'd been every kickass girl I could think of. No princesses, mermaids, or faeries for this gal. I was all about woman empowerment.

This year I was turning over a new leaf—sort of. What I had in mind for my costume was different from my usual characters, but it was going to be no less than amazing. There was only one problem…Lexi and I were on opposite continents when it came to shopping for our Halloween costumes. She wanted to hit every costume shop within a two-hour radius. I, on the other hand, was looking to scope out the craft and fabric shops. When I told this to Lexi, all I got was a blank stare.

"Why would you want to go there?" she finally asked, crossing her legs in the passenger seat, her black spiked boots nixing the dash.

I kept my eyes on the road, maneuvering my little white Fusion in the next lane. "It's like tradition. My mom and I have always made my costume. I can't imagine not doing it. It's part of the fun."

She looked unconvinced. Her blue-green eyes measuring me like I was the one who wasn't human—which was still totally debatably anyhoo. "You are like a dying breed. It's no wonder Chase is so enthralled with you."

I rolled my eyes. "He is not *enthralled* with me. He thinks I'm a nuisance."

"A sexy nuisance. I know Chase better than anyone, and let me tell you, *you* have changed him. You are the first person he's truly cared about."

"I'm not so sure about that."

"Are you telling me that you are not over-the-moon crazy about him?"

I shrugged. I wasn't admitting to anything, not even to myself.

"Do you even have ovaries?" she asked bluntly.

I rolled my eyes. "Obviously."

"Then trust me, you're more than interested. The girls in this town might treat him a like pariah, but they secretly dream about doing the nasty with him at night. Fact."

Flushing to the roots of my hair, I bit down on the edge of my nail. "Whatever."

She shook her head, sending her perfect blonde ringlets into a bounce. "The two of you are absolutely maddening to be around. I've never met more stubborn people. There is nothing Chase wouldn't do for you. Nothing. And I think you already know that."

I swallowed the large lump of emotion clogging my windpipe. It was a hard pill to swallow. I knew that without Chase, I wouldn't be here with Lexi getting ready to shop for my favorite holiday. Without Chase, my mom would be alone in the world. Without Chase, I wouldn't have the chance to find love.

We might always be at each other's throats, or drive each other insane, but he would always be there. He would never let me down. In my book, that spoke volumes. I knew that there were things out there in the world that I couldn't wrap my mind around, but knowing Chase was at my side made it all bearable.

"I know," I managed softly, risking a glance at her.

Her eyes shone seriously. "Just don't break his heart."

My chest felt heavy. What I needed to break was this somber mood that had settled over us. This was supposed to be fun. "I'm not sure I could. I swear he has a heart of stone."

"It was, until he met you."

She let me to stew over her words the rest of the trip until we'd reached our first destination, though her words never left me. Being the good friend that I was, I let her have the first pick. Well, that was one reason, but secretly I was also hoping for a miracle or an act of God that would allow Lexi to find her costume in the first store, anything to cut our shopping trip in half.

Every time we go out, I was reminded how different we really were. It was easy to forget when it was just us, but the moment we were out in public, I saw the strange way people reacted to them. It was so weird to me. Especially since there was a knot that formed in my stomach the further we got from home. The further away we got from Chase. I was trying hard to ignore the growing knot, and I did not want admit that I missed him, that he mattered that much.

I was blaming it entirely on the stupid mark on my hip, the one we both shared.

Lexi must have sensed my agitation because she repeatedly asked if I was okay. If I was feeling alright? Was something wrong? The only person I was fooling was me.

Thankfully, someone above answered my desperate prayers, and Lexi found her perfect hoochie ensemble at the second shop. "Do you think Hayden will like it?" she asked, showing a vulnerable side she did so well, yet I knew firsthand how incredibly fierce she could be. It still didn't stop all the guys in her life from protecting her.

"Are you kidding? He is going to blow a socket when he sees you." Then there was also the chance that Travis will incinerate him for looking at her so ravenously.

She giggled. "Good. I'm sure you'll knock Chase's socks off."

Lexi didn't have quite the vocabulary I did, but she usually said the first thing to pop into her perfect head. "What I have in mind doesn't have the same wow-factor as your costume. Plus, I couldn't pull off something this skimpy. You have a killer body—it was made to be seen."

"Angel, you really need to take a look in the mirror," she said, climbing into my car and tossing her purchase in the back.

"Trust me, I have," I muttered and hopped into the driver seat.

"I can't believe you didn't find anything you liked in either store. There must have been a thousand costumes in there."

I turned the key into the ignition, and my little Fusion purred to life "True," I smiled at Lexi. "But nothing screams originality like custom made." Custom sounded way better than handmade.

She looked unimpressed. "It just seems like too much work," she sighed.

"Maybe," I agreed. "But it is so rewarding."

"Yeah, so are chocolate éclairs, but you don't see me slaving away in the kitchen. That's why there are bakeries."

I rolled my eyes.

By the time we got to the fabric shop, I was ready to do my thing. Lexi however, looked lost, like a tear in the rain. "This will be fun," I tried to coax. She was definitely out of her element, while I was right at home.

"I don't even know where to start," she admitted, overwhelmed.

She trailed after me, her boots clicking on the tile floor as we meandered down the aisles looking for the ideal fabric. In my head I knew precisely what I wanted.

"Do you have a sewing machine?" Lexi asked, as I was pulling down rolls of material from the shelves.

"Um, yeah. My mom does. When I was little, she used to make all my dolls and Barbie's clothes," I said offhandedly, while I was trying to concentrate on fabrics.

"Wow. I can't believe your mom did that." There was

wistfulness and a young girls yearning in her voice.

"Yeah, no kidding. You should have seen her a few years ago. You wouldn't have recognized her she was so domesticated." It was then that I remembered Lexi never had a mom. I glanced at her leaning against a rack of plaid flannel fabric. She never looked more out of place, or more alone and like a little girl. "Hey, you should stay for dinner tonight. My mom is cooking, and I know she would love it if you came. She adores you."

The glint of sadness left her eyes and was replaced with one of mischief. "She also adores my dad."

I groaned. Mom and Devin had officially gone out on two dates. That was two dates too many in my book. "Ugh. Don't remind me. It is so weird." I gathered two of the fabric rolls I wanted under my arm.

Lexi beamed. "Maybe for you. I personally think it's great. Your mom is a-ma-zing, and my dad seems to really like her. I've not seen him this happy…" She pondered that statement for a moment. "Ever."

I didn't want to burst her bubble, so I just agreed. "I guess. So are you coming over?"

"Yeah," she said, nodding her honey highlighted blonde head.

We waited in line to get the fabric cut, paid for my purchases, and then headed home. As we entered the Spring Valley city limits, I couldn't help but notice how incredibly rustic and beautiful the woods looked, tangerine, candy apple red, and golden yellow trees were back dropped against the clear blue sky, or how the plowed fields were now dry and dead. Burning leaves scented the air and everything here moved with leisure. It was a nice change, and I hated to admit it, but I might actually be adapting to country life.

But I wouldn't dare tell a soul that.

Unfortunately my serene peace was cut short. Lexi was chattering a hundred miles an hour and fiddling with the radio stations, while I did everything I could to follow her conversation and stay on the road. It was not easy. Occasionally I would nod my head or give uh-huh remark. The sky was darkening, cutting down on my visibility. My car was cruising along the rocky road.

Lexi's voice cut through my concentration. Apparently I'd fallen behind on my appropriate responses. "Angel. Are you even—"

She never finished her sentence. There was a loud clunk, clunk, clunk noise vibrating under my car.

Slowing the car, I swore a colorful string of words under my breath and pulled over.

"Oh man, that doesn't sound good." Her brows drew together. "You got AAA right?"

"Triple what?" I muttered.

"I'm sure it's nothing," she reassured.

I wasn't convinced. If my car was clunking—it was bad news.

Getting out of the car, I walked around looking for...I didn't really know what I was looking for, something that screamed, *hey right here. I'm broken.* Well, as luck would have it, it didn't actually scream the problem, but my car was leaning very awkwardly to one side.

Good riddance. Now what?

I walked to the rear of the car. "Shit." One of my back tires was flatter than a pancake, and to make matters worse, there was an arrow sticking out of it. A mother freaking arrow.

That was definitely not normal, not even for the boonies.

Lexi stepped out beside me. She took one look at my poor tire and announced, "I'll call Chase. And Angel..."

I looked up from the mutilated rubber into her turquoise alarm-filled eyes.

"...get back in the car," she finished.

Oh mercy.

Chapter 4

All I could think of was, *crap here we go again.*

I hadn't even been back to my normal life for like two seconds, when shit decided to go south. Only me.

Huddling back into my car, I hit the lock button the moment Lexi slammed her door shut. The phone was already to her ear as she waited for her cousin to pick up. I knew that I didn't have any supersonic eyesight, but that didn't stop me from scanning the area like a crazy person. Someone or something was out there, and they had wanted to hurt us. This I was sure of, or we wouldn't be calling for backup.

My blood pressure spiked, and I felt a full on panic attack rising. Not knowing what lurked, hiding in the edges of the woods, was torturing me. Not knowing whether it was from Hell's gates or if it was human. The not knowing was killing me. I didn't know how Chase, Lexi, and Travis handled this. I wasn't cut out for this kind of life, yet the choice had already been made for me. It was out of my hands, and I better suck it up, put my big girl pants on, and calm down.

"Chase," she said into her pink rhinestone phone. "We need

you." Lexi glanced at the GPS on my dashboard. "We are a half mile from Burton's Bridge." She flipped her phone closed and glanced at me with big turquoise eyes. "He's on his way."

My heart started to beat irrationally fast in my chest. Just knowing that Chase was on his way did funny things to my belly—to all of me really. Those feelings of anxiousness I'd felt earlier, grew tenfold. I kept trying to tell myself it was because someone, or something, might be out there. Waiting. Watching. But in the end it really didn't matter how much I tried to delude myself. The fact still remained that Chase, and only Chase, made me feel this way.

Someday I was going to have to come to terms with that.

Someday was not today.

It took Chase less than three minutes to find us. Seriously—no joke. Under three minutes without a car. He traveled on foot faster than any mode of transportation. This was one of those times I loved that he wasn't entirely human.

There was a blur of color right before Chase materialized outside my window. My heart accelerated more as I stared at him through the windowpane, mesmerized by his half-silver, half-gold eyes. I completely forgot about my tire—forgot my fear—forgot to think. There was only him. I couldn't help but eat up the sight of him. In my head, I knew that I had just seen him a few hours ago, but the rest me felt like it had been days, weeks, years. There was no rhyme or reason—it just was.

I could tell by the way his eyes roamed over my face, that he felt exactly the same. The swirly mark at my hip tingled, and I instinctively put a hand to my side. It was always the same, and I wasn't sure I would ever get used to this.

Lexi cleared her throat, snapping me back to reality. I rolled down my foggy window.

"You got a flat," he said, stating the obvious. A piece of his midnight hair fell off to one side. It was so dark now, and he blended in with the night, except for his eyes.

The spell was broken, and I was feeling moody now. "Duh, it's the arrow sticking out of the tire that has us freaked out."

He inspected the tire and the nasty arrow embedded in the rubber, then he took off lickety-split.

Damn him.

"Where the hell did he go?" I asked Lexi who was completely unfazed by her cousin's sudden disappearance, leaving us stranded, again, I might add. Getting out of the car, I slammed the door with more force than necessary. This was more than I could take. "Ahhh!" I screamed.

"What? Are you trying to attract their attention? Or worse?" Chase asked, like a smartass, suddenly behind me.

I flinched, spinning around. Then my heart jumped as well, but for totally different reasons. He was close—extremely close.

On either side of my arms, his hands steadied me, and I laid mine fingers flat on his chest. A rush of security and ease washed through me. Inhaling, I breathed in his scent – sexy and fresh, as if he'd just stepped out of a shower. His heart beat strong under my palm, and I felt it quicken as I fisted a handful of his shirt, holding him in place. And I wished we were anywhere but here, stranded on the side of the road. I blinked.

He inched forward, and I held my breath.

"Can you guys do the whole sexual tension thing later? I want to get the heck out of dodge before one of them decides to come back and put an arrow in my heart," Lexi said condescendingly, clearly annoyed. She had gotten out of the car sometime during our burning exchange.

Taking a step back, Chase seared her with a dull look. "It's clear. Whoever was here is gone and isn't coming back, unless of course Angel starts yelling again. We might have to restrain her."

"I bet you'd like that," I sneered, feeling clear-headed again, instead of thinking with my teenage hormones.

He smirked. "I think I deserve a reward for rescuing you. I can think of a few ways you could repay me."

I arched a brow. "Me too. My foot up your ass sounds like a good one."

He snickered.

Lexi looked ready to slam our heads together.

We could do this all night, this sarcastic banter back and forth and not accomplish a darn thing. I crossed my arms. "Now fix my car so we can go home. I'm tired. I'm hungry. And I'm crabby," I complained.

"Yeah, yeah. Give me a minute. I'm still planning on collecting that reward," he added as he opened the trunk.

I knew all too well what his idea of a *reward* was. Not happening. However, that didn't stop my body from reacting to the insinuation. Traitorous body. The fact that he put the idea into my head was maddening. It would be all I thought about for the rest of the night. That was bound to get uncomfortable.

It was on the tip of my tongue to tell him he had exactly one minute, but one look in Lexi's direction told me that probably wasn't the best idea. She looked frazzled, and I wasn't really sure I had ever seen her frazzled. It probably wasn't wise to push my luck.

"Well, I got a reward for you," Lexi piped in, leaning on the car. "Angel's mom is making dinner, and I bet she would love it if you stopped by."

There was a good chance I might have to kick Lexi's butt. It was true that Mom would probably love it if Chase came over. Hell, lately half the time I thought she had a crush on him. My mom loved Chase, but I guess she wasn't thinking straight. The new romance seemed to have dulled her common sense.

I shuddered every time I thought about Mom and Devin. Together. Parents of teenagers should not be allowed to date until the teens have gone off to college. I'm thinking about starting a petition.

Chase popped his head out of the trunk, grinning slyly at me. "That is almost as good as what I had in mind."

I sighed. "Just fix the damn tire, would you?"

He mumbled something snide under his breath and got to work. Pretty sure it involved me being bossy and an ungrateful vixen. I watched as he effortlessly hijacked the back end of my car. His muscles flexed with his movements. I drooled. He might be the world's biggest ass, but he also had the world's hottest ass.

"You're staring," he said without lifting his head.

"So," I retorted unapologetically.

He angled his head up, meeting my gaze. "Didn't anyone teach you it's not polite to stare?"

"Didn't anyone teach you to be a gentleman?" I stuffed my hands into the back pocket of my jeans.

"You can tell me all about my flaws on the way home. Let's go," he stood up, dusting off his hands. "We're all good here."

No argument there. We piled back into my car, and I gladly let Chase take the driver's seat. "This wasn't an accident was it?" I asked, as he drove back home. Lexi was curled up in the backseat.

He glanced at me from the corner of his eye, the soft blue

light of the interior lights catching the silver hoop on his brow. "No," he stated simply. "I've come to realize that with you, I leave nothing up to chance."

I had my head rested on the back of my seat as I watched his profile. Everything about him looked dangerous, deadly. The hard set of his jaw, the steel grey eyes, the overly cocky attitude, but when I looked at him, I could see past all the BS he shielded himself with. I figured it was part bond and part my lacking the fear chromosome everyone else had, that I was able to see who he really was. And it was times like these, when I caught glimpses of his good side that my heart softened and melted toward him. It was easier for me to deal with the jerk, than to deal with the sweet side of Chase.

It was also safer for my heart.

Deep down I knew that if I gave him my heart, Chase Winters would have the power to destroy it. He could shatter my heart into a million, gazillion fragments. I was afraid to let myself feel anything for him other than annoyance and maybe friendship, but I also knew that I was deluding myself. The more time we spent together, the more he chipped away the barrier around my heart.

And I found myself powerless to stop it.

I tore my gaze from him and pulled out my phone. Sending a quick text to Mom, I hoped she was making a meal for an army, because dinner just got crowded. If I knew my mom, the whole

Winters clan would be at my house for dinner tonight.

Mom was a goddess in the kitchen. Once she found out we were having company, and that Chase had fixed my car, (making him a savior in her eyes) she pulled out all the stops—wine, her famous baked mostaccioli, and homemade garlic bread. Dinner ended up being boisterous, delicious, and surprisingly normal—like we were a family. Everyone talked at the same time, we all laughed at each other, and it was the most I'd ever seen my mom smile.

I might not be all that comfortable with her dating Devin, but he seemed to make her happy. I guess I needed to learn to come to terms with her having a boyfriend, but right now it was kind of hard. Chase was seated beside me, distracting me with his little touches. They looked innocent enough to everyone else, but to me they were unnerving. Numerous times when I was sure no one was looking, I swatted his hand or scowled in his general direction.

Toward the end of dinner, he caught my hand in his under the table. We were squished into our dining room table, putting us leg-to-leg. He laid my hand on his thigh, tracing lines on my fingers, and sending tendrils of tingles to each of my nerves. I wanted to close my eyes, and lay my head on his shoulder. He twisted my stomach into a ball of need.

The scraping of chairs against the hardwood floors knocked me back into the present. Chase dropped his eyes, hiding the flecks of yellow that had started to spark in his eyes. Devin volunteered to help my mom with the dishes and followed her into the kitchen, leaving just Travis, Lexi, Chase, and I.

Travis took one look across the table before announcing, "I'm out of here before the two of you starting going at it on the table."

Lexi pushed her chair, grinning. "Me too. See you tomorrow, Angel."

I was left opened-mouthed and alone with Chase and his wandering, skillful hands.

The corners of his mouth lifted. "I'm ready for my payment," his whispered in my ear.

"I just bet you are." I shivered. Swallowing, I was afraid to ask, yet intrigued. "What did you have in mind?" I turned in my seat so our legs were intermixed and one of my knees was in-between his legs.

The way he was looking at me, I thought for sure it was going to be something wicked and downright scandalous. "Just a kiss…for now." His hands gripped either side of my waist, cutting off any plans of escape, not that the thought had entered my mind.

Staring at his lips, I pondered the idea. Did I or didn't I? The longer I thought on it, the wider his smile grew. "Just one," I murmured, as I was closing the distance between our lips.

"One is never enough with me," he said right before his mouth touched mine.

Holy sweet pitchforks.

I swear you had to be part of Hell to kiss that mind-blowingly hot. Nothing this tempting, this soul-shattering could be a hundred percent good. It wasn't even a long kiss, but it didn't matter. I felt it all the way to the very tips of my toes.

Afterwards, I bit my lip. It was all I could do to keep from going in for seconds. He had warned me. Once was never enough. God I hated when he was right. It was such a deplorable quality.

~*~*~*~

Monday was blah…

But tomorrow was Tuesday. The day I had been anticipating for months—the release of Black Ops II. As any true gamer would know, there was a midnight release. Guess who was going to be first in line? Probably not, since I had to drag Chase with me. He was picking up Travis's copy for him. What a guy. I am sure there were ulterior motives, for example, keeping an eye on me.

Whatever.

Nothing was going to spoil this night. Not even douchebag's negative attitude toward video games.

Mom was at work, as I anxiously awaited Chase. I pulled a Love Pink hoodie over my tee and stuffed my earbuds in the pocket. It was going to be a long, chilly night, and I was going to need something to keep my mind off Chase.

I was pacing the family room in circular patterns, when I

HUNTING ANGEL

heard the crunching of tires on my driveway.

Finally.

Chapter 5

"I can't believe we are really doing this," Chase complained as he drove us into the city.

His luxury car hugged the road effortlessly. It was like we were gliding over the pavement, but even with the smooth ride, I was antsy. I just couldn't seem to sit still and get comfortable. "I can't believe *you* are here instead of Travis," I countered.

The plan had been that Travis and I would go together. I was still a little miffed that he had bailed on me and sent this lug in his place, but I wasn't going to let it overshadow my exhilaration. I wasn't sure anything could—not even Hell and all its cronies.

Chase stole a glance at me as I uncrossed my legs. Again. "God, you are a bouncing ball of energy tonight. How much coffee did you drink?"

I tucked my dark hair behind my ear and out of the way. "Umm, I don't know, like six cups with extra shots of espresso. Is there a Starbucks around here?"

The headlights from a passing car glinted off Chase's eyes. "Are you trying to overdose on caffeine? It would really piss me off if you died after I just saved your butt." His hand tightened on the wheel, as if the thought angered him.

"Funny. I'm pulling an all-nighter," I said, to explain the caffeine overkill.

"Why?" he asked, genuinely mystified. "We have school tomorrow," he added.

"Do you really need to ask? Two words, Chase. Black. Ops." I always got a weird tingle when I said his name. "Besides, I'm ditching school tomorrow. It's like a holiday."

"Let me guess, that was Travis's idea?"

"No. Maybe. Does it matter? It's a brilliant idea."

His brows drew together. Clearly he didn't think so. We arrived to the game store shortly after, which gave him a whole new onset of things to complain about. This was totally out of Chase's element, and he hated it. I tried not to let the fact that he came anyway with me, seep into my heart. He made it a little easier by being a complainer.

"Is this really worth waiting in line at midnight for?" Chase asked, falling in line behind me, staring at the long line of about a trillion people in front of us. I might have been exaggerating considering this was the boondocks, but apparently even in the backwoods people play video games.

I didn't even bat an eye. That question wasn't even worth answering. "Um yes."

"There is something wrong with the two of you. With all of

these people." He indicted to the line of fellow gamers (mostly guys I might add) standing in front and behind us.

My geekdom skyrocketed in his eyes. He just didn't understand. This was like the holy grail of games. This was Black Ops II. Enough said.

I don't know how long we were standing there before I got a creepy prickle on my neck. The kind that makes all the little hairs stand straight up. It could have been five minutes or an hour. With Chase next to me, I lost all track of time. He was razzing me once again about being here when I felt the first inklings of trouble.

Instinctually I huddled closer to him in line, staring out into the dark parking lot. The moon was just a small sliver tonight, illuminating barely any glow. It made the night that much darker and scarier. Chatter of excitement traveled down the shopping center sidewalk, but I couldn't shake the feeling that something was out there. Spying. Waiting. For me.

Either fatigue was starting to set in, or this was me being a complete paranoid schitzo. Or maybe I was having a caffeine crash. Right about now, I was wishing for a steamy cup of coffee. Snuggling deeper into my hoodie, I shivered. The temperature had dropped tremendously. Chase came up behind me and wrapped his arms around me, engulfing me with his warmth. If my teeth hadn't been chattering, I might have protested, but truthful his body offered a blissful heat. He was like a furnace.

"Thanks," I muttered, leaning the back of my head against his chest. I felt him stiffen, and I knew that eerie feeling was more than just my being paranoid. "Something is watching us," I said softly, burrowing myself deeper in his arms.

They tightened around me. "Or someone," he proclaimed, his eyes scanning farther than my human, well, mostly human eyes could see.

I was almost afraid to ask what he saw. "You think it's a hunter?"

"That or you have a secret admirer." The heat from his breath tickled my neck.

I jabbed him in the gut, unsuccessfully causing him pain. "I'm serious. You're so impossible sometimes," I proclaimed exasperated. Turning in his arms, I looked up at him just as he shook his messy dark hair.

"It's almost midnight, Angel Eyes. *This* is my time to shine."

Only Chase could pull off the whole I-just-got-out-of-bed look and still appear stunning. I hated him. Or so I keep telling myself. "Oh, great. That makes me feel loads better. Not only is there someone stalking us, but also you could possibly go on a demon rampage."

His eyes bore into mine. "I'm fine. Don't get yourself in a tizzy." The look on his face was starting to make me self-conscious. I felt like I was an experiment on display that he was studying.

"What? Why are you staring at me like that? Is there something on my face?" I wiped the back of my sleeve across my mouth.

His eyes held mine for a moment longer, and then shook his head. "Nothing. I think whatever is out there has me on edge."

"You don't think they'll try anything, do you?" I couldn't imagine an ambush with all these people about, but what did I know.

"I doubt it. They wouldn't risk hurting anyone." He wasn't exactly overly convincing.

Luckily, the line started to move. It was finally midnight. I lost all thoughts of hunters as the excitement for Black Ops II, almost at my fingertips, bubbled inside me.

By the time we made it to the register, Chase was clutching his jaw in impatience and annoyance, while I was close to squealing like a little kid on Christmas morning. The people around us gave us a wide berth, wary of Chase, but I was sort of getting used to being secluded.

We approached the counter, and I gave the guy behind it our receipts. Ethan, his shirt had stitched in the right corner, smiled brightly at me. "Wow, we don't get many girls during a release. Is this for your boyfriend?" he asked.

How cliché. What I really wanted to say was, *cut the chitchat and give me the game, newb.* But instead I said, "No, it's for me."

Ethan grinned. "Impressive."

"You should see my KD ratio," I bragged.

"We should play together sometime." He scribbled something on the back of my receipt before handing it back to me.

It was his gamertag. *Really?* Was I seriously getting hit on by the guy at the video game store? I shoved the little slip of paper in the back of my pocket. "Sure," I replied, being friendly.

Chase scowled beside me, drawing Ethan's eyes to him.

"I take it your boyfriend doesn't play," Ethan commented at the menacing figure hovering over me.

"He is not my boyfriend," I declared smartly.

"Yes, I am," Chase countered, giving him a demon glare. Poor Ethan cowered, fumbling my two copies of the games in his hand. "Let's go," Chase growled. Someone was definitely on edge.

I snatched the games from the counter and sent Ethan an apologetic smile. The second we were out of the store I gave into the urge and did a happy dance, right there on the sidewalk.

Chase was staring at me with a lopsided grin. "I think that is the biggest smile I have ever seen on your face."

I hugged the games to my chest. "I just died and went to heaven. Hurry, we need to get home. Now!"

"No arguments there." His eyes did a sweep of the parking lot perimeter.

"Are they still out there?" I asked, remembering we weren't alone.

He shrugged. "Doesn't matter. They won't be able to catch me," he said smugly with a devilish grin. His over-confidence was staggering. Someday, he was going to meet his match.

Walking me to the car, he opened the passenger side door. "Hang on," he said before I had a chance to get in. I turned around and looked up at him with a quizzical glare. This was not the time to stall. Before I even had a chance to figure out what he was plotting, his hand snaked into my back pocket like a thief and grabbed the receipt. "I don't think you'll be needing this," he said right before he tossed the little slip of white paper in the wind.

I watched as it skipped along the blacktop. "Mature," I replied.

He just grinned and got into the car. "Are you and Travis really staying up all night playing that ridiculous game?" he asked as the car hummed to life. The engine was so quiet, you could barely hear it.

I snapped my seatbelt buckle into place. "I'm going to let that slide because right now, not even you can bring down my fantastic mood. And to answer your question…yes. Absolutely. We've been planning this for weeks." I had the game still clutched in my hand as I hoped for an uneventful drive home. I wasn't deceiving myself into thinking whoever had been watching us was gone. In this world Chase and his family lived in, that theory wasn't plausible. I just prayed we got home.

My prayer was answered when Chase's sleek car pulled into my driveway. The porch light I'd left on still shined, casting shadows over the lawn. I exhaled a sigh of relief. There was just something in the cool night's air that had a spooky ambiance. I was more than ready to get inside to the safety of my house. Kind of ironic since half the time I was convinced my house was haunted.

He walked me inside. "Do you want me to stay? I could find ways to distract you." His voice went low and did all kinds of funny things to my stomach.

"There is no way you could distract me tonight."

His silver eyes lit with a challenge.

Oh shit. What have I done?

He stepped forward bumping our bodies. "I promise you, Angel Eyes, that game wouldn't stand a chance against what I could do to you." A flicker of topaz sparked inside his smoky eyes.

I gulped, knowing that deep down he was right, and that pissed me off. "I'll take a rain check."

He trailed a finger over my bottom lip, and it quivered on contact. "If you change your mind, you know where to find me." His tone left no room for doubt.

I opened the door quickly before I changed my mind. The

longer I just stood here, the more certain I was becoming that I didn't want him to leave. All the more reason he should. "Don't hold your breath," I mumbled, and shut the door before he had the chance to suck me in with those unusual eyes and his sultry voice.

I leaned against the door and just breathed. Then I heard his laugh, so I pushed off the door steaming mad. I hated that I'd let him get to me. Worse, that he knew he could. It was like he had some kind of power over me—over my body.

Stomping up the stairs, I flung myself on the bed and immediately tore open the game. I swear a ray of light beamed down and angels started to sing. It was that holy.

I wasted no time inserting the new disc into my Xbox. Time ceased to exist while I played. I had no idea how long I was absorbed or what time I closed my eyes. The last thing I remembered was the sweet sound of gunfire blasting in my surround sound headset.

I must have fallen asleep mid-match, with my Turtlebeach headset still on and the remote clutched in my grasp. Waking up to the theme of Black Ops II in my ears, was a great start to the day. I propped up on a mountain of pillows, thinking a few hours of sleep were just enough. The game was calling me.

From the corner of my eye I spotted something glowing, hidden in the shadows. By the time my brain processed that it was a guy, I started screaming. As the first piercing note hit the air, a hand closed around my mouth, silencing me. Looking up into eyes the color of liquid fire, I swallowed back the rest of my scream, and my stomach fell back into place.

Chase.

Slouching into his body, I smacked him on the chest. "What the hell? You scared me to death. Why the hell are you creeping in my room like some peeping tom watching me sleep?" *Now* I could feel the mark at my hip prickling, a moment ago I'd been too frightened to feel anything.

He snorted. "Don't flatter yourself."

"So you weren't watching me sleep?"

"And if I was?"

"I don't know. It's weird."

His eyes flirted over me. "It's hot, and you are totally turned on by it. Admit it."

I rolled my eyes and tried to ignore that I was alone in my room with him.

His hand ruffled my hair, reminding me that I'd just woken up. "You are such a she-devil in the morning. Hmm, I like it."

Good Lord. "You would. Don't you have someone else to torment?" I tried to hide my morning breath, but there was nothing I could do about the bedhead.

"You are always at the top of my list," he said, eyes sparking.

I attempted a bored expression. "Is there a point to this conversation because you are costing me valuable game time?"

"You and Travis need to get a life. I don't think he has moved an inch off the couch since I brought him the game last night."

The corners of my mouth tilted. "I know. We must have played most of the night together. It was glorious."

"Sometimes I think he should be the one stuck with you for all eternity," he grumbled cutely.

A faint smile crossed my lips. "What fun would that be for you?" I teased.

He looked at me in my leggings and tank like he was undressing me with those silvery eyes. "True. I am much more fun than he is."

I pretended to gag.

He pretended not to notice. "Come one. It's breakfast time."

"Wait, I—" The air swooshed out of my lungs as Chase hoisted me over his shoulders. I hadn't seen that one coming. "Chase, put me down!" I demanded.

Of course he ignored me. "I promised Lexi I would invite you over for breakfast. So, this is me inviting you. It is because of you and that damn game that she skipped school as well. She was afraid she would miss out on all the fun."

That didn't explain why *he* wasn't at school. I squirmed in his arms to no avail, and my efforts only got me a slap on the butt.

HUNTING ANGEL

"Chase?" I growled. "Try that again and I swear…"

Chapter 6

I was still slung over his shoulder when we entered the Winters house, but I wasn't making it easy for him. He dumped me on the couch beside Travis, who was sporting a silly grin. I pushed the hair out of my eyes and mouth. By this point, I was spitting mad. Not only had he yanked me from my bed, he had also deprived me of my Xbox.

I had been in the zone.

No one messed with me when I was in the zone.

I was going to show no mercy. My teeth were clenched so tight, my jaw started to throb painfully.

"Morning sunshine," Travis greeted, grinning like a fool. "When I told him to drag your butt over here, I didn't think he was going to take me literally."

"Damn it, Chase!" I yelled. "I am going to kill you!"

His lethal grin flashed at me from behind the kitchen counter. "You'll have to catch me first." Then he started making a ton of racket.

We both knew there was no way on planet earth I was going to be able to actually grab a hold of him, not unless he wanted to be caught. I cursed this stupid bond for not at least giving me inhuman speeds. Come on, was that too much to ask for? I mean, if I was going to spend the rest of my life running from Hell's minions and defending myself from getting butchered to death, I think I deserved a little compensation.

Apparently the universe and its order of balance had other plans. In my current state, the universe could suck it.

My raging pity party was cut short when Lexi bound down the staircase. "Oh goodie, Angel's here." She leaped onto the chaise. "Did you hear? We're playing hooky."

Sinking into the back of the black couch, I groaned. And just like that I saw my whole day going to hell. There went staying in bed all day playing the BLOPS II and lounging around the house in my jammies, which I just realized I was still wearing thanks to Chase's unwelcome arrival. Sometimes my neighbors could be so all-consuming.

"Here." Travis held out an extra controller. "This will make it better. And if we turn up the volume, we might be able to drown out their voices too."

Travis—my savior. "You read my mind," I sighed, breaking a grin for the first time since I'd woken up.

Lexi frowned at her older brother. "You are such a loser. Get a job, bum."

"I'm MLG, little sis," Travis retaliated, Lexi's burn doing no damage.

I couldn't help the smile that started to spread across my lips. First, I was pretty sure Lexi had no idea what MLG meant (major league gamer) and second, the look on Lexi's face was priceless. She looked like he had just told her he had some highly contagious disease that would slowly eat the flesh from her face.

Or that the mall was closed.

"You should see a doctor about that," Chase called from the kitchen, unable to miss a chance to take a jab at Travis.

Lexi crossed her arms and gave Travis a smug smile, glad to have someone on her side.

You think after the rough start, breakfast, well it was closer to lunch, would have been awkward and uncomfortable, but the one thing that made this dysfunctional family envious, was their ability to forgive and forget. A grudge never lasted long between Chase, Lexi, and Travis—the whole short temper demon thing. They might razz each other relentlessly, but at the end of the day…they were family.

And they made me feel part of it.

Even if I wasn't entirely convinced Devin was my biggest fan. He might be…ugh, it was still so hard to think about, *dating* my mom, but that didn't mean he necessarily thought I was the best thing for Lexi or Chase. I got the impression he thought I was more trouble than good.

And then there were the strange glances I kept getting from Chase. I'd been trying to convince myself that it was me. But lately, I've been catching him staring at me more and more, and not with the usual swoon-worthy gazes. These were more like he was dissecting me or waiting for me to grow a third eye, and whatever he saw had him thrown off balance. As soon as we were alone, I was going to grill him. He was hiding something from me.

I could feel it.

I guess this connection was good for something after all.

After we ate, I assumed I would be free of my imprisonment and head home. I should have known better. Chase had other plans. Plans that involved the two of us. Alone. In his bedroom. My heart was going to need a jumpstart—it had stopped beating.

He pulled me up the upstairs, and surprisingly, I let him. I could only resist the pull between us for so long, and I don't know why, but it felt like days since we had been alone. Really alone. The fact that I was secretly looking forward to being shut off from the world with just him was alarming.

His fingers interlaced with mine. "If I hadn't insisted that you come over, you would still be shut up in your room withering away to nothing," he said, as we climbed the stairs.

He was probably right, but I was definitely not going to admit it. I wouldn't give him the pleasure. "If you hadn't shown up, I probably would have prestige again."

"What?" The look on his face was comical as we walked over the threshold of his room.

Sometimes, I forgot that he knew next to nothing about games. My mouth twitched as I tried to hide my grin. "Nothing."

"How about we make *nothing* into something about me and you…preferably on my bed?"

"I don't think there is room for me with your inflated ego in the way," I commented, yawning. Still, I climbed into his bed, happy to lay my head on his pillow. His dark and erotic scent flirted with my senses from the sheets. Sighing contently, I inhaled deeply before I even realized what I was doing.

His head joined mine on the pillow, and he was smirking. "That's not the only thing that's inflated."

Color morphed into my cheeks.

The look in his eyes was full of pure wickedness. "Did I shock you, my virginal angel?"

"What makes you think I'm a virgin?" I knew I was skirting a fine line toward danger. A part of me must like to walk right on the edge of a rocky cliff. Chase could be unstable and hazardous, yet I didn't care.

"This," he murmured, brushing his thumb over my lips. "You blush every time I touch you."

I sucked in a sharp breath. The heat from his thumb was like magic. "I do not."

He arched a brow, his way of calling me a liar.

Blast him.

"That doesn't mean anything," I huffed.

"Really? Let's put it to the test." I didn't like the gleam in his eyes. It radiated trouble. "I bet you've never been kissed here," he challenged, and I watched stupefied as he lowered his head, slowly kissing my shoulder. "Or here," he murmured against my flushed skin.

I watched as his dark head traveled to my collarbone. Then his lips were kissing the sensitive alcove of my neck. But nothing prepared me for his mouth nibbling on my bottom lip, or when his fingers skirted the edge of my cotton waistband. My eyes were steamy. My insides turned into mush. And I didn't think I was going to last another ten seconds without moaning.

Then he whispered in my ear, "Your turn." He wanted me, to do to him the same in return.

I knew I was playing with fire, but what fun was it if you didn't get burned once in a while. And while I was at it, why not kick it up a notch. Straddling him, I kept my eyes glued to his, fascinated by the change of colors. Bending down, I whispered in his ear, "You asked for it."

His silver eyes darkened to coal laced with the most mesmerizing streaks of glittering gold. Pressing my lips softly to the spot where his neck and shoulder met, I felt his pulse quicken under my mouth. It was an empowering feeling, knowing that I could do that. I let my lips trail down his neck taking little nibbles at the rapidly beating vein. This time it was him who sucked in a sharp breath, and I smirked. But it wasn't long before I found myself caught in my own web of seduction.

Tilting my head back, I'd lost the ability to breath. His eyes were completely topaz and shimmered with passion. It was overwhelming, unsettling, and made my blood rush. Those perfect lips whispered my name right before I seared them with mine. Then the room shattered with electrifying heat. His hands were under my shirt, tugging it over my head before I could even register it was gone.

"Hmm, I love the way you smell, the way you taste," he murmured dreamily. "Like fresh peaches and wild berries from the vine. It lingers on my lips for hours after I kiss you, taunting me. Your scent follows me everywhere. On my clothes. In my car. In my room. In my dreams. It doesn't matter what I do or where I go, you are everywhere. You're a part of me."

I stared at him like I didn't recognize him. His words touched my very soul, and I didn't even know where to begin to explain how he made me feel. I wasn't good with caring and sharing—I just plain out sucked at it. With my luck, I would ruin what was the best moment of my life. So I didn't say anything.

Instead, I fused my lips to his again, trying to show him what

I was unable to say. What I was still unable to admit to myself.

I was falling for him—hard.

I had no more than touched his lips with mine when I heard his bedroom door swing open, followed by a low groan. His hands kept me from moving as I glanced over my shoulder.

Lexi stood in the doorway. "Ugh," she complained. "Can't you two get a room? The whole house doesn't want to see you sucking face twenty-four seven."

"This *is* my room," growled Chase, literally growled in his throat, eyes illuminating in the semi-dark room. A shudder of fear and excitement raced through me as he teetered close to the edge of no control.

"Oh," she exclaimed as if just realizing where she was. "God, you guys are worse than rabbits. And I thought Travis was bad."

"Out!" demanded a very annoyed Chase. "And lock the damn door."

Ten seconds after the door clicked, I started giggling. The moment was ruined.

"I am going to strangle her," he vowed, staring at the ceiling with his hands streaked through his messy hair.

That only made me laugh harder.

"You think this is funny?" His hands gripped my waist and yanked me against him.

The giggle perished in my throat, I gulped. Nope. When he

looked at me like that, there was absolutely nothing humorous about it. Instead I felt...

Hot.

Excited.

Achy.

"Your eyes..."

"What about them?" I asked feeling entranced.

He shook his head. "I keep trying to convince myself that I am seeing things, that it couldn't be possible."

"Is this what you haven't been telling me? What you've been hiding from me?"

He cocked a brow. "What makes you think I've been hiding things from you?"

I gave him a droll look. "You really don't think that this link we have is one only sided, do you?"

He shrugged. "I guess that was too much to expect. I was really hoping that you wouldn't be...affected by what happened."

"Okay, you are starting to scare me now. What is wrong with my eyes?"

"They change."

The eyes in question widened like alien saucers.

"No, not like mine," he said, reading my thoughts. "They remind me of a mood ring Lexi once wore. She was going through one of her phases and never took the damn thing off. Your eyes…they change colors with your mood. Not drastically, but enough that I notice."

"Meaning, my mom could notice. Anyone could notice," I added somberly.

He nodded his head.

"On the up side, you seem to be the only one who pisses me off lately. Maybe no one will notice."

"Maybe…" But he sounded anything but swayed. It was more like he agreed for my benefit, to make me feel better.

I was sure this wasn't good. If my eyes were changing because of our shared bond, what else did I have in store to look forward to? What other surprises awaited me?

Chapter 7

Halloween was like the best holiday ever. Hello free candy. Who can turn that down? I might be a senior in high school, but that didn't stop me from dressing up and enjoying my inner child.

...Or having to take crap from Chase.

Apparently the sight of me in my costume was hilarious. He probably didn't even know what I was. I was reluctant to admit how intoxicating his laugh was, realizing how little I actually heard it.

However, he was still a complete jerk. Some things never change. Chase might be incredibly gorgeous and I might be the teeniest bit attracted to the clad (okay more than a tiny bit,) but that didn't mean that most days, I didn't think he was a douche.

He looked me up and down, taking in the patched block dress I made myself, the red wig, and the stitches I'd drawn on my face. While he took his fill at the whole package, I tried to ignore what his gaze was doing to my body. Whenever Chase was near, it defied my wishes to be unaffected by his presence. Damn, uncontrollable body.

"Are you supposed to be homeless?" he asked, grinning

widely. There was still a chuckle in his voice.

I started to shut the door in his face only to be stopped by his foot in the threshold. I glared, crossing my arms. "For your information, bucko, I'm Sally Stitches."

He just stood there looking blank.

I sighed heavily. Did he ever watch movies? "From *A Nightmare Before Christmas*."

"Never seen it," he said, looking unimpressed.

"You're in luck," I declared, yanking him inside. I secretly grinned. "We can rectify that immediately."

He looked me from head-to-toe again, and once more I tried to ignore what his eyes did to me. It wasn't easy. Especially since not that long ago we had been horizontal, on his bed, doing things that still made me blush. He needed to stop affecting me like this. After all, I was only human, well mostly human I think. The jury was still out. "Why didn't you go for something more girly?" he asked seriously.

"You mean slutty." I was going to dropkick him. Soon.

He shrugged. "Your words not mine."

I rolled my eyes. "It's what you were thinking."

"I'll tell you what I am thinking," he purred. His voice had suddenly gotten low and seductive.

That was the signal that I was in trouble. My body responded instantly to his insinuation. "Nope," I said, waving my finger in the air. "Not tonight. Don't even think about it. Tonight, you are not distracting me with your sexual prowess."

"My what?"

"Just sit down. And keep your hands to yourself."

He gave me a crooked grin. "I thought you liked my hands."

"Don't flatter yourself." I knew I was giving off mixed signals, but I just couldn't help it.

"Do you want me to prove you're a liar?" he challenged.

One day I was going to make Chase Winters eat his words. I ignored him and popped the movie into the DVD player. Snuggling onto the couch next to him, I kept an ear out for the trick-or-treaters I was pretty sure weren't coming. There was a giant bowl of assorted candy by the door. The good kind, it was brimming with chocolate goodness. Since we pretty much lived in the boonies, I don't even know why Mom insisted we buy candy. Really, how many trick-or-treaters did she honestly think we were going to get?

I'll tell you.

Five. And two of those were Lexi and Travis. At least they understood the fun in dressing up.

The upside—I got all the leftover candy. Not that my hips needed the extra pounds, but my sweet tooth wouldn't be able to ignore the temptation. It was kind of like my body being unable to ignore Chase. He tasted so good, but afterward you felt guilty.

HUNTING ANGEL

On most days I thought my house was haunted. On Halloween, I was absolutely certain. All night I'd heard eerie noises. So when the ceiling above my head creaked, I should have expected it. Instead I acted like a scared little mouse and jumped into Chase's lap, so much for the hands off policy.

His arms prevented me from tumbling off the couch. "Don't worry, Angel Eyes. I'll protect you from the scary ghosts." He smirked, mocking me.

"Hilarious," I replied sarcastically…on second thought… "But seriously, are there such things as ghosts?" I asked hesitantly. It was plausible, right? I mean, I had a half-demon on my couch.

His sparkling silver eyes studied me, and then he burst out laughing to my exasperation.

Was that a yes or a no?

Luckily he was saved from my fists of fury by the doorbell. I'd been contemplating using them on him if he kept laughing at me. Trick-or-Treating had ended, but I figured there might be a few stragglers. Turned out, the straggler was Lexi.

"Am I interrupting something?" she asked, peering over my shoulder. "Or are you guys ready to go?"

Ugh. How could I have forgotten?

The sacred Spring Valley Halloween Bash.

It wasn't so much that I had forgotten we were going, it was that I had been so caught up in the movie and not passing out candy. "Um. Yeah, totally ready. Right Chase?" I turned around expecting to find him stretched out on the couch, but he was right behind me. "Damn it. You know I hate it when you sneak up on me."

He gave me a snarky grin. "I wasn't sneaking,"

"Whatever. Let's just go," I muttered.

Spring Valley's Halloween Bash consisted of an empty cornfield, piled with more pickups than I thought possible, a mile high, very unsafe looking bonfire, and the scent of un-chaperoned mischief. Stalks of dried and shriveled corn blanketed the ground. The bed of one of the many pickups blasted the newest Taylor Swift song, and there were red solo cups littered everywhere. The only source of light in the otherwise blinding night was the out of control fire and, of course, KC lights.

"Are you sure you are ready for this?" Chase asked, close to my ear.

I refrained from elbowing him.

Lexi, the sexy Grecian goddess, walked on the other side of me. Her hair tumbled in perfect pale ringlets down her neck. Her costume was a maxi-mini in glittering aquamarine, the same color of her eyes. She looked more Hollywood than horror.

"How the hell did you get Travis to let you leave the house wearing that?" Chase rumbled, getting his first real glance at his cousin. Travis and Chase more than often thought of Lexi as twelve-year-old girl. They could be domineering and fiercely protective to the point of suffocation. Sometimes the only course of action was blackmail.

Lexi's smile was anything but sweet. "I threatened to snap one of his games in half."

I gasped.

Chase looked like he was about make some form of overbearing and controlling suggestion. I butted in. "Give her some slack. It's Halloween."

"The day of the damned… I think I have a right to worry," he retorted.

"Look, we don't need a babysitter all the time. You're stifling me. Us," I corrected. He had me on edge. I don't know why I said it, but I regretted it the second the words flew from my mouth. Everything between us was so intense now. I didn't know how to deal with all these emotions I was having, and I knew taking it out on him wasn't the answer.

I was going to have to apologize. Later.

"Yeah," Lexi punctuated. "We are here to have fun, dance and drink. Not necessarily in that order," she said, plucking a fruity wine drink from one of the coolers.

Chase scowled. He barely spared me another glance before he took off. I lost sight of him in the crowd and sighed heavily. The look on his face stuck in my mind. I tried to convince myself that I imagined the quick streak of hurt.

"Come on," Lexi grinned, grabbing my arm. "Let's mingle."

I do not mingle. I don't drink due to daddy issues that have completely sworn me off alcohol. And I most certainly do not dance. But it was kind of hard to say no to the strength of a half-demon pulling you along.

Kailyn and Brandy spotted us and waved wildly.

"What took you guys so long to get here?" Kailyn asked at our approach. She was dressed as Pocahontas. With her dark hair in braids and her olive complexion she fit the part perfectly.

"I promised my mom I would pass out candy while she was at work," I informed her.

Brandy looked like she belonged in a harem. Her midriff was bared, and the material covering her legs couldn't have gotten any sheerer. She looked like a genie in a bottle, but with a lot less class. "You haven't missed much, that's for sure."

Shocker. In a town this small, we would have already heard about it if something had happened. Everything moved slower than snot here, except for gossip. That spread faster than the flu. "The night is still young and in Spring Valley, you are more likely to see a UFO than something of real importance happening," I said, unable to help myself. Poking fun of this town had become like second nature to me. Sort of like my love-hate relationship with Chase, though lately it seemed like we had come to some kind of truce, tonight excluded.

The world must have frozen over.

Brandy and Kailyn giggled.

"Ain't that the truth," Lexi agreed. "And trust me. Alien sightings are a common occurrence here."

No doubt, with the high demon activity they have running amuck. We chatted, but I sort of checked out of the conversation. Since I'd lost sight of him, Chase had been on my mind even though I tried to forget him. Scanning the crowd again, I looked for those silver eyes. Nothing. My heart sunk a little.

It's your own fault, I reminded myself. You wanted space. Suddenly I felt like I had too much space.

Lexi took a long swig of her bottle. When she turned her bright eyes on me, I knew I wasn't going to like what she had in mind. She grabbed a hold of my hand. "I love this song," she declared in a voice much louder than necessary. Someone was feeling a little buzzed.

Before I had a chance to protest, I found myself in the middle of what felt like a mosh pit. Bodies were bumpin' and grinding, in what I guess what was called dancing. Someone elbowed me in the ribs, my toes got trampled, and I hadn't even started moving yet. Not that there was much room to really move. I was so out of my element.

If I survived tonight, I was going to strangle Lexi.

I lost track of how long we swayed our hips to the bass. Somewhere between Tim McGraw and Miranda Lambert, Lexi brought me back to earth. She was also the reason I was wedged like a pickle.

"He's watching you," Lexi sung, twirling in a circle, the crystals on her dress catching in the firelight.

I was pretty sure that wine cooler had gone straight to her head. She wasn't making much sense. What a lightweight. "Who?" I asked, trying to concentrate on the movement of my feet.

She rolled her turquoise eyes. "Chase, dummy. Who else?"

My heart sped up in triple time. "Oh. Whatever. He is probably waiting for me to trip over my feet and fall on my ass."

She looked over my shoulder. "Hm. I don't think so. He is looking right this way."

"Lexi, stop," I growled.

"He is…wait…" Her eyes narrowed.

"What?" I screeched, barely able contain my exasperation.

"He's scowling," she finally said.

I relaxed. "Why is that abnormal?"

She had stopped dancing and looked around. I continued to move with the music, trying to blend in with the crowd. "Everyone is staring at you," she said, her eyes connecting back to me. "You're magnetizing."

"What?" I said again in disbelief. This time I stopped what

might have passed as dancing. What kind of mumble jumble was she going on about? Note to self: *Lexi and liquor don't mix.*

"Chase is going to go ape shit," Lexi informed, like I didn't already know.

Somehow, a circle had formed around Lexi and me, making us the center of attention, exactly what I hadn't wanted. People were still dancing, but they were more or less dancing around us. It was as if a spotlight was shining down on us.

On me.

I was going to puke.

I was going to faint.

Maybe both. I had to get out of here.

Leaving Lexi to her dancing, I pushed my way through the crowd, looking for some space and air. I couldn't breathe. I kept walking and walking, until the music was just a low hum. Leaning against a beat up, rusty red truck, I drew in huge gulps of the cool breeze. It washed over my heated cheeks. I laid my head back and closed my eyes, enjoying the moment, the low music in the distance, the smell of burning wood, and the crickets singing in the fields.

Away from all the gawking eyes.

I didn't hear the footsteps until it was too late for escape. My solitude was over. A cornstalk snapped, and I expected to see Chase's surly face bulldoze into the clearing, even deadly with anger he looked devastating. But it wasn't. Instead, I saw a very unwelcomed, wobbly Brody.

"Oh my God." My hand flew to my chest. "You scared the bejesus out of me." I didn't even try to hide the annoyance from my voice. The hammering of my heart pounded under my hand.

He stepped in front of me with a red plastic cup in his hand and like most of the guys, forewent a costume. "Sorry, I didn't mean to. I was being as loud as possible, I swear." He drew a sloppy X across his chest and smiled at me.

What a dork. "I think I'm just jumpy. Too much caffeine, or not enough."

He laughed with brown eyes that looked glazed, like melted ice. "That's what I like about you, you're funny. Not like the other girls at school."

If he only knew how different I was.

"I've been waiting all night to talk to you." His words sort of blurred together into one.

"You have?" I was utterly clueless as to why he wanted to talk to me.

He took a step closer, our shoulders brushing. "Of course. You look great by the way. Who are you supposed to be?"

I rolled my eyes and tried to ignore the sketchy feeling his lingering gaze was giving me. Did no one in this hick town watch movies? "Sally from *Nightmare Before Christmas*."

He blinked.

"It's a movie," I added.

"Oh. Well, it's by far the best costume of the night." He drowned the rest of the contents in his cup, wiping his mouth with the back of his hand, and set the empty cup on the bed of the truck.

Attractive.

I was waiting for the epic belch to follow and maybe even some belly scratching. It would have made my night.

Yet for whatever reason, my body suddenly went on alert.

Maybe it was the fact that he was clearly drunk.

Maybe it was the funny, slurred speech.

Maybe it was the scary gleam in his eyes.

Regardless, for his safety and mine, I knew that I didn't want to be alone with him. I was feeling very unsure about this whole situation, unsure about this whole night. Everything seemed off, bizarro.

"I didn't think I would get a minute alone with you," Brody slurred his words.

Touching. Can you believe this guy?

Suddenly he was in front of me, his arms boxing me on either side of the truck and pinning me in with his bulky body. I got that icky, sick feeling and swallowed my first taste of fear. It left a bad taste in my mouth. I realized I was trapped between his much larger-than-mine body and the side of the truck.

Shit.

This was an unexpected turn of events.

Not good.

"Brody," I said, trying to make my voice stern. "Don't do this," I warned, risking a glance up into his glassy brown eyes.

He angled his moppy brunette head. "Why not? I know you want to. I can see it in your eyes."

What an asshat. The only thing he saw in my eyes was disgust and fear.

"Brody look, I am sure you are a nice guy." My voice was tight, fear gripping me. I flattened my hands on his chest, pushing. He was an immovable force. I couldn't breathe. That pause was just the opening he was waiting for and then his mouth was on mine. He smelled like a brewery and tasted worse. I hated beer. An assault of memories flooded me. I was frozen in absolute panic.

This wasn't happening.

What was happening?

I couldn't believe it. I knew that Brody could be a jerky jock, but this...

It just goes to show you how horrific my judge of character could be.

I knew in my head I should scream, but nothing came out. His hand grabbed me at the waist, digging painfully into my skin.

His mouth was rough, bruising my lips with sloppy, wet kisses. I wanted to puke.

I needed to do something. Now.

I did the only thing I could think of. I brought my knee straight up in-between his legs with as much force as I could muster.

And I got just the results I was looking for.

His hands instantly released my waist as he moaned, clutching his groin. I wasted not a second of the reprieve I was given, knowing that it wouldn't cripple him for long.

I scrambled away from the truck. "Chase!" I called, breathing heavily, knowing that I only needed to say his name, and he would hear me.

Or so I hoped.

He stepped out of the dark shadows, eyes glowing like the Las Vegas strip. His movements were deadly quiet and dangerous, and he looked a thousand times scarier than Brody.

Chase.

"What took you so long?" I snapped, all my fear turning into rage, that and the fact that I wanted him to wrap his arms around me and take me the hell away from here—far away.

Chase's mouth thinned and his jawed ticked. "How was I to know that you weren't into it? You wanted space, remember? Well, I gave you plenty."

Ugh. He would have to bring that up now of all times. "I think I was making it pretty damn clear I wasn't interested. This fucktard was just too drunk and stupid to listen." My mouth tends to get filthier when I'm scared out of my wits.

Brody groaned again. In a flash, Chase reached down and hauled Brody up against the truck one-handed.

He wiggled his brows. "So you are admitting that you need me after all?" Smugness oozed from his whole entire body.

Brody made a grunting noise, causing Chase to remember he was still there and stiffen. Seriously bad move. He should have kept his trap shut. Now I was sure Chase was going to murder him. His eyes lit like embers against the starry night, and they were definitely filled with a murderous glare. Brody was toast.

I had to intervene.

Well, maybe not until Brody learned a lesson. No meant no, and if he needed the bejeebies beat out of him to get that, then by all means, who was I to begrudge him that lesson.

The first crunch of knuckles cracking against Brody's cheek wasn't pretty. I caught a glimpse of Brody's head swinging back right before I hid my eyes, no longer thinking that this so called *lesson* was a great idea. Especially with the kind of fists Chase packed. It wasn't exactly fair. Chase had been itching for a fight, and I just handed him one on a silver platter.

A trickle of blood seeped from Brody's nose, but that didn't stop Chase. He seemed to be out for more than just blood as he hit Brody again and again. If I didn't do something now, Chase might lose control. I have had my fair share of run-ins with both half-demons and the nasty stuff from the underworld. And though Chase never hurt me, that didn't mean I still didn't fear what lied hidden inside him.

I would be a fool not to. And mama didn't raise no fool.

Well, most of the time I wasn't foolish. There were those few times where desperation overrules reason.

"Chase!" I yelled from behind him.

At first I didn't think he heard me. Then his hand stopped midair—clenched and suspended in barely restrained fury. The fact that he had been able to stop wasn't lost to me, or the fact that I might be one of only a few people who could have actually gotten through to him. Later, when I wasn't feeling so exposed and vulnerable, I might realize the kind of power I had with him. For now, it just washed right over me.

Muscles taunt, he had Brody slammed up against the truck again, eyes glowing brighter than the moon. Brody's were full of fear and the fog of booze. He looked close to tears. "Touch her again, I dare you," Chase said in a haunting voice.

Mental eye roll. I hoped that was more of a threat than a challenge. The last thing I wanted was Brody to give Chase another reason to beat him to a bloody pulp. His face already looked like it had a horrible meeting with a meat grinder.

I gasped, as Chase's fist found the center of Brody's belly for one last punch. Brody crumbled to the cold, rocky ground. Chase turned to me, and a slice of fear rippled through me. Sometimes I forgot how scary he could really be. His hand grabbed mine, tugging me through the overgrown brush of the field.

I sighed, suddenly tired of being manhandled. "Are we just going to leave him there?" I asked, leaves crackling under our feet as I scrambled to keep up with Chase and his superior speed and long legs.

A hopeless endeavor really.

He stopped and my legs thanked him. "Do you really want me to go back there?" he growled.

I swallowed. "Um, definitely not—"

No sooner had the words left my mouth, when I felt the air sucked out of my lungs, and I was flying in the air. I never saw it coming. Somewhere in the distance, I heard a faint whoosh and humming, but it didn't register in my brain. When you are sailing through the air, there was only one place to go. Down.

My back hit the ground with a jarring force, and my chest felt like it was crushed by a giant boulder. That giant boulder turned out to be a body. It seemed like minutes before I was able to breathe again. In reality it was probably only seconds, yet time seemed to have slowed.

Disorientated, I stared above me, looking into Chase's glittering topaz eyes. He had tackled me, literally to the ground.

Now what?

Chapter 8

"What the hell, Chase? What is wrong with you?"

He looked down at me, pushing the hair out of my face. Both of us were breathing hard from the unexpected fall. "You ungrateful little brat, I just saved your life—again I might add."

I followed his gaze above our heads where I used to be standing. There, embedded in the grainy tree bark was a long sleek arrow with yellow feathers at the end. Someone had shot at me, or us, I wasn't certain.

"I was being shot at?" I asked in disbelief, peering back at his looming face.

"It looks that way."

I tried to ignore the way his body covered mine. You think after a death defying moment, I wouldn't be thinking about how glorious his rippled chest felt against mine, or that even when he was tossing me to the ground, I rarely get hurt. "Who would want to shoot me? With an arrow?" I asked, when I could think clearly again.

His eyes were studying mine. I could only assume that my eyes were doing that color changing dohicky. He had that look on his face. "Hunters. And it looks like they have figured out my kryptonite."

Kryptonite? Did he mean me? I was his weakness? "I thought you said you weren't a superhero?"

He snorted. "Angel, you're impossible." Then he kissed the tip of my nose before pushing to his feet. With a rough hand, he brushed his fingers through his windblown hair.

My chest felt lighter without his weight, though I missed the zing. I just laid there on the ground, looking at him hovering above me. He looked gorgeous and powerful with the moonlight at his back. He blended perfectly with the night. Yes, I was totally ogling, but so was he. We just couldn't seem to help ourselves. We probably should have been running for our lives from whatever was hunting us, not spending an eternity eyeballing each other.

The side of my hip tingled in hypnotic bliss.

It was Chase who eventually broke what was becoming a sizzling spell. He held out a hand. "We need to go."

Nodding, I took his hand and let him pull me to my feet. I couldn't have agreed more. Though, a tumble on the ground would have been fine too. Just saying.

But I knew he was right. We were sitting ducks out here in the open field. Whoever was out there had the trees and the twilight as their cover. But I had a half-demon. I think I win.

So far this Halloween was becoming too much real life horror for me. It wasn't my kind of fun. I'd like to leave the life-threatening situations to the movies. However, it seemed that wasn't in the cards for me.

Not now.

I needed to be a realist here.

I was going to be hunted.

My life was going to be in constant danger.

And one day, Chase might not be there to save me.

"Let's find Lexi before they decide to take a second shot," he said, sounding stressed.

I could see it in his stance, how much he wanted to go all demon gung-ho and get us out of here much faster. It riled him to have to resort to human speeds, especially when our lives were at stake.

He wrapped his around my shoulders, pulling me close to him, using his body as a shield. I felt his biceps bunch in barely restrained control. Things were not looking promising. At least if anyone asked about the glowing eyes, we could say they were contacts. No one would question it on Halloween.

We found Lexi in the same spot I'd left her. Dancing.

Chase literally plucked her from the man-made dance floor and hauled her through the sea of people. "Party's over. It's time to leave, cuz."

I followed swiftly beside him. Lexi, even in her slightly

hammered state, knew better than to argue. That didn't mean she went without style.

"Why does every party end with us dashing off? I just wanted one night to be free." There was pain and anger in Lexi's rant.

"You can throw a pity party at home. Get in the car. Now!" Chase demanded harshly.

He slid into the driver seat, immediately throwing the car in to drive and took off at mach ten. The wheels spun, squealing and leaving black rubber on the road behind us. I gripped the edge of my leather seat. A dense dust of gravel kicked up behind us, making it impossible to see.

No one said anything on the ride home. Lexi sulked in the back, and I was afraid that if I opened my mouth, I might lose it. Tears were already burning the back of my eyes, and my throat felt closed up.

The whole night hit me like a blizzard.

We dropped Lexi off at her house, and she went storming inside, giving Chase the cold shoulder.

He sighed heavily. "God, I hate this holiday."

Leaving him downstairs to stew on his personal hatred, I headed upstairs for the bathroom. The need to get out of this costume was stifling. Striping the patched dress, I tossed it haphazardly into a corner of the bathroom. In nothing but my skivvies, I started scrubbing the cracking make-up from my face.

Minutes later it felt like I was trying to scrub away the events of the night, but it hadn't worked. Looking at my reflection in the mirror, I could still feel Brody's hands piercing into my flesh. I could still see the arrow sticking out of the tree instead of my chest. I stared in the mirror at a girl who looked traumatized; my blue eyes were wide and an unusual shade lighter.

Gripping the side of the counter, I heaved and shoved the tears back down my throat. I refused to go postal and give into the useless tears that were threatening to spill all over my cheeks.

Tossing on a t-shirt, I opened the bathroom door and was hit with a wave of aftershocks. My entire body started shaking. Before I could register that I was about to have a mental breakdown, Chase was there.

So much for the brave face.

He pulled me against him, wrapping his strong arms around me. I was encompassed by his warmth and the scent of dark sin. My body, still trembling, pressed up to his even though in my mind I knew I was safe.

One thing was for certain, I didn't want to be alone. I knew all it would take was for me to ask and he would be suction-cupped to my side. In my present state, I wouldn't mind.

"Don't leave," I murmured quietly. So soft that anyone else wouldn't have heard it.

His fingers ran down the back of my hair. "I'll be here for as long as you need me."

Eternity, I thought.

Whoa. Where had that come from?

I knew our lives and future were tied together by forces outside my control, but eternity? Could I really see myself with Chase forever? We didn't even have any real concrete information about what linked us together. It was always possible that this bond could be broken. Who knew? And here I was thinking about being saddled with Chase for the rest of time.

I don't know what came over me. Maybe it was the sincerity in his words. Heck, it could have been a thousand different things. Yet, right now my brain was fried, and I didn't want to think about it. I just wanted him close. Sliding my arms around his waist, I clung to him as the last of the trembles left my body. I was afraid to let go—afraid to let *him* go.

How had he suddenly become so important?

I could feel tiny chip of defense around my heart crumbling. If I wasn't careful, I was going to lose my heart to the one person who could destroy it.

And maybe more than just my heart.

I was becoming too dependent on him.

Doomed, was what I was.

Time sat suspended as we stood there in each other's arms. It was Chase who finally pulled back. "Come on, let's get you in bed."

The mattress shifted under my knees as I climbed into my bed. "You're not leaving, are you?" The question tumbled from my lips.

He got under the covers beside me, eyes never wavering from mine. I scooted back, making room for him. He held his arm open and without a second thought I snuggled into his warm and secure embrace. "No, I told you I wouldn't," he whispered, drawing lazy circles on my back with his breath tickling my neck.

I sighed, contented. "I'm sorry about earlier tonight."

His hand paused on my back. "Which part?"

I restrained form pinching him. He wasn't going to make this easy. Apologizing to Chase was not on the list of things I'd ever thought I would be doing. "When I said you were stifling me...it's not true. Well, mostly not true."

He snorted. "That was the sorriest excuse for an apology."

This time I couldn't restrain myself. I pinched him in the side. "Don't make me take it back."

He laughed under his breath at me, and then his chest heaved. "It's for your own good."

My fingers played with the material of his navy t-shirt. "I know," I agreed.

"Sometimes I can't help but wonder if I did the right thing by saving you." There was regret in his voice, and I didn't like hearing it. "It was completely selfish, I know. But in that moment, I couldn't live with your blood on my hands. I couldn't live without y—"

He didn't finish that sentence, though I was pretty sure I knew how it ended. *He couldn't live without me.* The feeling was mutual. I couldn't say a month ago I would have felt the same, but since that night, I knew that my life was nothing without Chase, whether I was ready to admit it to myself or not. I was certainly not ready to voice it aloud, and apparently, neither was he.

It was both a scary and exhilarating revelation.

He took a deep breath, my head rising and falling with his chest. "But I'm not sure if this life I've now damned you to is worth the sacrifice. What kind of future have I given you but danger and fear? I don't want that for you. You deserve better." His fingers played with the ends of my hair.

I lifted my head and looked down into his silvery eyes ringed in gold. Putting my finger to his lips, I silenced him from anymore guilt and remorse. I wanted to do more than just silence him. I wanted to absolve him of those feelings. "Stop," I pleaded. "Stop blaming yourself. I won't have this dark cloud always over our heads."

"Are you really ordering me to not feel responsible for what happened to you?" he asked astonished, smirking crookedly.

"And if I am?"

He propped his head behind his arms. "Some days I think an angel sent you to me. And then there are days like today…and I am sure that Hell is laughing at me. When Death said that it would affect my life, I had never imagined this."

"Do you want me to pinch you again?"

His laugh sounded like sweet candy to my ears, especially after the night we'd had. I fell asleep in his arms, my head tucked under his chin. I didn't have a single nightmare, but my dreams were anything but peaceful. They were all of Chase and how he was slowly melting my heart.

~*~*~*~

I awoke in the morning stretched out in my bed. Rolling to my side, still half dazed with sleep, I reached for him. A small smile crept on my lips as I recalled falling asleep in his arms. He had turned a dreadful night into a memorable one and had been nothing but sweet, cuddly, and endearing, exactly what I had needed. And it's not like we haven't slept in the same bed before, but this time it meant so much more to me.

So when my hand reached across the bed and found nothing but cool sheets, my disappointment was immense. That sinking feeling settled in my chest, and I squeezed my eyes shut, waiting for it to go away. The thing was…I wasn't so certain it would just disappear, no matter how much I willed it.

Finally, I gave up, telling myself I was being irrational. It's not like he left me at the altar. He was just next door, probably still asleep and snoring like a pig. Staring at the empty space beside me, I could still see his face on the pillow. It didn't help that I could smell him everywhere.

On the sheets.

On me.

His essence lingered.

Memories of our evening together fluttered through my head. If there was one thing I learned from last night, it was that our bond allowed me to break through his demon haze easier. I'd sort of been able to before we were joined at the hip, but not like last night. Just remembering made my heart patter faster. It was convenient and a little empowering. I would totally be lying if I didn't say it secretly thrilled me.

Dragging my conflicted butt from bed, I could hear movement going on downstairs. I headed into the bathroom, splashed cold water on my face, and threw my hair up into a sloppy bun.

Mom was in the kitchen as she often was on her day off. Bacon sizzled on the stove. "How was the party last night?" she asked, flipping a perfectly golden piece of French toast.

My stomach growled loudly. "Surprisingly terrifying," I said dryly, taking a seat on one of the breakfast barstools.

She arched a brow. "See, and you thought this town was

going to be dull and boring. Good things come in small packages."

I choked on my OJ. She had no idea how true her words were. Spring Valley was anything but dull and boring, well, in the sense that my life was constantly in danger. The people in this town hadn't the first clue of what *really* went on in their quaint little hometown. "If you only knew," I muttered. Luckily my voice was muffled by the searing of bacon grease.

"Did you say something?" Mom asked, peering over her shoulder from the stove.

I just shook my head.

I didn't see Chase at all on Sunday and spent most of it hanging out with my mom. We could use some girl time. It was nice to pad around all day in knee-high socks, veg on junk food, and catch up on bad reality TV.

As much fun and relaxation I had on Sunday, I couldn't shake the fluttering in my heart, like little blips of panic. When that feeling only increased as night drew near, I knew Chase wasn't home.

He had gone out.

Those scattered feelings of unease I started to notice only happened when we were apart. The longer he was gone, the more it increased, a squeezing pressure in my chest. What was even crazier was I knew the precise nanosecond he got home.

Sighing in relief from the persistent and annoying ache in my heart, I wasn't very happy with this new development. I seriously did not want to be stressed out every time he decided to go somewhere.

The bigger question was, do I, or do I not, ask Chase if he had the same reaction. There would be nothing more humiliating and awkwardness if this was a one-sided byproduct of our bond. I didn't want to appear desperate and clingy.

I was not that girl.

Chapter 9

Monday came and Chase was in a mood—a dark mood. We hardly talked on the drive to school and once we got to the parking lot he took off, leaving Lexi and me behind.

"What's his deal?" I asked.

She just shrugged her dainty shoulders, blonde hair spilling over them and stared at her cousin's formidable back. "Who the heck knows. It's Chase. He doesn't need a reason to be pissy."

I'll say.

By the time I made it to chem class, I was actually feeling anxious. Today was the first time since Halloween night that I would see Brody. I wasn't sure how I should feel about that.

Chase was in his usual seat behind me, scowling and looking as grumpy as a bear. His eyes were zeroed in on Brody, and they were doing some weird eye-pissing match. Occasionally Brody would glance in my direction and I swear I heard Chase growl.

After the third time, I spun around in my chair, oblivious to the attention I was drawing. "Will you stop," I hissed at Chase.

He reclined in his seat, crossing his arms over his broad chest. "I warned him," he said darkly.

I heard my name just as I was about to go postal. "Ms. Morgan. Is there a problem I am unaware of?" Mr. Edgington interrupted my scolding.

Chase smirked and arched that damn brow with the silver hoop.

Right then, he was darn lucky I resisted the urge to pluck it from his eyebrow. Giving him a quick glare, I turned back toward the front of class and replied, "Nope. No problem."

A few kids snickered, knowing Chase and I had a history of getting on each other's nerves. "Good. Then let's proceed, shall we," Mr. Edgington said, pushing his dorky glasses back up the bridge of his sweaty nose.

I wasn't making excuse for Brody, but I was trying to protect Chase. Maybe Brody too. I wasn't entirely sure that Chase wouldn't literally rip his head off. I felt Chase's hands grip the desk behind me and Brody's eyes, like a red-handed thief, darted to the blackboard.

I rolled my eyes. This was going swell.

Peeking from under my lashes to my right, my eyes clashed with Brody's. I'd done a pretty bang up job of ignoring him since I walked into class, but here it was. Our first contact and Chase wasn't having it. Quickly, I shot my gaze back to the doodlings on my desk and tried with all my might to forget Brody even existed.

Chase was making that very difficult.

I was so hyper aware of Chase and the anger rolling off him that the room suddenly felt suffocating, as if the walls were closing in on me. The air was harder to breathe, and I couldn't wait for this class to end.

I don't know what happened. Maybe it was some kind of dominance power trip. Maybe it was some Neanderthal BS marking me his. Or maybe he just read the tense lines in my body. Whatever it was, it caught me off-guard.

I heard Chase exhale and shift forward in his seat, leaning close behind me. I practically jumped out of my seat when I felt his hand at the nape of my neck. He parted my long hair and started drawing lazy circles on the back of my neck with his finger.

Tingles shot down my spine, and I had to bite my lip to refrain from closing my eyes and sighing. Just his touch was enough to ease the tension and worries I'd been feeling. Conscious that we were smack dab in the middle of a chem lecture, I tried to ease away from his reach to no avail. It didn't matter how many times I swatted his hand away, he would chuckle low and start again. Finally, I just gave up.

Huge mistake. Monstrous.

It became distracting to a near point of explosive lust. I bit my lip – hard, just to keep from mortifying myself. It was definitely starting to get uncomfortable, and the second class ended I was going to pounce on him. Clarification – pounce as in I was going to give him the verbal lashing of the century, not pounce as in slamming him against the lockers and devouring him with just my mouth.

Damn him.

If he started to blow on my neck, I was going to lose it right there in the middle of Mr. Edgington's lesson on...shit. I had no idea what the heck we were supposed to be learning.

Before I had the chance to do anything that couldn't be undone, the bell rang—my saving grace. We were going to have to evoke a no touching in class policy ASAP. Grabbing my books, I stood up ready to give Chase an ass chewing. I sent him my signature evil glare with the promise that he would answer for his actions later, preferable when we were alone. Though maybe *alone* wasn't such a good idea.

Everyone shuffled out of class, practically pushing our way out. No one wanted to be in class longer than possible, but at the same time no one was overly eager to get to their next class either.

I should have seen this coming, but I guess he could still surprise me. The signs were all there. I knew them well now. I knew Chase.

No more than a foot out the classroom door and Chase had Brody pinned up against the lockers. Chase's fists clenched tight on Brody's shirt, his muscles tense. I hadn't even seen Chase move, and if I had to guess, no one else had either. The fact that he had used demon-speed in school was enough to be alarming. He knew damn better than to draw unwanted attention on himself.

I was starting to seethe right along with him, but for entirely different reasons. His were unreasonable and irrational, mine were sound and just. Yes, I got that Brody was a creep, but subjecting him to a thrashing every time he so much as looked in my general direction wasn't going to solve anything, except Chase getting expelled possibly.

A vein at Chase's neck ticked, and his jaw clenched. He was extremely pissed and struggling not to lose it. At this point it could go both ways, he was that close to the edge. "You look at her again and I'll rip your eyes out," he threatened a stunned Brody.

Beads of sweat glistened at Brody's hairline. "Look man, I don't know what you're deal is." A group had started to gather around us, like we needed to draw any more attention.

"I think you do. This is my final warning," Chase said.

From my angle I could see the flecks of amber melting into his eyes like liquid gold.

Shit on a shoe.

Fear encompassed Brody's brown eyes, and he shifted those pleading eyes to me, then back to Chase. "I swear. I don't even remember what happened on Saturday."

Convenient. But I actually believed him. There was too much distress and confusion in Brody's sappy eyes to be lying. Still didn't excuse him from being a bigger asstard than Chase. I frowned.

Chase on the other hand was a little harder to convince. "Let me refresh your memory," he said, tightening his grip.

Brody held up both his hands. "Whoa, wait. I assume that I must have done something worthy of your anger, but I swear, I'm sorry." When Chase didn't look remotely convinced, Brody added to his plea, "Really I am."

I touched a cautious hand to Chase's shoulder. "Chase," I warned, in a firm yet soft tone. I had to stop this now.

Chase flinched. He eased his clutch on Brody, but not without a good shove into the wall first for satisfaction. "Next time, not even Angel will be able to stop me from wiping the floor with your face."

"Was that necessary?" I asked, as we turned down the hallway.

"Define necessary?"

I huffed and hurried to my next class. Sometimes crossing words with Chase was so exhausting, and it was one of those days.

By the time school ended, I was fried. The more I simmered about what could have happened in the hallway, the angrier I got. He could have exposed himself. Lexi. Travis. Me. The drive home was utter silence. We were each mulling in our own parties of rage. Fun.

The moment my foot crossed over the threshold of my front

door, I rounded on him. "What the hell was that?" I demanded.

He wasn't the least put off by my disapproving tone. "I'm sick of him looking at you like you were a hot piece of ass. Not after what happened."

I rolled my eyes walking straight into the kitchen with him fast on my heels. "You didn't need to get all Rambo on me."

"That was for his benefit, not yours." His tone dropped below freezing, but I was too self-involved in my own anger to notice.

"Err!" I screamed, whipping around to face him. "You are the most frustrating guy in the universe, Chase Winters. You can't control who looks at me for God's sake. It's not your business."

Suddenly he was in my face, eyes gleaming like fiery meteorites. I gulped and raised my chin. He was not going to intimidate me.

A brow rose. "That's where you are wrong. It is my business. You. Are. My business."

I wanted to punt kick him in the nuts, and then stomp my foot down on his, except I couldn't see his foot. There was no space between us. "Just because I share your mark doesn't mean you control my life." Things were getting heated. Things were spinning wildly out of control.

He burned me with his eyes and said the most barbaric words that sent my world out of orbit. "You. Are. Mine."

We stood there toe-to-toe breathing heavily. I searched his eyes, unable to believe what had just come out of that gorgeous mouth. My entire body tingled. Oh, so not a good sign. "I'm not a piece of property," I said, taking a step back.

He angled his head, tugging on the sleeve of my cardigan. "Where do you think you're going?"

I smacked at his hand. "We're done." I wasn't sure if I meant that figuratively or literally.

His hand wrapped around my wrist, pulling me against his chest, eyes snapping with a ring of topaz. "We're just getting started," he countered, in a dark and sexy voice. The hand at my wrist slid under my sleeve. Sparks hummed as he touched my skin. There was nothing in the world I could compare it to.

I didn't want to be affected by this. Not by what he could make me feel. My body was screaming yes. It was like what happened in class today. He was always finding ways to touch me. "Why do you keep doing this to me?" I asked, flustered and flushed.

"Because I like to."

That wasn't really an answer. I drew in a deep breath, his scent infusing my senses, making me lightheaded. God, I like it too. "Chase," I whispered his name. It was my final attempt to stop this before it got out-of-hand, or maybe it was just the opposite. A plea for what I knew was to come.

Whatever it was, Chase took advantage. I tipped my head back, watching him with dark blue eyes. His breath stroked warmly against my lips, and I felt his lips curl right before he pressed them to mine. Both my hands were pressed against his chest. They fisted the front of his cotton t-shirt as I tried to catch my breath. I meant to push him away, but I only pulled him closer.

My brain had shut down.

Chase kissed like it would be his last, long and breathless. There was an overload of emotions mixing around inside me. As easy as it would be to blame this link between us for these berserk emotions, I knew it was a lie. Usually, I'm pretty good at lying to myself, really lying in general. But this time, I knew that these intense feelings had been there before the night I died.

Oh sweet mother Mary and Joseph. Lips like his should be forbidden.

He left me moonstuck.

My back hit something solid. Unperturbed, he lifted me, and I wrapped my legs around his waist as he hoisted me on the counter with a disturbing ease. My new position gave me a vantage point I was thoroughly enjoying, making me just a smidge taller than him. I sunk my hands into his dark hair keeping those sinful lips locked to mine. His fingers dug into my upper thighs.

Wa-wowzers.

The electricity between us charged the air throughout the

kitchen. His hands slid up my thighs, past my hips, and under my shirt. Simultaneously mine trailed down his spine and into the back pockets of his jeans. Lips smooth, his kisses were deep, scorching me to the very depth of my soul. Our tongues tangled in a dance as old as time. We were so caught up in each other that we didn't hear the squeaking of hinges until it was too late.

The front door creaked open followed by a girlish giggle that broke through our passionate cloud. Pulling our lips apart, I looked toward the door. Lo and behold, there was my mom entangled around Devin like a trollop. Forget the fact that I was in a similar position. This was my mom.

"Mom?"

"Angel?"

We both said in stunned unison.

Chapter 10

Mom's back hit the front door, and she rubbed the tension from her neck. Devin frowned. Chase grinned. And I jumped off the counter, utterly mortified.

"What are you doing?" I asked.

Mom ran her fingers down her caramel colored hair, trying to smooth away the tousled look courtesy of Devin. "I should probably be asking you the same thing, but it's pretty obvious what *you* were doing. On my kitchen counter nonetheless."

My cheeks turned a shade darker than beets. I was just glad I still had my shirt on. *Ugh.* The embarrassment. "I thought you were working today." Truthfully, I never knew when she worked anymore. It seemed like she was gone more than she was home. And if she did have the day off, she went out with Devin.

"As you can see, I'm not." Her lips formed a thin line.

Could this possibly get anymore awkward? And Chase was so not helping. I was two-seconds away from kicking him in the shin, anything to wipe that smirk off his mouth.

"Chloe, why don't I take Chase next door so you and Angel can talk," Devin volunteered, his hazel eyes looking displeased at his nephew.

"Good idea." She turned to Devin. "I'll call you later?"

Devin nodded his sandy hair out of his eyes. Mom and I both watched as Devin and Chase sauntered out the door.

God, he had a superb butt.

Mom cleared her throat.

Slowly, I tore my gaze from the closed door and met my mom's soft eyes. She moved from the door to the couch, and I reluctantly followed. "I'm thinking we need to have a few rules about boys in the house while I'm at work."

I sunk into the worn cushions. "What if we use the sock rule? If you are going to bring Devin to get your freak on, you put a sock on the front door. That way I'll know not to disturb you."

She sighed. "That wasn't exactly what I had in mind, but now that you mentioned it—" she said as if the thought had merit.

"Mom, gross," I interrupted before this suddenly became a house rule. "I was kidding. The last thing I want to think about every time I see a sock is you and Devin naked."

"I see your point, but the reality is I am gone most evenings, and now that you and Chase are more...involved, I don't want you to end up pregnant. You are too young to get tied down."

I pulled my knees up against my chest, hugging them. "Mom, it's not like that."

Her brow waggled. "Really? 'Cuz what I just saw looked

pretty intense."

There was no denying that. I could have said the same about her and Devin, but I knew she would play the adult card. Forget that I was turning eighteen soon. I fumbled with my hands, trying to find the words to explain what was between Chase and me. Not an easy task, especially since I myself didn't have a clue. "It's complicated."

"You don't have to tell me how complicated relationships can be. I just want you to be careful, not just with intimacy but with your heart as well. Seeing the two of you together makes me realize how serious things are. At the same time, I know that you are safe with Chase. He would never let anything harm you, but I don't want him breaking your heart either."

"That makes two of us," I mumbled.

She casually brushed aside a piece of hair from my face, and then a huge grin bloomed on her face, followed by an escaped giggle. "That. Was. Hysterical."

I just stared at her like she'd lost her mind.

"Oh my goodness, the look on your face when I opened the door—priceless," she said, still laughing.

My own laugh joined hers. It really had been comical after the fact. I might have had a loser for a father, but my mom made up for it in tenfold. She was the best. I don't know what I would have done without her.

~*~*~*~

The next morning, I hopped into my little white Fusion and drove myself to school. It was weird driving alone, not having to fight over stations with Chase and Lexi, not having to listen to Chase ridicule Lexi's outfit choice for being overly sexy and inappropriate for school. It was peaceful.

I hated it.

Chase had plans afterschool like most afternoons lately. Slivers of curiosity and suspicion were starting to weave in my belly. Where was he going all the time? What was so important? It's not like he had a job…This whole sneaking off thing was getting tiresome.

And yes, I was being nosey.

Call it female intuition, but I knew something fishy was going on. And I was going to figure it out.

Lexi, of course was no help. If it didn't directly involve her somehow, she wasn't the least bit concerned. She just shrugged her shoulders and said, "It's Chase. Everything he does is a mystery."

Ugh.

Why was I the only one who was worried?

Then there was the voice in my head. *Because you are closer to him than anyone has ever been.*

Sometimes the voice in my head could be such a nuisance.

The final bell rang on what turned out to be a very long school day. I went to my locker first to drop off my books and fished out my car keys. Stepping through the double front doors of the school, I watched stupefied from the sidewalk as a flashy silver car zoomed by.

It was impossible to mistake whose it was. I knew that car as well as I knew mine.

What I hadn't been prepared for was the person seated comfortably in the passenger seat. Too cozy for my liking. The flaming red hair was distinctive.

Sierra.

The color drained from my face in disbelief and hurt. His eyes clashed with my own as I stood on the sidelines looking an idiot. And for a split-second, I swear I saw a spark of regret and maybe even pleading. But in that moment, I didn't care. The lancing pain turned rapidly into searing rage.

Then I caught Sierra's smirk as she noticed me. The gleam of satisfaction in her eyes made me want to go nuclear.

How dare he make me look like a fool? Make me think he cared.

I did the only sane thing a girl in my position would do. I flipped him off.

She was the last person in the universe I expected him to be sneaking off with. *She* was his so-called *plans*. For the first time since he saved me, I thought our bond truly, utterly, sucked ass.

It was a curse.

If he was fooling around with Sierra then this whole being linked crapola was a shamble. It didn't mean jack, and this *thing* I thought we had going between us was bogus, nothing more than my overactive sick imagination and Chase's cruel manipulation.

Damn half-demons.

He really was a heartless asshole.

In my head, I called him every colorful swear I could come up with. A sailor would have been proud.

How could I have possibly thought that a guy like Chase would be so infatuated with *me*? Would care about *me*? Would love *me*? Especially knowing he could have any girl he wanted. He could have Sierra. Why would he want to tie himself down to me for the rest of his life? It didn't make sense that fateful night, and it made even less sense now.

What an utter fool I'd been. Just the other day he had his tongue blissfully down my throat. Then he turned around and snuck off with Sierra. And what pissed me off the most was that he made me look like a sucker. So here I was surrounded by dust, staring after the tail end of his car, flipping him the bird. My eyes welled with tears I refused to shed.

Or more like, I didn't want to shed on the likes of Chase Winters. He didn't deserve an ounce of my hurt, but the heart wasn't easy to dupe. And right now, mine was shattering into a gazillion tiny, jagged pieces.

I wiped the sleeve of my blue cardigan over my eyes, erasing a few tears that had escaped. Through the smudge of my blurring vision, I saw the flashing of his red brake lights. My heart skipped, only to fracture again with an overwhelming new surge of agony when his silvery car turned onto the main road, full speed ahead.

The lying snake was going to pay.

As soon as I was able to pick my crushed heart off the concrete and piece it back together. Not only had Chase pummeled my heart, it was also the realization that *I* had cared. *I* had more than cared. *I* had started to fall in love with him. And that was as much a punch to the gut as seeing him go off with slutty Sierra was.

Suddenly, I couldn't breathe.

Pressure squeezed in my chest and everything around me went silent. My feet felt super glued to the sidewalk. I couldn't move. It wasn't until a girl in a lower class accidently bumped into me that I stumbled back into the present. Running a shaky hand through my hair, I walked to my car like a mummy wrapped in anguish.

The ride back to my house seemed to take hours. I was numb. All I wanted to do was crawl into bed, pull down the blinds, and wallow in self-pity. But the longer he was gone, the stronger the pounding of anxiety knocked in my chest.

My bed was the only thing on my mind when I walked through the front door. I hit the silver comforter like a sobbing hot mess. The tears couldn't be repressed any longer, and I needed to let go of all the hurt building inside me. It was like a flood of raw emotion.

Alone, I shut myself off from the world. I shut myself off from *him*. Ignored the phone calls. Dismissed the text messages. But as long as he was gone, my body wouldn't give into the sleep I desperately wanted. Sleep – the one chance to flee from the ache.

I watched the clock above my door, as the little hand clicked and clicked in slow motion around in a circle. The room darkened with nightfall, while I lay curled into a ball, wishing this connection between us was severed. Then on a sharp intake of air, I opened my eyes and the anxiousness was gone. Every muscle in my body relaxed, losing the tension that seemed to have increased with each passing minute.

Shitbrick was home.

What I wanted to do was get up, stomp across his yard, karate chop the door, and give him the lashing of the decade. However my worn body had other plans, lashes fluttered close as I pulled the covers to my chin and promptly fell in a deep slumber.

Tomorrow would be another matter entirely.

~*~*~*~

I was up at the crack of dawn, something that was completely unheard of, but the little sleep I'd gotten had been sound. It might have been completely naïve of me, but I had almost hoped that when I awoke, this gut-retching hurt would be gone.

It wasn't.

Bracing myself on the bathroom sink, I groaned in horror at the sight that stared back at me. I looked like I'd been ravished by a zombie. And these puffy, red, and swollen eyes weren't going to miraculous vanish.

I cursed him a thousand different ways standing there in the middle of the bathroom mirror before I decided that *I* wasn't going to let him see my pain. If it killed me, I was going to look fabulous. Nothing a shower, two frozen spoons, and some heavy makeup couldn't fix.

Or so I prayed.

After a long, steaming hot shower, I plodded to my closet. Tearing open the doors, I started to rummage through my clothes like a woman on a mission. Then I realized my wardrobe sucked some serious ass. That was all it took for a wave of heartache to bombard me again. I slid down the wall and put my head on my knees. Wet hair fell over my shoulders.

I needed to be stronger than this. It wasn't like we had a commitment to each other, but tell that to my bleeding heart. Why was what we had between us, so complex? I deserved better. I deserved respect and honesty. I picked myself off the floor with renewed determination.

I was one of the first to arrive at school, leaving before Chase had a chance to catch me. It would be impossible to not run into him, but snubbing was another matter entirely. And that was just what I had done. However, chem class was unavoidable and the few others we now had together thanks to his demon persuasion.

At the first whisper of his breath against my neck I nearly hit the class ceiling. "The silent treatment. Really, Angel? I thought you were more creative than that."

"Shocking. I always thought you were a douchebag. Now I know you are." So much for biting my tongue.

"Angel Eyes, it's not what it seems."

"Don't. Call. Me. That." I gritted my teeth.

"Meet me at my house, after school. I'll prove it." The end of his pencil outlined a pattern on the back of my shirt.

As if. Even as the thought fluttered in my head, I couldn't suppress the shudder that tore through me. *Damn him.* Leaning forward on my desk, I tried to stay out of his reach.

He chuckled under his breath.

I wanted to jam that pencil down his throat. He wouldn't be chuckling then.

As soon as the bell rang, I was the first out of my seat and through the door. I was surprised I'd made it so far. By the end of the day, I was split in half. There was no denying that a huge part of me wanted to tell him to stick his explanation where the sun don't shine. Another part of me, a slim part of me, wanted to hear him worm out of this without my hand connecting to his cheek.

When I pulled into my driveway, his car was already parked sleekly in his. *What the hell?* How had he beaten me home? It was now or never. It turned out, my feet made the decision for me.

I marched across his yard, each stomp getting heavier and heavier until I reached the steps of his white porch. I put a hand on the banister. No way was I meeting him anywhere. I was going to tell him off, lose his number, and forget he was alive. That was the plan.

The plan was blown to shit.

The door opened before I had a chance to knock. I stood on the porch seething with pent up rage. Before I even registered what I was doing, my hand was sailing through the air straight for Chase's perfect cheekbone. Unfortunately my hand never made the connection. And it burned my blood. It was the least he had deserved after the way he had made me feel.

His hand wrapped around my wrist, and his thumb rubbed over my pulsing vein. "You are a naughty girl."

I let a strangled cry right before I launched myself at him. Nothing beat a woman scorned. My fist beat against his chest wildly with unrestrained vigor and was anything but effective to my utter frustration. I wanted to hurt him as much as he had hurt me. But it was like hitting a solid wall, and I only ended up bruising my hands in addition to my already bruised heart.

To say I went ballistic was an understatement.

His arms engulfed me, holding me until the fight was drained out of me. My breathing was coming in quick pants having exerted so much energy. I expected him to laugh at me or tease me, anything but the harsh regret I heard in his voice.

"Angel, it's not what you think," he whispered in my ear.

I went limp in his arms, my heart squeezing. "I'm not an idiot, Chase."

"I never said you were, but you are acting like a fool." That was it. I clamped my teeth on his arm and bit down. His arm released me on a curse like hot coal. "Damn it, Angel." Firmly he spun me around to face him. "What can I say to you that will make you believe that there is nothing between Sierra and I? There never was and there never will be. Not now." There was desperation in his tone that I never thought possible.

I narrowed my eyes. "Why? Because of this stupid mark?" I snorted. "Please, don't let it stand in the way."

He groaned, running a frustrated hand through his midnight hair. "Ugh, Angel, you are such an impossible brat."

"Me!" I shrieked. He had some nerve. His hand reached out to me again. "Touch me, and I will make mincemeat out of you," I threatened through my clenched teeth. My jaw was starting to throb, along with my head.

Travis snickered from inside the house. I hadn't even noticed him or that we had an audience. My rage had disbursed all my focus on Chase. Nothing new, he always consumed me in one way or another.

Chase scowled, his whiskey rimmed eyes never leaving mine. "Travis, don't you have some brain cells to kill?"

I saw Travis lean over the back of the couch. "Are you kidding? And miss Angel tear you to shreds? This is way more entertaining."

"Fine," said Chase, a vein at his temple pulsing. "We're leaving."

"I am not going anywhere with you," I announced prepared to hug one of the porch columns if necessary.

His eyes flashed as he engulfed the doorway. "You can walk out of here on your own, or I can help you. And trust me, I would enjoy it."

"Why should I go anywhere with you, you two-timing low-life," I snapped.

"So I can show you what I've been doing…and it hasn't been Sierra."

I rolled my eyes. "Fine," I reluctantly agreed. He had piqued my interest. "Travis, if I don't come back…avenge me."

Dimples in full view, Travis laughed. "It would be my pleasure."

Chapter 11

"Where are you taking me?" I asked, grudgingly hopping into his overpriced car. He was keeping a close eye on me, and I knew that if I made a break for it, he would stop me before I'd even had the chance to take one step. Why had I agreed to let him hijack me without giving me any information?

After last night, he was lucky I was even speaking to him.

"To get some answers," he said short.

"Stop being so mysterious. It's annoying." His grip tightened on the wheel, and I secretly grinned inside. Good, let him get agitated.

"You aren't going to give up are you?" he asked.

"Not a chance in hell. You got me in the car, the least you can do is tell me where we are going. You owe it to me." I leaned against the door, putting as much space as the car allowed between us.

"You would see it that way." He sighed. "It's not what you think. Sierra has been helping me."

"Oh, I'm sure she has," I sneered, narrowing my gaze.

"You are utterly impossible," he declared, shaking his head, the light from the window emphasized his chiseled cheekbones.

I pivoted in my seat. "Don't you dare make this about me. I'm two-seconds away from jumping out of the car."

"You won't even reach the handle before I got to you," he heaved heavily, clearly unhappy with the direction this convo was going. "Look, before this turns into a full out combat, just listen." He looked over at me waiting to see what I would do or say next.

I did nothing.

Turning his eyes back to the miles of road stretched out before us, he took advantage of my silence. "Sierra's parents are both half-demons."

That was nothing new to me. Lexi had told me about her parents. I didn't really see what they had to do with any of this. Were they pushing Chase and Sierra together? The thought filled me with red hot jealousy. I bit my tongue and let him continue.

"They know a lot of people within the Divisa community. We've all heard rumors about humans being bonded to half-demons, but that's just it—rumors. I never really put much stock in any of that crap. Until you. Sierra however, totally bought into it mainly because of her parents. I asked her for help locating someone who might know more about our connection, about what might happen to you because of it."

Wow. I sort of felt lame.

He wasn't sneaking off and hooking up with that skank Sierra.

But even so, I absolutely hated knowing that they had spent any time together just on principal, even if it was for a good cause.

When the initial shock wore off, I asked. "And you found someone?"

His lips twitched. "I found an extremely knowledgeable Divisa on the outskirts of town. He might be able to shed some light on this whole connection we got going. That's what Sierra and I were doing, tracking him down. Her parents only had a name. When we found him, they made a call. He agreed to talk with us."

"And Sierra was just helping you out of the kindness of her black heart? Bullshit. What does she get? What did you promise her in return?" It was common knowledge that there was no love lost between Sierra and I.

"Look, I know that she can be…"

"A bitch," I supplied.

He grinned. A low beam of sunlight hit him through the window, highlighting streaks of midnight in his hair. "That's putting it nicely. But she just wants to help."

"You expect me to believe that load of crap?"

"I do. I've never lied to you, Angel. I am not about to start now," he declared.

I looked away, staring out the window as rows upon rows of dense trees rolled by. "Do you really think he will be able to help?"

I finally asked.

"I hope so. He is our only lead so far." He gave me a crocked grin. "Hold tight, this is going to be the ride of your life."

I crossed my fingers as he drove us out of Spring Valley and onto the highway. There was something relaxing about the way he drove. I shouldn't have felt that. Not. At. All. He didn't exactly have the best track record with cars. You'd think that I would have been scared to death to get in another car with him, but that wasn't the case. Somehow Chase always managed to make me feel safe and secure.

Even when I was pissed to the max at him.

I was totally going to blame that on this bond. Also, I couldn't help but notice that just being near him made me feel at peace. "So what's his name?" I asked, tucking my hands into the pockets of my teal hoodie.

Peering at me from under insanely thick lashes, he grinned. "Ives."

"Ives," I echoed, scrunching my nose. "What kind of name is Ives?"

Not long after that he turned off the main road and down what I wouldn't have even deemed a road. It was more like a path, a ghostly path. When he pulled up to a house that looked more like an abandoned shack, I figured we were lost. Boards twisted chaotically, falling off and the wood was miss-matched and different colors. "Why didn't you use the GPS?"

He gave me an odd look. "We're here. What do I need the GPS for?

"You're joking," I snorted. "He lives here? A rat couldn't live here."

"Angel Eyes, sometimes you can be such a snob."

I gave him the stink eye. *Me?* I'm not the one driving a car that obviously cost more than this guy's house. Reluctantly following him out of the car, I waited on the rattling and rickety porch as Chase knocked on the door.

"It's open," called a voice from inside.

"Are you sure this is a good idea?" I whispered. "I better come out of here alive," I warned unable to shake this eerie vibe.

Chase grinned devilishly. "Where's your sense of adventure?"

"I left it at home with my common sense," I replied surly.

The decrepit door creaked like an old woman as Chase pushed it open. When we looked inside the air swirled with dust particles through a tiny stream of light. The uneven floorboards groaned as Chase walked over the threshold. His body was taunt and on alert, looking for anything out of the ordinary. He might be here for answers, but that didn't mean he wasn't cautious. Chase was always on guard.

It was just one of his many annoying traits.

"In the back," yelled the voice again. It was deep and sounded like aged wine. Maybe he was as old as this dump.

I followed close behind Chase. Possibly too close. I could smell him over the musty, pine scent. Sexy. Wicked. Yummy. Unable to help myself, I inhaled deeply, forgetting where we were or why we were here.

He stopped abruptly right outside a doorway, and I bumped ungracefully into him, the whole arms flailing deal. "Did you just sniff me?" he asked with a lazy grin.

I regained my balance. "And if I did?"

He just shook his head and stepped through the door. The room wasn't exactly what I'd been expecting. Papers were scattered haphazardly on top a large mahogany desk. And the man behind the desk was an even bigger shock. He was maybe in his forties, with brown wavy hair, a day's growth covered his face, and...he was smoking hot for an old dude. Gently smiling, he indicated for us to take a seat in the two chairs.

I didn't move.

"Angel, you can close your mouth now," Chase whispered in my ear, pulling me from my gawking state.

I gave him an evil glare from the corner of my eye, and then planted my butt in front of the massive desk. Trying to ignore my flushing cheeks, I glanced at the rest of the room. Framed maps lined the walls along with a whole lot of other ancient mumble jumble.

"Wow. I was skeptical when Magnolia called." I said, looking me over. I assumed Magnolia was Sierra's mom. His green eyes brimmed with wonder. "You really do ooze his signature. Could I possibly see the marks?"

"I don't do show and tell," I snapped. No matter how hot Ives might be, I wasn't ready to lift up my shirt for any yahoo.

"Not going to happen," Chase refused, echoing my rude remark. "You'll just have to take our word for it. They're there and identical."

"I can tell you it burned like a mother," I said, offering that little tidbit. The memory still tortured me some nights, even some days. It was the kind of pain I never wanted to feel again. The marks were unique to the demon bloodlines. You could tell which demon had sired the half-breed by the mark they were born with. Travis and Lexi share the same symbol—the same demon blood.

Ives reclined from the desk, putting his hands behind his head. "Hm. That sounds about right. It's been quite some time since I have seen a bond such as yours—one linking a human with a half-demon. I will answer any questions that I can, but I must warn you, I am no expert. It's a phenomenon few understand and grasp even less."

Goodie gumdrops. It was our lucky day.

"But wow, what the two of you have is strong," he added.

Chase cut the friendly pleasantries. "How about you start with what you do know," he prompted, not entirely impressed with Ives. He was such a cynic.

Ives palm tree green eyes twinkled. "There are three various bonds. If the information I've gathered over the years is accurate, yours is a soulbond—a linking of souls. It is believed that the circumstances surrounding the connection play into factor as to the kind of link that is shared between the two involved. There must be an extremely strong desire for the completion to take place and also a sacrifice from the half-demon. Do you have any idea what your sacrifice was?" he asked Chase.

"Yeah, my sanity," he mumbled under his breath.

I kicked him.

Chase raised a curious brow at me.

Finding humor in our behavior, Ives lips turned up at the corners. He folded his hands together on top of the desk. "I can draw my own conclusions. Getting back to the connection…There is a contingent to the bond. The more time you spend together, the stronger your bond will become."

Oh crap on a stick.

I chewed on my bottom lip. "What do you mean by time?" I asked.

His clear green eyes met mine. "From what I've learned, each moment you are together tightens the link between you. Even just being in the same house, the same school can strengthen the connection."

"Err, what about being neighbors? Is there a radius on this together aspect? Are we talking few feet, a few miles?" I asked.

"Hmm, good question. I take it you live next to each other?" We nodded in unison.

"I can't pinpoint an exact distance. It doesn't work that way, but it is something that I would tell you to experiment with. A few miles would be my guess," Ives informed.

"So by us being neighbors…" I began, trying to put together the pieces and wrap my head around this. "We are potentially forging our connection to each other without trying?" *Dear God.*

"Potentially—yes. From what I can sense…most definitely," Ives confirmed with a serious expression.

Chase groaned and I squeaked.

After a few moments of sinking silence I heard Chase ask, "What happens if we are separated?"

The computer screen on his desk flickered black from inactivity. "For short periods of time—nothing. It's the long timeframes that you need to worry about. The tighter your link to each other is, the harder a separation can be, even crucially painful. It starts out with just a tightness in the chest and then progresses to difficulty breathing, only to get worse and worse the more drawn out the length is."

Pure panic filled me. Chase reached over and twined our

fingers together, offering me comfort. There he went again, trying to be sweet. But this time, it was appreciated and effective. The alarm I felt moments ago dissipated.

"Enough to kill us?" Chase asked what was in both our thoughts. Had he saved me, only to possibly send us both to the grave?

Ives tapped the end of a pencil on the desk. "Not that I have ever seen, but it can weaken you to the point of death."

"Well, that sounds fun…maybe if you were sadistic," I mumbled.

Ives mouth twitched. I could tell he was amused by me. Who could really blame him? I was just a ball of sunshine.

Ives pushed up the sleeves of his black cardigan. "Let's do a little test, shall we?" he sprung on us sounding like a scientist.

"I'm a sucky lab rat," I assured Ives. *A test?* I didn't like the sound of that and by the stiffening of hothead beside me, neither did he. We were both afraid of what the conclusions might be.

"I couldn't help but notice how upset you got Angel when I mentioned the pain you could encounter if kept apart. Then Chase, you reached for her hand. Why?"

Chase angled his head and looked at him calculatedly, like he was trying to figure out his angle. "I was trying to offer her comfort," he replied, shrugging like it was no big deal.

"And Angel, did it work? Was he able to take away the fear

you were feeling?"

I looked from Ives to Chase feeling exposed. "Maybe."

Ives grinned. "I'll take that as a yes. What I think neither of you realized is the depth of the connection that is already in motion." His eyes sought Chase's. "Chase, you can feel Angel's emotions. What she is feeling and in return act on what her emotions are telling you. When you touch her, you take away her pain, her fear, and give her comfort, solace. She can also offer the same to you. Together, the two of you are indirectly responsible for the other's well-being, for their happiness."

Neither of us looked convinced—or thrilled by this revelation.

I scowled, not liking the path this conversation was taking. I seemed to find myself more and more attached to Chase—without even trying.

"What are you feeling now, Angel?" Ives asked quietly.

"Like I want to stab him," I answered, attempting boredom.

"And Chase…"

A hint of smirk crossed Chase's lips. He reclined in his seat like he didn't have a care in the world, except of course for the little tick in his neck. It was little things like that I noticed and maybe more... He wasn't any happier about our little experiment than I was. At least we were in agreement on something. "Like she is stabbing me," he replied.

I rolled my eyes.

"Good. This is good."

Oookay. How he thought this was good was mind boggling.

"Now I want you to take her hands," Ives instructed.

Chase looked at him from across the desk like the man was insane. "So she can bite my head off. No way. I'm not stupid. I don't see what the point of this is," Chase argued, clearly not feeling this little *test*.

Ives lifted his brow challenging him. "I wouldn't have pegged you for a quitter."

Ding. Ding. Ding. Thanks Ives for pushing Chase's manhood button. Of course he wasn't going to back away from the test now. Turning in his chair toward me, he held out his hands. I didn't move and kept my arms crossed. No one said I had to cooperate in this twisted game.

"Angel," Chase growled.

This was stupid. My eyes were like little blue flames as they attached with his. There were tiny specks of gold breaking through the icy silver. "Fine," I spat and laced my fingers with his, expecting nothing to happen, except many more irritation. I couldn't have been more wrong.

Or maybe I was being difficult because I was more afraid of what would happen.

The instant his skin touched mine, a cool wash of calm

overcame me. I knew I should have been annoyed, but I couldn't think past Chase touching me, watching me so intently with those silvery eyes. Maybe if I was made of stone, instead of the pile of mush he turned me into.

"Did I mention that I hate tests," I said sulking, my eyes still captured in his.

Ives chuckled from behind his desk. "Success I presume." He seemed to be enjoying this a little too much. It was kind of warped in my mind. He propped his elbows on the desk. "With that out of the way, let me ask you…have you noticed any additional attention, Angel? Like making more friends, or guys suddenly noticing you?"

"Err, maybe," I replied, thinking about Brody and a few others. I wasn't sure I was going to like where this was heading.

"You know that Divisa ward off human contact, but Angel, in your case, it seems you give off the opposite—you attract them."

Chase straightened in his chair, ears perked and attention at full alert. "You've got to be shitting me. Is this some kind of cruel joke?"

"Afraid not," Ives reassured with just a hint of a smile, knowing very well what was going through Chase's head. "At least until the bond is fully complete. That is if you decide to complete. Until that time though, she will draw all manner of attention. It's proven to be different for each link."

Chase frowned.

"And to think I thought it was my sparkling personality," I said dryly.

Ives grinned, shaking his head at me. "If I was twenty years younger, I just might have given Chase a run for his money."

I felt Chase stiffen beside me.

Did he just make a pass at me? Stranger things have happened true, but this took the cake. I was starting to like Ives. At least he had good taste.

"But something tells me that he wouldn't let you go without a fight. I've heard the rumors swirling about you Chase Winters. I don't think I would like to die just yet."

Oh just dandy.

His reputation preceded him.

"You mentioned that there were three kinds of bonds," Chase said, moving things back to safer ground. I'd forgotten that little bit of info.

Ives nodded in affirmation. "Yes the triforce. We have already distinguished soulbond which is what you two have. There is also heartbond and bodybond."

Interesting. I'd like to know how the others varied from ours, but Chase rattled off another question before I had a chance to ask.

"Is there a way to break the bond?" Chase asked, moving

right on. I figured he didn't even want to touch upon Ives harmless flirtation.

My heart rate went through the roof. Chase's gaze slid to mine, and I knew he could sense my panic. This whole emotion sharing thing sucked big time.

"Death," Ives said simply.

Bummer. That put the atmosphere in a somber mood. My expression fell just as Chase's phone rang. He excused himself and walked to the back of the room.

"I don't know if I envy him or pity him," Ives commented in a low voice.

"I can't decide if I should be flattered or offended," I retorted.

He laughed, his eyes crinkling at the ends. It was a pleasant sound. "I can see why he made such a vast sacrifice. Most of our kind don't socialize with outsiders. Not to say it doesn't happen, but it's less complicated if we don't. That said, I don't know if there is another girl with the gall to stand up to Chase. He is enamored by you and you with him." He lounged back in his chair, twirling a pencil between his fingers. "To truly keep the other safe, you must bind more than just your souls—soulbond isn't enough. You need to complete the triforce—Heart. Body. Soul."

"Heart, body, and soul?" I mumbled confused.

"You got it. Otherwise, forces beyond your control will make it next to impossible to survive as you are, sort of in limbo. You aren't human, but you are tied to a half-demon. There are other things as well, abilities that could have been transferred from Chase. Your bond was forged by desperate love. Love is powerful. Don't under estimate its strength.

Stop the presses. There was too much going on in his words. He had me bouncing from left to right. What I did get was…he thought Chase loves me. I might have powers, and something about us being binding our heart, body, and soul. Was that something other than what our current state was?

There is one catch however…" Ives said.

Of course there was.

"It's never been done before," he finished.

I am pretty sure my eyes bugged out. So what I gathered from all that mumble jumble was that the binding triforce had never been completed before. Yet Ives thought that Chase and I should be some kind of magical guinea pigs and attempt all three bindings.

Yeah, I am not so sure about that.

Chase came back before I could bombard Ives with a gazillion questions. "Come on Angel, let's go. We're done here." There wasn't any wiggle room for argument in his statement, and I really didn't want to expel the energy to do so. Ives had given me much to think about, putting my pretty little head on the verge of information overload.

Chase thanked Ives and shook his hand goodbye, before ushering me out of the shack. "What we're you talking about before we left?" Chase questioned as he started the car. It purred silently to life.

I flashed him a sassy grin. "How magnificent I am and how extremely lucky you are to have me in your life," I replied smugly.

He snorted and put the car into gear. "What did he really say, because he most definitely did not spew that kind of nonsense?"

Crossing my arms, I glared straight ahead trying to pretend we weren't flying down the road at the speed of light. "That you're a dick and I should run now while I still have the chance."

This time he flashed me a grin that was mouthwatering. "You can run Angel, but you can't hide."

Chapter 12

After that it was pretty quiet in the car. I seethed most of the way home ready to bolt from the close confinements of the car. Being in a small space with Chase, Chase's ego, and my anger was becoming uncomfortably crowded.

"Are you done pouting, Angel Eyes?" he asked when we were almost home.

"For your information, I am not pouting. I'm pissed."

"Either way it's cute."

He was the most insufferable, narcissistic, jackass on the planet. Somehow that got me thinking about Ives. "How does Ives know about this stuff?"

"It happened to him."

"Seriously?"

"Dead serious."

"Cute. Is he still bound to a human?"

Chase shrugged. "I don't know. One of the conditions of him seeing us was that we didn't ask him personal questions."

Debating whether or not I should press the fact that I was dying to know what happened between Ives and the human he was linked to. It was going to drive me insane. Were they still linked? How did it happen? Was it a soulbond like ours? Were they dead? All of these questions were reeling in my head when I heard Chase swear out of nowhere.

"What the hell?"

Without any warning, he whipped the car to the shoulder of the road. Gravel spit out from under the tires as he slammed on the brakes. I followed his gaze to the woods along the side of the road and just caught a glimmer of red shooting through the dense trees.

Then I heard the handle of his door pop open. When I looked back to him, he was already out of the car. "What are you doing?" I demanded, my heart picking up.

"Hunter. Stay put. You got that?" Chase ordered, like he was the highest Supreme Court.

I blinked.

"Angel, I mean it," he added. Every muscle in his body was tense, and his eyes began to glow like shooting comets. It wasn't yet dark but it wasn't long before we lost all sunlight. There were just a few twinkling stars breaking out into the blue sky. It was one of the nights were you could see both the sun and the moon.

I sulked in the seat. "Fine," I huffed, sinking into the leather upholstery with my arms crossed. I stared straight ahead even as my heart leaped into my throat. He was leaving me alone. By my lonesome, while he went after a hunter.

Yeah, I wasn't a happy camper.

When the driver's side door clicked closed, I turned in my seat just in time to see Chase's image blur before my eyes into the barren forest. This time of year the trees were just a shell of bark, but the forest floor was blanketed in dried, crumpled leaves.

I despised the woods and all the spine-chilling, terrible things that seem to migrate there. And I wasn't talking about bears, lions, or even wood elves. There were much, much worse things lurking in these woods.

Another minute passed, I waited just to make sure he didn't circle around and check on me. I wouldn't put it past him. He might have thought chasing a hunter alone was a good idea, but I on the other hand, had a different opinion. He could be such a damn prickly thorn in my side. The longer I sat in this car, the more certain I was that he was in trouble.

Digging for my phone, I punched in the only number I knew would help Chase's stupid ass. He answered on the second ring.

"Travis, I think Chase is in danger." I said so fast that I wasn't sure he understood me.

"Where are you?" Travis's calm voice asked. He was probably used to Chase doing senseless and stupid things.

I gave him a quick rundown of where I thought we were, and how dumbass had gone after a hunter alone. He dropped the fbomb before informing me that he would be there in minute. And when one of them says *minute*, they literally mean minute.

But sitting in Chase's car like a morsel for any hellish thing to snack on, made the seconds feel like hours. When I saw Travis's car roll up next to Chase's, my heart thumped wildly. In my mind, too much time had passed since he had gone in the woods. Alone. We needed to go after him now. I couldn't explain the sense of hurry. It was just there, gnawing at my insides.

I jumped out of Chase's car the same time Travis jumped out of his. If I knew Travis, he would order me about just as Chase did, and I was having none of it. Not this time.

"*You* are staying here," Travis ordered.

As if. And so predictable. "I'm coming with you, or I'll go on my own. You can't stop me."

He saw the set of determination in my face. "If anything happens to you Angel…" He let his words linger gravely in the air. "There is no saving you this time. Hell takes your soul. For good. No bartering. Do you understand that?" He didn't wait for me to answer as he ranted on. "And I am pretty sure Chase will send me there after you if he finds out I let you come tracking in the woods."

I crossed my arms over my chest. "Tough shit. Plus at least I won't be in Hell alone."

"Cute, Angel. Real cute. I am not ready to die, so you are

141 | P a g e

staying put. This isn't a joke. He left you behind for a good reason." He stalked off toward the bare trees assuming the subject was finished.

Little did he know. Plus who the heck was laughing? I followed right on his heels before he decided to go all warp speed and leave me on my own. "Travis, please," I tugged on the sleeve of his arm. "I *need to see* that he is okay. I can't explain it, I just need to."

He let out a long sigh. The setting sun was at his back, haloing him in a soft glow. A gentle crisp breeze played with the ends of his blond hair. "You are only going to slow me down. I can find him faster on my own."

True. Tears of frustration and worry started to pool in the corner of my eyes.

He relented like a true guy, uncomfortable with a woman's tears. It was a low card to play, but it was effective. "Try to keep up," he grumbled unhappily.

We weaved in and around the trees as soundlessly as possible. It was much harder for me, and he kept the speed more to my pace, but I could tell he was itching to take off.

"Stay close," he whispered, turning his head over his shoulder.

We traveled deeper into the thick forest, cutting off some of our moonlight. I don't know how Travis knew where to go, but I just assumed it was one of his half-demon traits.

"I hear voices," I said quietly to his back.

He looked over his shoulder and gave me a strange look.

"What?"

He shook his gloriously blonde head. "Nothing, it's just that you picked up the voices the same time I did."

Odd. "Well, I can't tell what they are saying."

Travis grinned. "Chase is giving somebody hell."

Of course he was.

"Come on, we can't let him have all the fun."

Travis's idea of fun was subjective. I swear he thought his real life was a video game.

I stuck to him like bees to honey, so of course when he halted in his tracks, I rammed into his back. Travis's reflexes were faster than a jackrabbit and he avoided tripping. I wasn't so lucky.

Pushing the hair out of my face, I glared at Travis's back. "What the he—" A flash of red caught my eye cutting off my wicked tongue. It was the same shade of red that I had seen on the side of the road. A girl about my age stood a few feet in front of us. Her hair contrasted against her black clothing, a pretty blend of red and blonde, not bold like the hoodrat Sierra's. I was so stumped at first, I couldn't figure out what this girl was doing in the middle of the woods by herself, or what the weird contraption she had poised in her hands.

Then it hit me like a kick to gut.

It was a bow.

Following the line of her crossbow, I let out a ghastly gasp. Her arrow was pulled back tight and taut and centered on...

Chase.

My stomach dropped off earth. *Oh, for freak's sake.*

Travis and I had come into the small clearing to the right of the hunter and Chase was maybe twenty feet away, looking downright pissed the hell off. My eyes met his extremely displeased glare. Someone wasn't happy to see me. *Screw him.*

Unable to take Chase's murderous stare, I peeked over at Travis. He was zapped frozen beside me.

What the shit. Why wasn't Travis doing something? Why hadn't he gone all demon-berserk and taken down this girl? I didn't get it. He was like a statue with his mouth wide opened, staring at the red-headed girl like he'd just seen a ghost.

I elbowed him in the side.

No response.

Travis picked a hell of a time to check out.

I glanced back at Chase, hoping he had a plan.

"Angel," he rumbled. "I told you to stay put. Will you never just do what I ask?"

Can you believe this guy? Here I am, worried about him, trying to rescue him and he is scalding me. "Uh, it looks like you need me," I said, stating the obvious.

He was talking to me, but he kept his eyes on the so-called hunter. "Do you honestly think I couldn't have handled one little hunter? Your lack of faith in me is heartbreaking."

"As touching as this is, will you both shut up before I decide to shoot one of you," the petite hunter threatened, still poised to kill.

I shut my trap for once and chewed on my lip, trying to devise a plan to get us all out of here without an arrow sticking out of someone's flesh. Formulating a plan on the spot was hard stuff. I don't know how the hell Chase did this. He was definitely a more spur-of-the-moment kind of guy.

To make matters worse, my deep thought process was interrupted by the redheaded Pocahontas. "So you are the girl Chase Winters would do anything for…kill for even."

I didn't like her tone, or the way she spoke Chase's name, like she knew him. The tip of my tongue was burning with insults, all of which would probably get him shot, though I was pretty sure he was faster than the arrow.

She pursed her lips eyeballing me. "You are not at all what I expected."

Chase flinched, drawing her attention back to her mark. He had done so deliberately. Every bone marrow in my body told me so—to take her attention off me. "What does it matter to you?" Chase asked. His eyes were starting to change colors.

This girl had balls, I'll give her that. "It's my business to know everything about Divisa, including their weaknesses."

That was it. She'd done it now. I have to say, she wasn't the brightest hunter in the woods.

"You touch a hair on her head," he roared. "And I'll make you wish you had never stepped foot in this town again."

Again? What did he mean again? He knew her? How was that possible?

"I didn't believe the rumors. Chase Winters Achilles heel…a girl. Never in a thousand years would I have believed it if I hadn't seen it for myself. Does your girlfriend here know the truth about you? Does she know what you truly are, mutt?"

I shifted my gaze to him. A moment passed between us as I stared into eyes devoid of any silver. They hardened turning from steel to liquid fire.

Our exchange hadn't gone unnoticed. "Brilliant. So she does know. Which I'd already figured out. You aren't doing a very good job protecting your secret. She makes you sloppy. With her you drop your guard, forget what you really are." The sneer in tone was making me itchy.

Suddenly it hit me. It all made sense. She'd been the hunter stalking us. "What do you want?" I asked, tired of hearing her talk.

Her stance never wavered. She was tight like a sleek panther. "Hm. The question of the hour. I thought that was obvious…to kill him of course."

I rolled my eyes. Soooo not going to happen. It was plain that she didn't *really* know Chase. "Good luck," I muttered.

"Angel? That's your name isn't?" she asked. "Funny that your boyfriend is half-demon isn't it?"

I shrugged. "Not really. And he is not my boyfriend," I added just to clarify.

She laughed confidently. "The mark you have on your hip says otherwise."

My eyes narrowed at her. This bitch really had to go. How had she known about my mark? I had told no one outside our circle.

"You. Love. A demon," she said to me. Each word emphasized with hate. "It's wrong. They're wrong."

I wiped my sweaty palms on the legs of my jeans, still trying to figure out how we were going to get out of this. "Umm, love is such a strong word. I am not sure I would say love."

"Angel!" Chase growled like a grumpy grizzly.

I ignored him. "Like. I *like* Chase, though there are more days when I dislike him."

Again he rumbled my name with eyes burning like Time Square, followed by, "This isn't helping."

That was a matter of personal opinion. I sort of had a plan here. Really, I did. So I continued to pretend Chase didn't exist.

"Have you met the man? He would drive even the sanest person crazy in a week. Or less."

I tried to distract her with rambling, hoping that Travis would snap out of his stupor. At least long enough to get her focused off killing Chase and more on what blabber I was spewing.

I know, epic plan.

Problem was, Travis was still thunderstruck and not going to be of any help by the look of it.

"Look bitc—"

Travis's voice cut me off. "Emma."

Oh shit. Oh shit.

Please God, tell me I heard him wrong. *Emma? Travis's Emma.* No wonder he was standing there pale and in shock like the walking dead. The girl he was madly in love with had just returned from the grave.

This had just taken an unexpected twist. Why was I always the last to know what was going on? And what on earth had happened to Emma? From what I have heard about her, this was a completely different girl. Never once had Travis mentioned that his Emma was a hunter, which led me to believe this was a new development. A sticky-icky discovering for everyone involved.

Emma tilted her head toward Travis, really seeing him for the first time. And this was the distraction I'd been waiting for. Finally. Travis actually came through.

The world moved in slow motion, like everything was passing through thick glass, but at the same time it all happened in the blink of an eye.

I saw Emma with the crossbow aimed at Chase's heart and her eyes glistened with hate. I watched as they flickered for just a moment with confusion. If I didn't act now, she was going to kill Chase. My heart lurched from my chest, and I knew I was going to do something desperate and stupid. Chase must have known it too.

My name bellowed from his lips, but I was already in motion. I ran straight toward her.

Realizing that I was moving, Emma pulled back the arched bow, preparing to let the arrow fly. Chase was in action coming straight for us, but there was no way he was going to make it in time, even with his turbo speed.

At that moment, I didn't think about the bow she had in her hand or any other weapons this hunter could possibly have had on her. All I thought about was that she wanted to hurt Chase, try to kill Chase. That was enough to make me flaming mad.

I hit her with bone-jarring thump, and the two of us went tumbling to the stiff ground. The impact of the hit stunned me for just a second and then again from the fall, but I pushed all the pain aside and let adrenaline kick in. I went all commando on her ass. Unfortunately, she was just as quick on her recovery. Maybe more so.

I pinned her with my weight (thank God for that box of cupcakes I'd eaten earlier) and she went straight for my hair. My head snapped back and tears of pain lanced my eyes. I smacked whatever I could get to connect with my crazy hands, but mostly we were just wrestling pathetically on the woodsy floor.

Fighting wasn't my style, I was just mouthy. So the fact that I was doing so now was a joke. It was pitiable. This girl was a trained assassin. Her fist made contact with my lip and I swear I saw stars. Groaning, I could feel Chase glaring at me and hear Travis snicker above us, but none of it mattered. She was going to pay. I was feeling the height of bitchiness.

But I never got the chance to unleash the witch inside me. Chase secured his arms around me, pulling me to my feet and off Emma, while Travis secured her in his arms. She was flailing in his grasp like a mad woman. "Christ Angel. When did you become such a wildcat?" Chase asked after I stopped fighting in his arms.

I jerked out of his grasp. "The day I met you," I seethed, wiping the back of my sleeve against my mouth. Blood trickled from the side of my lip and hurt like a mother trucker.

Chase grinned now that he felt like he had things under control. "Yeah, I have that effect on people."

"Shut up," I grumbled and straightened my medusa hair.

He stayed plastered to my side and whispered, "I know

something we can do to help you alleviate some of the pent up energy you're feeling."

I tried to ignore the shiver of excitement. Damn him. "I just bet you do," I muttered.

He was suddenly in front of me and in my face. Like a switch being flipped he suddenly looked scary mad. "You could have been hurt. Don't try a stunt like that again." His voice had gone dark and ten octaves below freezing. There was no room for argument in his words.

I crossed my arms and glared.

Without giving so much as a warning, he gave a nod over my shoulder at Travis and then proceeded to pluck me off my feet. In seconds my stomach was in my throat as Chase raced through the woods. I buried my head into the soft cotton of his grey shirt.

"Let's go," Chase demanded, dropping me into the front seat of his car. My head was still spinning in dizzy circles.

I could hear Travis grunting and grumbling from outside the car. "I'm trying. I've sort of got my hands full," Travis complained.

"I just bet you do," Chase said under his breath.

Travis jumped in the back with his very uncooperative, kicking package.

"Are you sure this is a good idea?" Chase asked, looking at Travis in the rearview mirror as he made a very speedy u-turn. "This feels like kidnapping."

I snorted. "She deserves it."

Chase gave me a fierce look that said I better keep my trap shut or I would find myself in deeper trouble.

"I just want to talk to her. That's all. It's not kidnapping," Travis rationed.

Chase was totally getting off seeing his cousin riled. "You have such a way with girls Travis. It's astonishing."

Travis gave him a deeply dimpled grin. "That's what they all say."

"I'm gonna be sick," I mumbled.

Chase chuckled. "What the hell are you planning to do with her?"

Travis ran an unsteady hand through his blonde hair. "I don't know," he replied, looking a little lost and so unlike the charmer I was used to.

"We could toss her out of the car," I suggested.

Chase tried not to smile as he glanced at me from the corner of his eye. Then he shook his head. "You and I, Angel, we're not done yet. I am nowhere near finished with you."

I gulped. This time I was pretty sure there wasn't any sexual undertones in that statement, just plain, pure exasperation.

Err, maybe a little.

Chapter 13

As soon as Chase's car skidded to a halt in his driveway, he turned to Travis and a very livid Emma in the back. "What is the point of this Travis? Why bring *her* back here?" Chase asked, unable to hide the condemnation from his voice.

"What did you want me to do with her? Let her go, so she can try and kill you again?" Travis retorted.

Chase snorted like the idea was obscene. "I hope you know what you are in for. I understand it's got to be a shock to see her—"

"A shock!" Travis cut him off. "I thought she was dead. You thought she was dead."

"Looks like I was wrong."

"That's a first," I mumbled.

He shot me with a pair of silver daggers. "I'm getting to you, just give me a minute."

"Actually, I am beat. I was thinking about going—"

"Like hell you are," he retorted, stopping me in my tracks.

"Get that shrew out of my car," Chase ground with clenched teeth. He was pissed and was getting angrier by the minute. Not so good for Emma, he was seconds away from ripping her head off. He waited impatiently until Travis removed his difficult package from the backseat. I cringed as I watched Emma take a swing at Travis's pretty boy face, following it with a heel to the shin. Chase turned those glowing eyes on me. "What were you thinking?" he yelled, rattling my brain cells. His car just wasn't big enough for this kind of volume.

Wow, someone was ungrateful. "Last time I save your butt, you – you ungrateful ass," I spat right back and stormed out of the car, making a beeline for the house.

He was on my heels, obviously not done reprimanding me. "Damn it, Angel. You could have been hurt. Don't. Ever. Pull a fucking stunt like that again." His voice was cold enough to freeze Hell.

Whoa. He was really pissed. Like full on demon rager.

I swallowed a lump of my own anger and pivoted on my feet to face him just inside the doorway to his house. "And you would be dead!" I replied, matching my tone with his.

My rebuttal did no good. "*You* could have been killed."

And there it was—the root of his fury. Everything somehow circled back to me and him trying to keep me alive. It had to be exhausting.

A twisted laugh echoed from just inside the family room, drawing our focus off each other. "Unbelievable. I have never seen a half-breed try so hard to keep a human alive. Or for that matter a human who gets in as much trouble as you."

I was really starting to hate Emma. Right now, my hand twitched to backhand that smartass smirk right off her rosy-cheeked face. There was only room for one smartass in this town and I had already taken the job. "Why the hell is she here again?" The question tumbled from my lips before I even thought about engaging with the enemy.

"Haven't you heard? This town has a horrible demon infestation. I'm here to clean house," she smirked, completely unfazed by the fact that she was being held prisoner in a house full of half-demons.

I started across the room only to be pulled up short by Chase's firm arms around my waist. "Hey there my little hellcat, I think you have done enough for today. But I appreciate you defending my honor. I think we will let Travis take it from here. She's his problem now."

Emma's eyes flickered ever so slightly at the mention of Travis's name. "Maybe we should gag her," I suggested sarcastically. I was going to donkey punch her. Payback for the split lip she gave me. Tit for tat and all that jazz.

Chase, having gotten over his little hissy fit, chuckled. Having a common hatred helped. We both had it in for the little hunter. I was still having a hard time believing that this girl, who was my height and skinnier than me, could be a so called hunter.

It was ludicrous.

"So how long are we keeping her?" I asked, sounding like she was a stray pet. I couldn't help but wonder where the heck Travis had disappeared to.

Chase walked into the family room, never taking his eyes off Emma. He watched her like a hawk. "I think Travis is just looking for some answers, closure or some crap."

"And he thinks I'll cooperate?" Emma spoke, leering at Chase hovering over her.

I rolled my eyes. At least his anger was no longer directed at me. I guess I had her to thank for that.

Lexi and Travis shuffled down the stairs in a blur of motion, stopping at the bottom of the steps. Lexi gasped. "Travis! You tied her up?" she stated properly outraged. Her blonde hair was in a perfect sleek updo. "This better not be some kind of kinky foreplay," she added, scrunching her nose and looking adorable doing it.

Travis didn't answer. He was staring at Emma and she was staring right back. It almost felt invasive for all of us to be in the room. I had the urge to quietly slip from the room, and I was pretty sure neither of them would have noticed if a herd of elephants trampled through the house. They were too wrapped up in each other.

Finally Chase cleared his throat. Loudly.

"What in God's name is going on?" Lexi demanded, her hands on her hips looking to each one of us for answers. I sheepishly looked at the carpet pretending it was the most interesting thing on the planet.

"We were just about to ask Emma that. Weren't we, Travis?" Chase piped in. "Well, at least why she tried to kill me?"

Lexi's aqua eyes went wide. "I don't believe it. Emma wouldn't hurt anyone."

"Believe it little cousin."

"You're all nothing but an abomination," Emma hissed, digging her own grave.

Hurt and disbelief leaped into Lexi's eyes, and my heart went out to her. Lexi had a gentle nature despite the fact she was part demon.

"When I get out of here, I'll come after you again and finish what I started. I'll kill every one of you, including your little pet."

I couldn't seem to be able to control myself around her. I took a step toward her, but Chase was always faster. His arms grabbed my waist from behind and tugged me to his chest. They were like vise grips. "Angel, move again and I will tie you up next to her," Chase threatened in my ear.

I could feel his heart thumping against my back. "How can you just sit there and do nothing? She hurt Lexi and Lexi doesn't

157 | P a g e

deserve that." I was so dang frustrated.

He sighed heavily. "Angel Eyes, you never fail to surprise me. All in due time," he whispered.

"You can let go of me now."

"Nah, I think I'll keep hold of you for safe keeping."

Emma snorted. "Disgusting."

I jumped against the bonds of his arms, and they only tightened around me, anticipating my move.

"What happened to you?" It was Travis's soft voice that broke through the thickening tension swirling like a Kansas tornado in the room.

Emma's emerald eyes clung to Travis's stormy sea green gaze as he sauntered over to the couch and sat next to her. He waited patiently for her to answer, just studying her, trying to figure out where the girl he had fallen in love with had gone. Because surely this she-devil dressed in all black wasn't her. The silence lingered as we all waited on edge for her to say something. My bet was that she was going to inform us of the number of sick and twisted ways she planned to hunt us.

Sometimes it is nice to be wrong.

But that didn't mean she was exactly pleasant about it. "I came into the family business," Emma finally answered with indifference.

"Family business," Travis echoed, his brows drawing together.

"Someone in your family is a hunter?"

Emma didn't so much as blink. Lexi crept into the room next to where Chase and I were standing. His arms had gone lax around my waist, and I felt him relax some, which in turn had mind my wandering to his marvelous body pressed against me. Suddenly, I found it hard to concentrate on anything but the half-demon behind me.

Emma raised her head defiantly. "You know nothing of family."

I couldn't fathom how Travis stayed so calm around her. Deep lines of thought crossed his forehead. Then a light of understanding moved into Travis's blue-green eyes. "Your dad."

Her thin lips and her silence were all the confirmation we needed. Wow. And I thought I had mega daddy issues. At least mine didn't train me to be a killer all while pretending I was missing for over a year. That was some pretty heavy shit.

Her eyes shifted like a cat ready to bolt. "You think you got it all figured out." Everything about her voice and actions were filled with pride and sheer stubbornness. Not an ounce of fear. "You have no idea."

Sympathy filled Travis's expression. His hand reached out to smooth a strand of strawberry blonde hair out of her face. Emma flinched out of his reach, and he dropped his hand looking defeated and hurt.

"I looked for you, Emma." There was just the slightest fraction of emotion in her eyes when Travis spoke her name. "I never stopped looking for you, even when the police called off the search. Even when your parents stopped, I never did. I always knew you were still out there. I could feel you." He put his hand to his heart. "In here, I knew you were alive."

My heart wept for him, for his heartache. Poor guy. Travis was one-in-a-million. If Emma didn't recognize that, then she didn't deserve him. In my eyes, she deserved less than dirt.

Emma lowered her head. "You shouldn't have wasted your time."

Lexi and I both gasped at her harsh rejection. Chase had his own reaction. Leave it to him to spice things up.

Like a beam of lightning, he was suddenly gone from behind me and in Emma's face. He ignored the growl of protest from Travis. "Let's speed this up, shall we. I can't have you running around trying to kill people I care about, now can I?" His eyes got serious as they stared into Emma's green ones. They went weird opaque silver ringed in gold.

He planned to compel Emma. Intrigued, I took a step closer. I'd never seen Chase use his persuasion. Travis and Lexi yes, but not Chase.

"Chase," Travis pleaded, realizing what his cousin had planned.

"It's the only way," Chase assured.

Emma just smirked, meeting his gaze straight on. If she knew as much about Divisa as she claimed, then she had to know what Chase was going to do. Why didn't she fight? Turn her head at least? His eyes captured hers and his voice went deep and silky. "You never saw us today. You don't know who we are or what we are."

I was on the brink of my feet, gripping the back of the couch.

Emma giggled like a lunatic. "I can't be compelled. Nice try though tough guy."

Chase narrowed his eyes. "Well, that complicates matters."

Travis stepped between Chase and Emma before Chase took things into a different direction. I was afraid to find out what that direction might have been. Kidnapping was one thing, but murder… I shuddered.

"What else you got?" Emma asked with an edge.

I pretended I hadn't heard her. Lexi was next to me and the two of us stared at the guys. "Now what?" I mumbled.

Travis shook his head sullenly. "Nothing. I let her go."

"You what?" came a unified outrage from everyone in the room.

"What other options do we have?" Travis's aquamarine eyes begged his cousin to understand his predicament. No matter what had Emma said or done, Travis couldn't harm a hair on her head, not the girl he had loved, and probably still loved regardless of her hatred. Brainwashing at its finest.

We all waited as Chase weighed Emma's fate. Thank heavens Devin wasn't home or this might have been awkward to explain, but something told me that Devin was good with unusual. Chase might not be the oldest, but there was no doubt where the shoulder of authority lay. It went to his head 9.9 times out of 10. I could just hear him saying that it was the price for being a badass.

I snorted. Chase eyed me and cocked a brow at my sudden outburst. I returned the gesture.

"This is going to end badly," Chase predicted. Then he sighed. "Travis, take her home."

Chapter 14

The following day at school, chaos broke out through the halls. Cluster of students loitered in the halls in hushed whispers, stunned expressions, and even some tears. I knew something big had happened, and I didn't have to wait long to find out.

Strutting down the tiled hall like she owned the world was my worst nightmare.

Emma Deen.

Her hair, a perfect blend of blond and red, was tossed into a no-nonsense ponytail. She wore no makeup and managed to still look beautiful. Everything about her stood out like a sore thumb. There was just something about the way she carried herself. It wasn't like most high school girls.

I was almost sure that I hated her more than Sierra and that was saying something. Emma was unpredictable, a threat to my health, and seven different kinds of crazy. We needed to stay clear of each other, or one of us was liable to kill the other. But at Hall High avoiding someone was near impossible. This was the kind of school where running into someone several times a day was a given. Having a class with everyone at least once a day—

guaranteed.

This girl was going to my make life a living nightmare.

I slumped hard against the lockers and shut my eyes. Was it too much to hope that I could meld into the metal and disappear? I tried to make myself invisible, but no matter how much I wished she would walk right by me, it didn't happen. I had danced with the devil, and Hell was going to take every opportunity to make my life difficult...or so I told myself.

"Well, if it isn't my favorite mutant." She had this charming voice, but there was nothing sweet about her words.

My stomach fell. I opened my eyes to find a pair of emeralds that could cut right to your soul. Pulling from some inner strength I didn't know was there, I masked my fear with sarcasm. My weapon of choice. "Fancy seeing you here," I tossed back, wondering where my usual shadows were. Go figure, on the day that I actually wished they were here, they both decided to evaporate. "I'd say it's a pleasure, but I'd be lying."

"Such manners. Didn't your mama teach you that if you don't have something nice to say, you shouldn't say anything at all?"

The mentioning of Mom and all I saw was red. "Listen, you redneck skank—"

She cut me off before I could finish my verbal assault. "Do you kiss your boyfriend with that dirty mouth?"

I ground my teeth. "I told you. He is not my boyfriend."

She leaned in close to me, a hand propped on the locker near my head. It took everything inside me not to flinch. "Is that why he spends so much of his time with his hand up your shirt?"

I couldn't have been more thankful for the crowd of students around us. I push off the locker. "I don't have time for this," I fumed and walked away.

"Lucky for you, all I have is time," she sneered as I passed.

~*~*~*~

At lunch, everyone was in hoopla over Emma Deen returning from the side of a milk carton. My fake surprise was hard to keep in place, especially after our little confrontation this morning. I was still seething inside.

"I heard that she ran away with a drummer and went on tour with him. She only came home after finding him in the sack with a blonde bombshell groupie," Brandy shared what had to have been the tenth rumor I'd heard about Emma's unforeseen come back. Brandy's almond-shaped eyes were sparkling with animation.

Kailyn shook her chocolate curls that framed a heart-shaped face. "That's not what I heard."

Here we go again. I dropped my head on my hands, checking out of a conversation that was becoming quite old. I could care less that she had been missing more than a year. It could have been a hundred years and I couldn't have cared any more.

"So, are you going to tell me what happened earlier today?"

HUNTING ANGEL

Chase whispered in my ear. I never heard him, but he was just suddenly there, sitting beside me.

I picked at the plate of, what I guess was supposed to be mashed potatoes, in front of me. "No, not really."

"Angel," he said sternly.

My heart skipped. It happened every time he said my name. Didn't matter whether it was in longing, anger, or annoyance, the results were always the same. My name from his lips made my insides amuck.

"We need to talk."

By *talk*, he meant more than just about Emma being on the attendance list at Hall High. We still hadn't really spoken about what we learned from Ives. There hadn't been much time. Emma seemed to find a way to interfere in every aspect of my life lately.

I wanted to cause her bodily harm.

"Okay," I agreed. "My house after school."

"Is your mom working tonight?" he asked.

Strange. He never cared before. "Is that going to be a problem?" He hated when I answered a questioned with a question, but I couldn't resist irritating him. It was just too damn fun. His brows drew together, and for the first time, I noticed a glint in his eyes I'd never seen before. Chase looked tired. Reaching out, I covered my hand over his. "Hey, what's wrong?"

"Nothing," he assured, and sealed the deal with a dazzling

grin. Slowly he slid his hand from under mine, and I tried to hide the hurt from my eyes.

Folding my hands together, I tuned back to my friends at the table. The topic, of course, was still the lunatic Emma. Lexi smiled knowingly at me from across the table and arched a sculpted brow. She and I both knew that Emma was anything but what she seemed. As if she could sense we were talking about her, Emma walked into the cafeteria. Some joker whistled at her as she walked by. Thankfully Travis wasn't here. I would have hated to see what that guy's face would look like after Travis got through with him.

Emma might not be herself, but I was sure Travis harbored some kind of hope that she still loved him, because it was obvious he was still hung up on her. I just didn't want to see Travis get heartbroken a second time. From what I've heard, he couldn't survive another blow like losing Emma the first time had been.

Brandy flipped her long black hair over her shoulder. Her eyes like everyone else in the lunchroom were on Emma. "She's different."

Chase shot me an amused grin. I rolled my eyes.

"We used to be friends, before…" Brandy's voice trailed off.

My ears perked up like a golden retriever. "You knew Emma?" Why did I not know this?

"We both did," Kailyn added. "We used to hound her to join the cheerleading squad."

"I wonder if she even dances anymore," Brandy added.

"I doubt it. She looks more like a tomboy. Did you see what she was wearing?" There was just a hint of envy in Kailyn's tone. My guess was that she was jealous of the attention swirling around Emma's reappearance.

My eyes followed her as she gracefully weaved through the cluster of round tables. Her black cargo pants sat low on her waist and on her they looked sexy. Chains of silver hung around her neck in a variety of lengths down her white t-shirt. Gathered at the nape of her neck was her strawberry blonde hair in a low ponytail. Looks like someone had hung up her ballet shoes and traded them in for a bow and arrow.

Our eyes meet across the crowded and chatty room that smelled of baked chicken, watery mashed potatoes, and icky, lumpy brown sauce, but all I could taste was my own unease. Emma winked at me from where she sat, straight and rigid in her seat. Chase snarled low in his throat.

Emma, Chase, and I together under one roof was going to be extremely hazardous for everyone.

~*~*~*~

I sat at the edge of the couch arm and crossed my feet. "You wanted to talk, so...talk."

His form dwarfed the room with his commanding presence. Leaning against the wall, he couldn't have been any farther away from me. "Now that we know Emma and her dad are out there hunting us, I need you to be more careful than usual. We can't afford any mistakes."

He was telling me stuff I had already figured out on my own. "I'm not going to do anything stupid," I assured.

"Really? Because I am pretty sure that stunt you pulled yesterday in the woods was pretty stupid."

I rolled my eyes. "Are you telling me that if roles had been reversed, you wouldn't have done the same?"

He lifted his silver hooped brow. "That's the difference. I could have handled the situation. Hell, I had it under control."

"It didn't look that way from where I stood."

He pushed off the wall and in a blink he was standing in front of me. My breath caught in my throat as I slide off the couch to my feet. We hadn't been this close in days, not close enough that I could feel the heat radiating off him, or his body brushing up against mine. Eyes flashed the color of lightning, smothering the silver. "Then there is something wrong with your eyes. Or maybe it's just your judgment. You forget all too easily what I am." He cocked his head.

I took a step forward and watched his eyes widen in surprise. He'd expected to frighten me. When was he going to learn that I wasn't afraid of him, of what he was? No matter how many times he threw it my face. "I know who you are. You're the guy who is constantly saving me."

The look on his face said he was expecting a different reaction. Anger. Fear. Retreat. Not intrigue, desire, respect.

I'd always had an aggressive streak, but this was unchartered territory for me. And it was totally freaking Chase out. That turned me on. It gave me this girl-power feeling that went to my head. I'd never tried to seduce someone before, and I wasn't sure why I wanted to, or what had gotten into me. Flatting my hands on his chest, I peeked up at him under my lashes. His eyes had gone brighter, and my heart thundered.

"You play a dangerous game."

Heard it before. I bit the inside of my cheek and said, "I like danger." I was testing him, testing myself. Things felt different since yesterday, since seeing Ives. He had pulled away from me, and over the past few days he had put a wall between us. I didn't understand why. What happened? What changed?

Looping my arms around his neck, tingles of excitement and eagerness unfolded through me. Lifting up on my toes, I closed the space between our mouths fully intending for our lips to lock. My eyes fluttered close, and—

I stumbled.

Chase had removed himself rather quickly from my embrace. He cut me a look and took a step back, then another, running a hand through his dark locks. I tried to ignore how magnificent he looked in those jeans. And the disappointment that spun in my belly. He shook his head, looking overwhelmed by me. I had become the aggressor, flipping the tables on him, and it looked to be messing with his head.

Served him right. Someone needed to flatten him on his superior rump. I was just glad it was me, even though I was hurting from the rejection. "What's your deal?" I asked, taking a step in his direction.

A mask of indifference clouded his eyes still glowing. "I don't know what you mean?"

I rolled my eyes. "Bullshit. For weeks you put on the moves, making my head spin. And now, you can't stand to be next to me. Don't play dumb with me. Ever since Ives and then the Emma thing, you are different. What gives?"

His lips turned down in annoyance. For a brief second, the mask fractured and sadness shaped his features. I couldn't be sure I actually saw it. I squared my shoulders, prepared to hear the worse. He was treating me like I had leprosy.

"Look, you heard what Ives said. The more we are together, they deeper we get, the stronger our bond becomes. I can't take the chance of that happening. I've seen what it did to Travis when Emma left. I need a clear head or someone is going to die. My number one priority is to keep you alive, not get in your pants. It would help if you didn't constantly put yourself in danger and throw yourself at me. I've already given up enough for you."

Ouch. Pain exuded in my eyes. My fists clenched at my sides, nails digging into my skin. What I heard was *he'd given up his life to be tied down to me in a bond he didn't want.* "Don't do me any favors. I don't need you. And as sure as hell don't want you."

Lie. Lie. Lie.

It was all big fat lies.

Anger zapped into his demon eyes. I guess that wasn't the right response. A muscle popped in his jaw. "You are so frustrating," he snapped, eyes blistering with increased irritation. "Why do I care? Have it your way." Long purposeful strides carried him across the room.

"Good. That's the way I like it! My way!" I yelled to his rippled receding back.

Ugh. Why did I have to notice how he looked all the time? Why couldn't he be repulsive and an ass, instead of just being the biggest ass in the galaxy.

Right before he slammed door, he looked over his shoulder for one last long glare. I gave him the timeless one finger salute. Some things never change. The door vibrated on its hinges, and I swear I heard wood split.

Sinking into the couch like a slug, I could barely believe we were back to this.

Fighting.

Slamming doors.

At each other's throats.

I had really hoped that we had moved past this, talk about a giant leap backwards. Was this what being linked to Chase would be like? Extreme highs and extreme lows? Were we forever stuck in this cycle of devouring and despising one another?

Only time would tell.

Well, time could kiss my scrawny ass.

Chapter 15

The following afternoon I'd successfully avoided Chase. It helped
that he seemed to be doing the same. Lexi continually gave us
exhausted glances. I could tell she thought we were being silly and
didn't enjoy being caught in the middle of our hateful glares.

Poor Lexi.

I was going to have to make it up to her, a shopping trip or
some other torturous excursion like a spa day. Gag with me a
spoon. I must really like Lexi if I was remotely thinking of agreeing
to let someone smear mud masks on my face, paint my nails, or
touch my hair.

She was my best friend, and lately we haven't really spent time
together. I must be feeling guilty. It was all Chase's fault. This
stupid soulbond and his mood swings were driving me berserk.
What I needed to do was get my life back. Back before every
thought was consumed with my overbearing yet drool-worthy hot
neighbor.

I needed counseling.

Or worse, shock therapy.

Something—anything, to rid me of my obsession with Chase

Winters.

Parking my little white Fusion in my driveway, I swung the car door shut behind me. As I lifted my bag higher on my shoulder, a movement at Lexi's house caught my attention. Chase's shadowy form lurked in the doorway, and our eyes fastened. I couldn't make out his expression, but his lazy stance leaning up against the door frame made my heart sputter.

I blinked.

That was all it took for him to disappear. One blink and he left me wondering if he had ever really been there, or was my mind now imagining him. Steaming, I stomped into the house cursing and banishing thoughts of Chase Winters from my head. I refused to admit that after only twenty-four hours I missed him, no matter what games my subconscious was playing on me.

Walking into the house, I ignored the pangs that plagued my chest. Rejection was a bitch no matter how you sugarcoated it. Just as I was about to flip the light switch on in the hallway, I noticed what looked like a figure sitting in the dark on my couch. Complete panic set in and a scream bubbled up my esophagus. I swallowed it down the back of my throat before I got myself killed. Gazillion of gruesome thoughts and images spiraled through my brain. I really needed to lay off the video games, but in my defense, my real life wasn't that far off from fantasy.

Run, warned an impatient voice in my head. *Get out of there while his back is to you.*

But following directions was never my strong suit. I pretty much did things to the beat of my own drum and forget about doing what normal, rational people would have done. My brain wasn't wired on the same frequency as everyone else's. If it had been, I would have retreated quietly from the house and ran next door. Nope, instead I stood there frozen like a time capsule.

The shadowy figure must have heard my gasp and turned toward me before I had a chance to bolt. I expected to see hallowed eyes without a soul or the eyes the color of blood not aqua eyes brimming with sadness.

"Travis?" I expelled on a rush of air. Stepping closer into the room, I could make out his sharp cheekbones, his frowning mouth, and his moppy sandy hair. "What the hell? You literally just shaved off ten years of my life. Between you and Chase, I don't know how many I have left."

"Sorry," he apologized, his voice falling flat, not at all like the usual carefree disposition I was accustomed to.

Plopping my badonkadonk down on the sofa beside Travis, I didn't bother with the lights. Darkness seemed to suit both our moods. Misery really did love company, and he looked like he could use a friend. Why he chose me was mind-boggling. I could only assume this surprise visit was about Emma.

I looked at my friend and for the first time since I had known him, he seemed deflated. Not at all like the Adonis God I associated him to. His shirt was wrinkled as if he just threw on whatever was lying on the floor. His eyes were ringed in puffiness and dark circles. And a single whiff said he desperately needed a shower. Travis looked like crapola.

"Talk to me, what's going on?" I kept my voice soft.

He ran both hands through his already wild hair. "Nobody gets it. Not what's running through my head, or how I am feeling inside. They've tried to pretend nothing is different, but that's just it. Everything is different. To make matters worse...the one person I want to talk to...the one who would get it. Well, I can't be sure she won't try to stake me before hearing me out." He dropped his head into his hands.

I scooted closer to him on the couch. My heart lurched inside my ribcage for him, for his evident pain. "Travis," I said gently. "I can't pretend to understand what you are going through, but I'll listen. I won't judge you for what you're feeling. Trust me, if I can be tied to your dumbass cousin, then I must have the empathy of a freaking saint." My jab at Chase got me the smallest of a smirk. It was a start.

Emma's return had messed with his head. "I've never experienced a shock like that. It jolted through my system, I was useless against it," he said, bringing the memories back to life. "A part of me never expected to see her again. Never see her face.

Never hear her voice. Touch her. It was surreal. Just the sight of her stole the breath from my lungs."

I thought about what he said, seeing someone you thought was gone from your life forever. I knew that if my dad suddenly appeared one day, I would drop dead on the spot. All things considered, I thought Travis handled the situation as well as was expected.

His voice quivered ever so slightly. "Emma and I don't have the kind of link you and Chase do, but I would have given my life for hers a million times over. That has to count for something."

"It does," I assured with compassion.

He lifted his head, meeting my eyes with so much pain swimming in them. "I feel like I should have done something. I should have known she was in trouble, that she needed me."

His guilt was monumental. It stifled the air. He blamed himself for what had happened to Emma, for her transformation into a vicious hunter. How did one absolve that kind of blame from his shoulders? I couldn't stand to see Travis take such a gigantic heap of fault onto him. It was unfair, unjust, and plain out bullshit. "Travis, you couldn't have known. This guilt you're carrying around is going to eat you up inside, and it's not what Emma would want. Not the Emma you knew."

He didn't look convinced. "Maybe," he conceded, but I could tell that he was just being polite, he didn't really believe it. I wasn't sure there was anything I could have said that would have made a difference.

Of course I wasn't one to give up.

"Emma showed up at school this week," I said, unsure whether it was a wise decision to tell him. I took the chance.

"She was?" There was a touch of hope in his voice. It killed me to have to crush it.

I nodded and pulled my legs under me. "Yeah."

He took a deep breath. "I'm guessing by your tone, it didn't go well."

"Depends on who you talk to. School was definitely buzzing, that's for sure. I'd never heard so much outlandish gibberish in my life."

"That's a small town for you. News like that is the biggest thing of the year. It tops Fall Harvest."

Good Lord. The peeps of Spring Valley needed to get a life.

Travis's lashes lowered. "Did she...?"

"Try to shank me in the hall?" I supplied, only partially joking. "No, but I got the impression that she would have liked to cut out my tongue." That might not have been the smartest answer, but sometimes my mouth is flapping before I realize what I was saying.

"I don't know what to do," he admitted, sounding more saddened than ever. Some friend I was. "This is a disaster. I know

Chase. He will stop at nothing to protect you."

I swallowed, getting an idea of where his mind was leading to. Travis was worried, and probably rightly so, that Chase would harm the girl he was still in love with to protect me. The girl he was secretly hoping he could save. I didn't know if I should pity him or condone him for his perseverance, because there was a very good possibility that Chase would do just that.

And I wasn't positive I would try to stop him.

He must have seen the doubt in my eyes. Pivoting on the couch faster than my eyes could follow, he grabbed my hand. "Angel, I can save her. I know I can." There was hysteria bubbling in his voice. He desperately wanted me to believe. "I just need the chance, and I know that I can get through to her. Somewhere inside there is a girl who loved me once. I know that she is still in there. I can feel it."

Squeezing his hand, I held his gaze and looked deep into his wide-eyes. I had to do something. Say something. Quickly. During his saving Emma speech, Travis's eyes had started to glow brighter than the sun.

"Travis, hey. Listen to me." My eyes never wavered, and his were intently captured with mine. I watched a little staggered as his irises slowly calmed. *Slap me silly and call me crazy, but that was weird.* "Everything is going to be okay. I promise. I won't let Chase hurt Emma." I don't know why I made such a declaration, because honestly it was far from the truth. No way did I know that everything was going to be fine, or if I could actually prevent Chase from slicing and dicing Emma. She made it pretty clear she was trying to kill us. But I had to say something before he went into demon-freak-out-mode.

His eyes were still locked on mine, unblinking. It was like I had him captivated under my spell, but I was mostly certainly not a witch. Well, I was ninety-nine percent sure I wasn't. At this point, even the impossible was probably possible.

Then in a snap I saw clarity come back into his expression, like a cloudy haze had been lifted from him. "D-did you just compel me?" Travis accused.

"What?" I shot, taken aback.

"This is bad, I got that blank spot in my head, though this is the first time I've ever experienced it. I had no idea what it felt like. You just got inside my head," he told me.

"Na-uh. I did not." I sounded like a five-year old.

He just stared at me oddly. Shifting uncomfortably under his astonished gaze, I couldn't take the suspense any longer. "Okay, say that I did," I conceded. "Is it a big deal?" I'd never done anything like this. Heck, I didn't even know that I had done it or what exactly I had done.

He shrugged, finally waking from his daze of wonder. "Depends, I guess. We're not supposed to be susceptible to compulsion, so I can only guess that some Divisa won't take well to knowing you can manipulate their minds."

I cringed. Sierra's name popped into my head. "Great," I muttered dryly.

"Chase has no idea how incredibly fortunate he is to have you. I'm gonna kick his ass later for putting that shadow of pain in your eyes."

I rolled my eyes.

"By the way...did you know your eyes change colors?" he asked offhandedly.

Damnation. What next? Was I going to sprout horns and blow fire? Fortunately this wasn't a surprise. Chase had already confirmed that my eyes did that freaky-color-fluctuating-thingy.

I hugged one of the couch throw pillows, averting my gaze to the mocha carpet. "Just one more of the many perks of being brought back from the dead," I mumbled.

A corner of his mouth lifted. "Well, it's kind of hot."

I grinned despite myself, and then promptly hit him with the pillow.

He dodged it of course, chuckling. "And if that leaves this room, I will deny, deny, deny until I'm six feet under. I really don't want to mess up this face." He rubbed a hand under his two-day growth chin. "It would be such a damn shame if that happened."

And I saw a hint of sparkle in his teal eyes, just like the old

WEIL

charming Travis.

There it was. What I was looking for.

A ray of hope.

Chapter 16

"Angel!" Mom bellowed from downstairs.

I just barely heard her through my headset. Flipping the off switch on my Xbox, I put aside the controller, and opened my bedroom door. "One sec!" I yelled back as I started to descend the stairs.

It was the start of Thanksgiving break and that meant quality time with Mom. Seeing her in the kitchen, mixing a bowl of what I hoped would be pumpkin pie, I realized how much I missed her. Between my school, her job and now Devin, we hardly saw each other. Sometimes it felt like we were more roommates than mother and daughter.

She had an atrocious apron tied around her waist, a jazzy CD on low in the background, a streak of flour on her cheek, and her honey hair piled like a nest on top of her head. She looked beautiful. For the first time my house didn't feel old and creepy. It felt homey.

I jumped up on the corner of the counter, the only one without clutter and food ingredients, and Mom grinned at me. I tried not to think about the last time I'd been up on this counter.

How I'd been wrapped around Chase. Pangs of longing I couldn't control stabbed my heart. Days without him were taking its toll, but my stubbornness won out.

"What's up?" I asked, sticking my finger in the bowl.

She swatted my hand, but not before I scoped some batter. "So, I wanted to run an idea by you," she began. Her spoon paused.

Uh-oh. What now?

"Please tell me you're not preggers," I said. Apparently I had sex on the brain, and it wasn't wasted on me that there was probably a good chance my mom was doing the deed with Devin.

I shuddered at the thought. Ick.

"Angel, you'd make a great big sister. But no, there are no little babies in our future." She gave me a pointed look. "Right?"

"Funny."

"Just checking. Anyway, that is not what I wanted to talk about. I was thinking about having the Winters clan over for Thanksgiving dinner. Devin isn't much of a cook, and I thought it would be good for them. And us. A family dinner." She looked at me with her big brown eyes, waiting to see how I would respond.

At the end of the day, I knew that what I wanted was all that really matter to her. So if I made a stink about this, we would be having Thanksgiving with just the two of us, the way it had been the last few years and I liked it that way. But I also knew that things never stayed the same. Change was inevitable. I looked into Mom's warm eyes and I saw, really saw that Devin made her happy. She sacrificed so much for me. Didn't she deserve happiness?

"That sounds great," I heard myself say.

"Really?" she asked like she couldn't believe that I was being serious.

I jumped off the counter. "Really, Mom," I assured and gave her a hug.

"Devin and I weren't sure. He thought that you and Chase had a lovers' spat. Is everything okay?"

My mom usually lacked the normal internal motherly instinct, so I wasn't surprised that Devin might have mentioned something to her. I still wasn't pleased by it.

"We aren't lovers," was the first thing out of my mouth. "And we're fine."

Lie, screamed a voice inside my head. He still hadn't spoken to me.

"Well it should be eventful," she said, squeezing my shoulder. I didn't doubt that.

~*~*~*~

Thanksgiving with a bunch of half-demons, my mom, and her boyfriend…sounded like a recipe for disaster. The dreaded holiday was upon me in all its anticipated emotional conflict. "This is going to be worse than a root canal," I mumbled to my bedroom ceiling. We had the kind of ceilings that had the little popcorn balls on them. Sometimes if I stared long enough, I could make out creepy shapes and faces. To say my house more than often gave me the willies was an understatement.

Laying there on my back, my thoughts drifted to Chase, and how I would be forced to be in close quarters with him. We had successfully eluded the other like pros and the space was bittersweet. Now, the thought of seeing him filled me with a mixture of apprehension and impatience. Whether I wanted to admit it to myself or not...I missed the jerk.

What was wrong with me?

I'll tell you. It was the damn curse that bound my soul to his for all eternity. *Lord help m*e.

Swinging out of bed, I headed into the bathroom to steam in a very long, indulgent hot shower. Afterward, I threw in some hair product and dried my dark locks. I guess since it was a holiday, I could attempt to look nice, but that still meant no dress. Scurrying through my closet, I tugged on a pair of skinny jeans with no holes and a blouse with the tags still on.

My mom was going to be so impressed.

Butterflies buzzed in my belly as I rounded down the stairs. I knew before I even left my room that *he* was in the house. It might have been why I lingered upstairs for as long as possible, not yet ready to face him, and at the same time bursting to see him. I couldn't explain. It wasn't logical.

Mom's gentle humming could be heard over the clattering of pots and pans. I stepped into the kitchen. "Glad you could join the living," she said when she saw me. "Oh, Angel. You look lovely."

"Thanks," I mumbled, a ball of nerves moving through the room. And then the smell of something familiar tickled my nose, and it wasn't turkey. Sharp tingles frolicked along my skin. My heart rate spiked.

Chase.

I had to fight every crazy and irrational instinct to turn around and throw myself into his arms. Knowing D-bag, I'd probably end up on my butt. Deliberately, I spun around ever so slowly. When my eyes latched onto him, I immediately forgot to breathe. Sooty lashes, fanning the tips of his cheeks hid his eyes as he looked me over. I found myself impatient to see the color of his eyes. Silver or gold? Which would they be?

Was his heart beating a thousand miles a minute like mine was?

Had he suffered as I had the in last week?

God, I hoped so.

The room around me vanished and the suspense was killing me. I willed him to look at me. And then our eyes met. A burst of sunlight exploded inside me, filling my entire being with warmth. I took a step forward. Wanting… Needing…to be closer to him. It was unfair that only this guy could make me feel so crazy, *him* of all people. A lazy smile crossed his lips as his eyes ran over my face, eating up the sight of me.

I shivered.

"Angel."

That was all he said. Just my name and I was melting faster than an ice cream cone on a hot summer's night. The sound of his voice tore through me. I never wanted anything so much in my life as I wanted the touch of his hand and to feel his arms around me. My control was only so great, I had to close me eyes against it, and my hands balled to fists at my side.

Still it wasn't enough.

As if he understood what I wanted, his hand moved toward my face. I leaned forward and—

"Angel." Mom said my name behind me like she was disciplining a bad puppy. "Why don't you offer our guests something to eat or drink while I finish up with dinner," she suggested, breaking our enthralled contact.

That had been close. Too close.

He hadn't even touched me and I'd made a complete and utter idiot of myself standing there like I was awestruck by his hotness. Okay, let's face it, I had been. That was irrelevant. What I needed was stronger willpower for frickin' sake. There was no reason we couldn't have a nice *family dinner* without ripping into each other or jumping each other's bones on the dining room table.

Or so I hoped.

With one long deep breath, I turned and grabbed a platter from the island. Smiling sweetly I walked into the family room, stopping in front of Chase. My eyes glittered with sarcastic humor. "Devil egg?" I asked, holding out a tray of the little white halves with gooey yellow tops.

Travis coughed covering a laugh. Devin frowned. Lexi giggled. The corners of Chase's mouth tilted, and I tried not to stare at his lips, failing miserably.

This was going horribly fabulous.

Setting the platter down, I joined the others. There was a football game on the TV, occupying the guys' attention. I caught Chase glancing at me as much as I snuck glances at him. Lexi was thumbing through a few of my mom's magazines looking bored.

Excusing myself for a moment, I needed air. Being within arm's reach of Chase was making my insides go bananas. So I snuck off into the hallway thinking I could cure myself of him with some distance. But he was like a deadly disease. There wasn't a cure. No pill. No remedy. No medical procedure. I leaned my head against the wall and blinked.

Chase popped in front of me and I shrieked. My heart

pounded in my ears, and I swung at him, hitting only air. He moved to the side. "Christ. I hate when you do that. I swear you do it just to piss me off."

"Which isn't hard to do, Angel Eyes." His eyes were laughing at me.

I made a face.

"Are we going to kiss and make-up now?" he asked, blocking any escape with his powerful body. It was rippled, chiseled, and toned in all the right places.

I gave him an uninterested expression. "Don't hold your breath."

The ghost of a smile lurked on his lips. "Doesn't hurt to try."

I stood as still as possible with the wall pressed to my back and tried with all my might to not be effective by his close proximity. My teenage hormones had other ideas.

I hated them.

A moment passed between us and he must have seen it in my eyes, because he took a step back. "How about a truce? For Devin and your mom. What do you say?" A brow arched.

It was a dirty trick to play the mom-card. He knew I wouldn't do anything to upset her. "Like I have a choice, but this doesn't mean I forgive you."

His hand reached out and twirled the ends of my hair. "What exactly am I supposed to be forgiven for?" The sound of his voice was like dark silk.

I socked him in the chest.

He grinned, not budging an inch. "I've missed you, Angel Eyes."

My eyes flashed to his. I knew that he said it offhandedly, jokingly, but that didn't stop my breath from hitching. I fumbled with something smart to say. "Devin seems a little on edge. What gives? Did you piss him off too?"

He snorted. "You wish. Actually, he is worried about what is between us now that he is shacking up with your mom."

I cringed. "Do not ever mention shacking and my mom in the same sentence."

He grinned, his eyes dancing with mischief. Someone was in a playful mood, a complete turnabout from the other day. He made my head spin. "My uncle is afraid that we will either get too close or have the explosion of the century. Both in his mind are not good outcomes."

I relaxed into his body without realizing I was doing it. His fingers played with mine as we talked. "He should stop trying to knock her up and spend more time worrying about our current hunter pollution."

He chuckled. The sound hit me straight in the gut. "Whether you believe it or not, Devin has your mom's best interest at heart. Yours too. He wants to protect her from all this. He doesn't want her to be touched or tainted by the dealings of the underworld."

Like me, I thought. And so did Chase. I could see the guilt and blame reflecting in his smoky eyes still. It was in his voice. He still believed everything that happened to me was his fault. I sighed. "We should get back before someone notices we're both missing."

"They probably think we're kissing and making-up."

"In your dreams."

"I know I'm in yours."

"Do you always have to have the last word?"

His face was expressionless. "Is a frog's ass watertight?"

I groaned. This was going nowhere fast. Pushing off the wall, I brushed past him. "Jerk," I muttered under my breath, but grinning inside.

"Brat," he countered just for my ears alone.

By dinner we had waved the white flag—a ceasefire. Well, at least through the holiday. After that it was fair game again. Dinner was loud, boisterous, and chaotic. Everyone talked over everyone. Chase and Travis ate enough to feed a small country. There was so much laughter that I actually swore water came out of my nose once. The muscles in my mouth were sore from grinning so much.

It felt normal.

Seeing my mom that happy was worth putting up with Chase. It was worth every horrible, painful, and scary thing that had happened to me since moving to Spring Valley. When dessert was served, I was positive I couldn't stuff another bite in my gorged belly.

"You going to eat that?" Chase asked, eyeballing my piece of pumpkin pie piled with cool whip. Just the way I liked it.

I shoveled a heaping spoonful in my mouth, looking like a chipmunk.

He chuckled, sneaking a fork full of my pie. I slapped at his hand. "Do you want to lose a finger?" I threatened my mouth still full of pumpkin goop.

Moving closer to me, he pushed aside a fallen piece of hair behind my ear. The intoxicating scent of him fluttered over my face, overriding the sweetness of the pie. From across the table, Mom raised an eye, and I quickly swiped at his lingering hand.

"Knock it off," I scolded, only to be rewarded with one of his dazzling smiles. Pushing my plate in his direction, I knew that if I ate another bite, I would hurl. He ate the whole darn thing. Bottomless pit.

Lexi and I retired to the couch after dinner in a practically comatose state. Food does that. I played with the sleeves of my cardigan. "What are you doing tomorrow?" I cringed even as I asked. Tomorrow was the biggest shopping day of the year. Duh. Lexi was going to be riding high on caffeine and start shopping before the sun even cracked.

From the other side of the couch, she looked at me over the

pages of Black Friday ads. "Probably check out the sales."

"So, I was thinking of tagging along." I regretted the words even as they tumbled from my mouth. I wanted to be a good friend, best friend, but this was just going too far. If it had been Travis, none of this would have even been an issue. But Lexi was my best friend, so…

"I'm sorry, what did you say? You want to shop? With *me*?" she echoed in disbelief.

I nodded and swallowed, knowing I have already dug my own grave.

A mile wide grin lit up her face. Sparkling blue-green eyes the color of the sea shined at me with genuine glee. "Pedi," she shrieked in delight. My poor ears rang, even as I found myself engulfed in a giant smothering Lexi hug.

Who said anything about getting my nails done? I thought she would drag only my butt to every store known to man.

Chapter 17

Black Friday.

The biggest shopping day of the year.

Most people spent the day getting up at the butt crack of dawn, fighting crowds and long lines trying to find the deal of the century.

The whole concept made me cringe.

Me, I spent the day running for my life. Well, first I'd gotten a pedi and mani with Lexi, a fat wad of good that was going to do me now.

The morning started out normal, as most mornings do, if you could call this morning. The sky was black as night, the air was brisk and crisp, and the woods surrounding Spring Valley were sleepy and quiet. Lexi drove us into the city as my eyes were unusually droopy. I couldn't think this early. It was unnatural.

I pulled my pink hoodie closer around me, letting the ends fall over my chilled hands. "Need. Coffee," I demanded like a zombie with bloodshot eyes and blood thirst.

"Hold your horses," Lexi grumbled. "If I had known you were such a crabass in the morning, I would have left you at home.

Jeesh."

"Please, you live with Chase. Nobody can be worse than him."

"True, but you come in close second." Lexi's aquamarine eyes glinted off the passing headlights as she quickly pulled into a 24-hour Starbucks.

I could have kissed her. Taking a sip of my raspberry mocha I burnt my tongue, but I didn't care. I sighed in heavenly appreciation. "So where is our first target?" I asked as the caffeine started to pump through my system.

"You are going to love this. And it's a BOGO."

The pirate smile on her lips said all I needed to know. I was going to hate it.

When she pulled up to a nail spa, I just about died. "Please tell me this is a joke."

"I would never joke about my nails."

That's what I was afraid of.

Getting both pedicure and manicures was the pits. I don't get how girls enjoy it. Sure the soaking was relaxing, but once they broke out the file, I was as wiggly as a puppy. The coffee wasn't helping. I felt sorry for the tech who worked on me. She kept giving me the stink eye. I really couldn't blame her. I was totally being a pain the buttocks. In my defense, this was my first time, and I wasn't the girly girl type. Painted nails were a luxury I just didn't have the tolerance for, or a steady hand. My nails usually looked like they were hacked by a chainsaw.

I stared down at my fresh glossy black cherry chutney (who makes up these names?) nails. "These will be demolished by tomorrow," I announced.

Lexi tsked her tongue and lead us onward to the next stop—a boutique. She sighed beside me. "You must lack a female gene, the one that gives you fashion sense."

That should've offended me, but it didn't. "I have fashion sense," I argued, thumbing through a clothing rack as if I knew what I was looking for. One glance at the price tag and I dropped it like hotcakes.

"Umm, maybe for a ten-year old. Face it Angel, jeans and converse aren't exactly fashionable." Her fingers expertly searched through the rack, knowing exactly what she wanted, the complete opposite of me.

"I beg to differ. Fashion is subjective." Okay, so high fashion wasn't my thing and yeah, maybe I only wore the bare essential of make-up, but that didn't mean that I didn't like to look hot. Lexi was going to give me a complex, on top of the ones I already had.

"Here, try this." She handed me a midnight blue top with a cutout in the back. "This will make your eyes pop."

Did I want my chameleon eyes to pop? Turning the tag around, I gasped. "No. Thank. You."

She rolled her eyes. "You need to use your womanly wiles and get Chase to spoil you once in a while."

"Why would I do that? I don't want his money."

She snickered. "Just his body."

I gave her a dry look and screwed up my nose, absolutely uncomfortable talking about Chase's magnificent body with his cousin.

"Because dummy. Chase is swimming in a trust account. The last thing he needs is another car or another toy." She shrugged. "I am sure he would be plenty happy to spend it on you."

"Lexi, I couldn't do that. I don't want a sugar daddy." Lexi never failed to throw me for a loop. "Is that what you want? A sugar daddy?" I asked.

She shrugged. "It beats being alone."

Even though she was acting like it wasn't a big deal, I could see that under the surface there was old pain and uncertainty about her future. Being a senior in high school could do that to you, even the ones who look like they have everything together. Being a half-demon that most human's outcast was…lonely and sad. That was what I saw lurking behind those startling aqua eyes. "Lexi, you're beautiful. Any guy would be lucky to have you. Money isn't as important as your happiness."

"It's easy for you to say. You have Chase."

"I don't really have Chase. And anyway he's been…weird

lately."

"Weirder than normal? I find that hard to believe."

I snorted. "I know right? He just seems to be pulling away."

"I know my cousin. If he is putting up walls, then he thinks he is protecting you somehow. Smash the wall down. Look…" She turned toward me, forgetting all about the racks upon racks of clothes. "Chase thinks he always knows best and sure most of the time he does, but he hardly ever put his feelings first. He is always battling everyone else's fights. Chase needs you, whether he likes it or not. You are the first real good thing that has ever happened to him, and I don't think he knows what to do about how he feels for you. He is exceptional at keeping people safe. He is not so good at expressing himself. It might take him forever to tell you that he loves you, but I am telling you that he does. Don't let him slip away. You'll regret it."

"Just because our souls are bound doesn't mean—"

"That is the worst copout. You were crazy for each other before that. It never would have happened if he wasn't in love with you. Chase would never make himself vulnerable like that for just anyone."

"I'm not so positive that what he feels for me is love," I replied, feeling too exposed.

I watched her eyes spark in annoyance. "I've never met two more clueless people. It is obvious to everyone that you guys are absolutely gaga over each other. So why don't the two of you see it? I know you feel it."

I wanted to deny, but I couldn't. But I also wasn't ready to admit it to myself, and I surely wasn't ready to say it out loud. "Maybe."

"I get that bearing your heart is scary. Giving your heart to someone like Chase is probably terrifying. Rejection sucks. But the reward is so much greater. It just has to be. Love is power, not that he needs anymore power, but you get what I am trying to say. When he takes a step back, you take two forward. Eventually he will have nowhere to go but to you."

"Did you ever think about writing poetry, because that was some seriously beautiful stuff? It brought a tear to my eye." I pretended to wipe at my eyes.

She bumped me playfully with her hip. "You're so lame."

"You aren't the first Winters to say so."

Her face softened. "But I am the one that matters."

It had been a long and exhausting day when Lexi finally called it quits, but I had expected nothing less. I sunk into the cushiony fabric seat of her car with every inch of my body aching. How did she do this? I felt like I just finished boot camp.

While I looked like I had been wrung through the trenches, Lexi looked fabulous. "Thanks for coming with me. It wouldn't have been the same alone. I'm really glad we're friends."

"Best friends," I supplied.

She gave me a smile bright enough to light the galaxy. I met hers with one of my own. We might not share the same taste in clothes, hobbies, or dating expectations, but somehow it worked.

Split-seconds passed from the time I looked from Lexi to the road. Literally seconds, but here in Spring Valley, seconds was all it took for trouble to find you. When I glanced back up my eyes clashed with a black and furry something, a highly unwelcomed sight. There smack dab in the middle of the road, was a hound. I couldn't suppress the gulp or the fear that quaked through me.

On the brink of my seat I waited, breath held, poised to see those horrible blood-red eyes. All I could think of was that I didn't want to die on Black Friday. It was too ominous. Lexi hit the brakes in a knee-jerk response, bucking us against our seatbelts. Her brakes protested against the asphalt in an ear-piercing scream.

The dog, at the shattering sound of her car coming to a screeching halt, turned its head. All I saw was crimson. I stopped breathing. I stopped thinking. My eyes locked on the black dog, frozen in terror.

"It's not a hellhound," Lexi said, but the roaring of pure panic in my head made it impossible for me to comprehend her words. In my book, hellhounds only ever meant more evil and dangerous things from the underworld were close on its heels.

My mind was clouded, living my own private nightmare. I

blinked and rubbed my eyes, trying to coax myself from going into a full-freak-out. It took many deep breaths before I saw the chocolate eyes, innocent and lost staring at me through the glass shield.

Just a dog. A normal dog. Nothing demonic in its eyes.

Fido gave one short bark and then paddled off the road, its tongue lolled to one side. I slumped all 125 pounds of me into the seat, shaken. "Christ, I think I just shaved a decade off my life," I said as Lexi regained her composure much faster than me and hit the gas.

"You don't have to tell me. I think I just got my first gray hair," she stated.

Just when my heart rate was almost normal and I could breathe sweet air again, I heard the roar of a powerful engine, like one of those monster truck sounds. I half expected to see a giant truck with teeth painted on the grill behind us.

If only.

God, now what?

Lexi's eyes darted to the rearview mirror, her knuckles tightening on the steering wheel. A SUV pulled up beside us driving like a bat out of hell. What a maniac. It was people like this guy who caused accidents. The SUV rumbled its engine as it rode alongside us on the wrong side of the tracks. At first I thought they were just going to pass us by obviously in a hurry, but they didn't. Steadily, the SUV kept pace with Lexi's little car. Every now and then it gave a roar of the engine.

My blood pressure went through the sunroof as the knowledge that this SUV wasn't friendly sunk in. I watched as Lexi's eyes melded in gold, making every hair on my body stand up. Normally Lexi was the epitome of control. If she lost it, then we were in some serious dog poo.

"Oh shit," I said under my breath.

Lines of concentration creased on her mouth, and I could tell she wanted to be anywhere but trapped in this car, unable to tap into her demon strength. And then she had me to worry about— the frail whatever I was. Gripping the edge of my seat again, I prepared myself for the absolute worst, and my mind was very imaginative.

I watched stunned as the blue SUV jerked toward us. Lexi's eyes got huge. "Angel, call Cha—"

Her voice was broken off. Like something from the Dukes of Hazard, the monster truck sideswiped her car. It caused quite a chain reaction.

Her poor car crunched under the impact, metal screeching against metal.

Lexi's car fishtailed, swerving out-of-control.

And we screamed bloody murder.

Chapter 18

By the time I cleared my rattled brain the SUV had recovered and was coming at us again. My eyes adjusted just in time to catch a view of the lunatic driver. She was female and had hair the color of strawberries and spun gold.

Emma.

That skankbag. I should have known.

Leave it to Emma to be a buzz kill. What looked to be the perfect end to an exhausting day was ruined by none other than my newest enemy. And the sad part, she wasn't even supernatural. What she was becoming was a nuisance, extremely bothersome, and a giant pain in my arse. And I don't think I needed to mention that she was also life-threatening.

You'd have thought I would have been prepared for the second impact. I wasn't. I knew it was coming and there was nothing I could do about it. Bracing myself, with my feet against the floorboards, I prayed we wouldn't spin off the road and end in the ditch. I had no desire to be flipped in a car. Again. It wasn't that I didn't trust Lexi's demon abilities... It was that I thought Emma would finish what she started. Kill us while we were incapacitated by shards of car parts.

On the second hit, my skull crashed into the passenger side window, spidering the glass. My head split in blinding pain, and I felt the sticky substance of blood drip down the side of my forehead. Black stars colored my vision and I heard Lexi call my name through the tunnel of blackness. When the fuzziness cleared, the nightmare wasn't over as I had hoped.

Neck and neck the two vehicles raced down the deserted road. Stupid Spring Valley and its country roads. There was never anybody around when you needed them and really how much more of playing bumper cars could Lexi's take?

"Hey, you okay?" Lexi asked for what I was certain wasn't the first time.

"Yeah, I'll live another day." At least I thought I would if we managed to get out of this sticky situation.

"Good. 'Cuz Chase would fry my ass if anything happened to you." She looked a tad concerned.

We didn't really have time to chitchat or formulate a plan because the SUV was relentless and coming at us again. To make matters worse, if we hurt Emma, we would directly be hurting Travis and nobody wanted it to come to that. But that didn't mean we couldn't play a little dirty.

Oh my God. Chase must be rubbing off on me.

"Hit her!" I yelled.

"Hang on. I have a better idea. I've grown tired of these games." Lexi said in an eerie voice, very unlike her usual tone, and slammed the brakes. The sound of rubber screeching pierced our ears. Smoke burned from the tires and my seatbelt dug into my chest as we came to a harsh stop. My head hit the head rest in a jarring thump.

The SUV went flying by.

"Now what?" I questioned, unsure what the plan was.

"I'm going to go buckwild on her boney butt," Lexi informed. She had that same crazy pitch to her tone.

It was starting to scare me.

The SUV's brake lights flashed red, and before I had the chance to object, Lexi vanished in front of my eyes. Her door was wide open, letting in the chilly November air. I jumped from the car just in time to see Emma step out of the SUV. I don't think she ever saw Lexi coming. Heck, I didn't even see her until she had Emma pinned against the car with one hand at Emma's throat.

This was bad.

I stared to jog toward the SUV hoping that we would be able to settle this without any more bloodshed. My head was still throbbing like a snare drum. The cut on the side of my head was sticky and covered in dried up blood, not to mention it was painful. I just wanted to get home.

I rarely see Lexi with her demon eyes, but right now they were set aflame. The hand wrapped around Emma's neck squeezed as she struggled to breathe. I approached cautiously not sure what I was supposed to do. Did I try to stop Lexi? Or do I sit back and do nothing, potentially letting Lexi do irreversible damage to Emma?

Turned out I didn't have to decide.

Lexi looked fierce and wicked. She eased her grip, but held Emma in place. "My brother might be blinded by the past and what you used to be, but I'm a realist. I know what you are. I can't believe we used to be friends." Her words hung in the air and an emotion I couldn't identify flickered over Emma's face before she sealed it behind an expressionless glare. "Is there even a fraction of who you used to be underneath all that hate?" Lexi questioned with the sincerity of a friend trying to reach out.

"That girl is gone. Nothing I can do will bring her back. I can't turn the hands of time," Emma wheezed.

"No, I don't suspect you can. But you aren't the only one who has changed. My brother's never been the same since you disappeared. He was crushed, frantic by your sudden departure. I want to ensure that he doesn't feel that kind of pain again." Lexi angled her head, trying to get her point across.

"You want to kill me. So, what's stopping you?" Emma baited like she had a death sentence. This chick wasn't afraid of death. It made me wonder what kinds of hell she had endured. On second thought, I wasn't sure I wanted to know.

"My brother. Unlike you, I care about him."

"You don't know jack about how I feel," Emma spat, anger fueling her words.

This was going nowhere. Lexi must have realized it too. "Get in your beastie truck and do my brother a favor. Ride out of Spring Valley and never come back." She released her viper grip from Emma's white neck. She'd lost all the color from her usual peachy complexion.

Emma's eyes were twin blazing cut emeralds. Oh, she had a lot more she wanted to say to Lexi, but also knew this was one battle where she was out numbered. Flinging off the car, she got behind the wheel and spun the gravel under her tires as she revved the engine.

The two of us sat there in silence staring at the back of the SUV until it was no longer visible. Our ride home was somber. Irritation still radiated off Lexi, and I wasn't going to be the one to push her over the cliff, figuratively speaking. We pulled into her driveway with half her bumper dragging on the ground. She had to hold her door closed while she drove. Thank God for demon strength. Her pathetic car clanked the whole way home like it was barely holding together. It would have been safer if we had walked home, and we probably should have called a tow truck, but she didn't want what had gone down reported to the police. It was best to keep the authorities out of Divisa business. The less the authorities knew the safer they all were.

I should have known Chase would be able to feel that something was wrong. What surprised me was that he hadn't come barreling down the road searching for us. It wasn't like him to sit back and be idle. Standing in the driveway, he examined Lexi's car with flames leaping in his eyes. If she noticed her cousin's battle stance she didn't show it. With her head held high, she grabbed her mounds of shopping bags from the back and swung her door open, leaving it ajar. There was no point in trying to latch it. The darn thing looked like it was only attached by one tiny bolt. It was hopeless.

"Lexi!" Chase rumbled.

I cringed at his firm and cold voice.

"Why is Angel bleeding? You were supposed to keep her out of trouble." He accused, being such an insensitive boar. I wanted to throttle him.

"Ah!" cried Lexi, frustrated to a point of no return.

Here we go, I thought.

The packages in her hands waved wildly as ranted, "I have had a day from hell, and I can't do this with you right now. Angel can explain."

Travis's laugh echoed from the porch. "What did you hit with your car? A dinosaur or your fist?"

"Ha. Ha. Ha," she mocked with her blonde locks flying. "I should have hit your girlfriend with it when I had the chance and if you don't stop laughing I'll hit you with my fist."

Oh boy.

"You saw Emma?" There was a desperate hope in his voice.

She leered at Travis. "Yes dear brother. We had a lovely chat, catching up on old times."

His eyes flashed." Lexi," Travis warned.

"No. I've freaking had it," she dropped her bags and threw her dainty arms out. "I'm done being nice. I'm done doing what I'm told. I'm done taking orders from the two of you," she raved like a woman fed up, then picked up her stuff off the floor and stormed off.

My friend just flipped her lid. It was the first time I've seen her completely frazzled and about to unravel. I'd never seen them fight like this. It was…intense and scary.

Travis intercepted Lexi from walking into the house, lips curled and the muscles on his back flexed. "If you hurt her—"

"You'll what?" Lexi baited in abandoned rage. "Eliminate me? I'd like to see you try." Okay, I am pretty sure that was going a little overboard. Travis would never hurt Lexi. *Right?* Not even to save Emma. But as I thought it, I began to have doubts. As I am sure Lexi did as well. How far was Travis willing to go?

Travis was silent, only further infuriating Lexi, not that I blamed her. She spun on her three-inch heels and gracefully stomped into the house with Travis nipping at her heels.

There was however, an obscene amount of yelling, door slamming in every direction, and in general stuff crashing.

I kept waiting for Chase to intercede, but he never did.

Nada.

Instead, he sauntered over to me and leaned on the car beside me like there wasn't World War III going on inside his house. A panel on the side of the car thumped to the ground. Neither of us so much as twitched.

"Wow. Talk about going out with a bang." My throat was scratchy from all the excitement. It was too much for one day, so I resorted to sarcasm. It was my crutch.

He shook his head at me. "Let's get you inside and take a look at that nasty gash. Then you can tell me what in God's creation happened."

It was sad, but right now I'd follow him anywhere, even into the fiery pits of Hell. I just didn't want to let him out of my sight. I nodded and let him lead me next door. He carefully cleaned the wound as I grimaced like a baby.

He grinned at me. I scowled at him. "You're enjoying this," I stated.

He shook his dark tousled head. "No, not really."

"Liar."

His gunmetal eyes sobered. "I don't like seeing you in pain."

That I believed. I swallowed, trying not to get lost in his velvet eyes. "It hardly hurts anymore."

"Liar."

Our smiles mirrored each other. Tonight was the first night in two weeks that I felt like the barrier he'd been building around himself was gone. Our eyes locked, and something passed between us. My tattoo tingled frenziedly, and I knew he was as captivated as I was in this moment. I wanted to close the space between us, but was too chicken shit. Why didn't he make the first move? At least then I would know what to expect.

He cleared his throat. "So what did you do this time?" he asked teasingly.

Leave it to Chase to shatter a perfectly good moment. "Emma went mental and tried to run us of the road, then Lexi choke-slammed her. It was awesome." I was never good with details.

He arched a brow. "Awesome, huh?"

I grinned, loving that the jab went to his ego, the desired effect. He could be so predictable. "Well, she is pretty kickass for a girl," I retorted.

Leaning back on the wall, he crossed his arms smirking like he was hot shit. "Oh, yeah. I happen to think I'm pretty awesome."

I rolled my eyes. "Why am I not surprised?" I made the

mistake of blinking, because suddenly he was in front of me and I was staring into a pair of glittering eyes the color of platinum.

"Speaking of awesome, I hear you've acquired a new trick," he said. The low and sexy tone of his voice tickled my belly.

I tilted my head back. "Travis told you, huh?"

He brushed my hair back from my head, feathering lightly over the cut on my head. I expected pain, but felt nothing but a dull ache. "It looks like you got more than a tattoo from being soulbond to me. You heal as well. Fast."

My hand immediately went to my head where the cut should have been. There was nothing but tenderness to the touch. No bumpy raised skin. "Why couldn't I get anything cool like super speed or inhuman strength?"

He snickered. "Well, on the flipside you aren't as breakable anymore."

I punched him in the side which only rewarded me with a chuckle. That was what he got for standing so close.

"Brat," he uttered under his breath and laced his fingers with mine.

My stomach back flipped.

"I better get you off your feet. Who knows how much blood you've lost. I wouldn't want you fainting on me," he said, leading me toward the family room.

I snorted. "I've never fainted in my life."

Raising that damn brow with the hoop in it, he called my bluff.

"Fine. Before meeting you," I added.

He laughed. "Angel Eyes, you just don't give up graciously." He collapsed onto the couch.

I stared down at him. "Where would you like me to sit? I'm the patient here and you take up the whole thing with that Viking body."

Grinning, he tugged me down beside him. "Right here," he whispered, weaving a secured arm around my waist. Heat grazed over each part his hand touched before settling cozily on my hip.

In his arms the gut-dropping fear from the day dissolved. I rested my hand on his beating heart. "Do you think they will get past this?" I asked, thinking about Travis and Lexi under the same roof with boiling tempers.

It was scary how in tune we were. He didn't need to ask who I was talking about. We apparently were wired into the same frequency. "Eventually."

"By eventually, do you mean once we figure out what to do about Emma?"

"Don't worry about that now. Just rest."

That meant yes and I'll handle it. I didn't press him, but I wanted to. My droopy eyes won over. I guess I was just too worn out to think about all that right now. I just wanted a few stolen moments in his arms while he wasn't pushing me away. So I took advantage of being in his embrace and snuggled deeper into his chest, closing my eyes in serene peace.

When I awoke sometime in the middle of the night, sprawled out on the couch, I was alone. He had snuck out on me again. Probably best. But my heart didn't agree and that worried me.

Chapter 19

"I saw Emma last night," Travis confessed.

He showed up on my doorstep Saturday, soaked to the bone, looking lost. It had started pouring buckets and buckets of rain early in the morning, pelting the roof in a rain dance. I had every light on in the house and it still didn't chase away the gloominess. What a cruddy day. Thunder rumbled the old wooden floorboards, lightening cracked, casting bursts of light through the windows. It was so dark and depressing outside you would never know it was late afternoon. Mom had just left for her shift when Travis knocked on the door. He was the only Winters who didn't just let themselves in.

"Funny, so did I," I replied wryly.

He gave me a dull look. Apparently this was a serious conversation, and I was being my normally flippant self. "I thought if I could talk to her…" He stood up from the couch and started pacing, restlessness vibrating off him. Locks of dark blonde hair were plastered against his face and he was leaking puddles all over my mom's floor.

My heart went out to Travis. It was impossible not to notice how much he had changed since Emma's untimely appearance. The string of emotions that crossed his face daily was a yoyo of hope, confusion, determination, and anguish.

I hugged my knees, just listening to him struggle. What could I really say to ease the jumble of emotions he was feeling?

"There are moments when I break through that thick barrier and see the girl I loved behind it," he continued. "But it's just glimpses. Nearly as quick, she puts that tough girl chip back in place and I don't recognize her. How do I break through? Really break through to her?"

A bolt of lightning crackled across the sky. "I don't know her, not like you."

"I used to think I knew her better than anyone, better than myself. But now…I'm not sure of anything except that I can't give up on her."

Of course not. Travis was not that kind of guy. Well, apparently before Emma he was *that* kind of guy and much worse, or so the stories go. "I don't really have any profound words of wisdom that will magically turn her back. I'm not a wizard." And I royally sucked at trying to cheer him up. It boggled my mind why he trusted me. "Neither of you is the same anymore. I think you both need to somehow rediscover each other."

He turned away from the cloudy window and looked at me. "And how do you propose we do that? She has suddenly declared herself my enemy. I can hardly get her to talk to me."

"Every couple has their challenges. Yours is just…different."

The corner of his lip twitched, exposing one of his dimples. "You really suck at this."

Duh. I rolled my eyes. "So what happened when you saw her last night?" I couldn't help but ask, curiosity getting the best of me.

"Not as much as I would have liked."

"Was she surprised to see you?"

"You could say that. She didn't see me coming, that's for sure. After she got over her shock, it felt like old times for a minute. Then she started ranting about her dad, me being at her house and how he would kill me."

Yeah, that all sounded about right. And unnerving. Travis was a braver man than I. It helped he was half-demon I guess.

"When she realized I wasn't budging, she started to threaten me. Said she would kill me herself if I didn't get off her property."

If I wasn't mistaken, it actually sounded like Emma was protecting Travis. Protecting him from her batshit crazy father. "I think she was trying to save you, warn you that her house wasn't safe, Travis." I was giving him more hope. I just prayed it wasn't false hope.

He considered that for a moment before his eyes filled with sorrow. "I miss her so much. There is this giant, gaping hole in my heart that can only be filled by her. I don't know how to fix it. Fix us."

Oh lordy. We already established he was definitely coming to the wrong peep for advice on relationships. "I'm no expert here." I can't believe what I was about to say. It was no secret that I was no big fan of Emma. I kept thinking if it was Chase, what would I do? What lengths would I go to, to protect him? And the answer was simple. What wouldn't I do for Chase was more the question. There was nothing I wouldn't do. Nothing I wouldn't endure. No price I wasn't willing to pay to keep him alive. I'd never give up on him.

The scary part was, I just realized the depth of how I truly felt about the jerkwad. "You just can't give up," I said softly.

Travis's eyes clashed with mine and surprise overrode the sorrow. He nodded. "You're right. Thanks. I knew you we're the only one who would understand. Black Ops later?"

A round of search and destroy cured everything. "You know it. Hey, can you tell Chase I want to talk to him?"

"Yeah, no prob. He's lucky to have you. If he hurts you, I'll pulverize him."

We stepped onto the porch; the sun was peeking behind a sheet of black clouds. The ground was drenched and smelled of earth and worms. I clung to the damp banister as I watched Travis cross the yard between our houses.

His situation left me realizing again how short and precious life really was. I didn't want to live with regrets and what ifs. Lately I'd been suppressing feelings I didn't want to admit were there. They scared the living piss out of me. Now, suddenly as I found myself staring into Chase's silver stone eyes, I knew what I was going to do.

No regrets.

I must have been out of my mind or glutton for disappointment, because there was no way this was going to turn out like I envisioned.

How could it?

We were so different, besides him being part demon, I mean. Night and day, we were.

Seeing him strut over toward me caused my heart to somersault. He looked homegrown and delicious in torn jeans and a t-shirt that only made his biceps look that much more edible. "Hey," he greeted. "You look better."

I shuffled my feet nervously on the porch. "Better than what?"

"Do you always have to argue with everything I say?"

It was on the tip of my tongue to say something snappy, and my anxiety wasn't helping in any way. "Maybe."

The wood of the porch supports creaked under his weight as he leaned a hip into it. "I didn't get a chance to mention it last night, but I think it would be best if you didn't let it get out…what you can do. Not everyone will like the idea that you can get inside their head."

"They'll think I'm a threat," I stated, reading into his suggestion. Immediately I thought of Sierra. She would love any excuse to wipe me from the planet. "I don't plan on broadcasting it over the six o'clock news."

He gave me a come get me grin. "Okay, with that settled, you can stop the nervous shuffle and just spit it out."

I frowned. "Why would you think I have anything to say to you?" Dumb question, but my brain wasn't processing properly.

I got an arched brow.

My insides were a giant jittery pile of gnats. I looked down at my joined hands, knowing I just had to spit it out. There was no other way and if I didn't do it now, I was going lose my nerve altogether. I sighed heavily. "Fine," I said crossing my arms. "I don't understand what is going on between us. One minute you are all over me, and the next you can't get far enough away. What gives?"

"Nothing gives, except your bad taste in company."

"Did you and Travis have some kind of falling out I don't know about?"

He shrugged. "We just have different ideas of what's right. This Emma thing hasn't got him thinking straight."

"Let me guess, your way is the right way."

He gave me a pearly grin. "Of course."

"That still doesn't explain why you are acting all weird." I called bullshit. "I feel it remember? Ever since we got back from seeing Ives you've been acting strange. What could he have possibly said to make you bug out?"

He looked out over my shoulder staring into the woods behind my house. "I'm not bugging out. And it's not so much what he said, but our situation."

"Situation? You're talking about being strapped to me for all eternity?"

"It's not like that and you know it."

"What is it like, Chase? Because I'm not getting it. If you are having second thoughts—"

His eyes returned to mine. "I don't regret the outcome of what happened that night I saved you. I would do it again in a heartbeat. I just wish that I had been able to save your soul. Knowing that it's been darkened by Hell kills me. Then there are all these feelings that I don't know what to do about. When I'm not near you, it feels like there is a gaping hole in my heart. The further and longer I'm gone, the bigger it gets. Suddenly, I find myself unable to get a grip on my control. It gets more difficult every day I see you."

Oh wow. Oh God. Oh wow.

Something happened that only happens once in a blue moon.
I went tongue-tied.

"Angel…say something."

I couldn't believe it. My head was whirling. I demanded to
know what was going through his head, and to my great surprise,
he just admitted more than he had since I met him over the
summer.

"Your eyes are doing that weird voodoo thing again," he
commented, filling the void.

He totally stole my line. And hey, I'm not the one with
voodoo eyes. He was. I'll admit there might be something different
about mine, but they didn't glow neon. That constituted as way
more weird.

He stood there beside me waiting, while I was trying to pick
my mouth off the ground looking stupefied. "You've always been
in control around me." That was all I could think to say. I guess it
was better than, *what did you say?* That had been my initial response.
Classic.

He rose off the banister, watching me intently. "Then I put on
a good front. The truth is, I've never felt more out of control than
when I am with you."

Something inside me snapped. I don't know what came over
me, but I knew it was now or never. This was it. I was balanced on
the verge of a pivotal moment, teetering on the edge of a gigantic

mountain—the point of no return. The fact that I had just come to this conclusion myself and really hadn't processed it thoroughly probably wasn't the best possible time to share, but I knew me. If I didn't do it while I had the kahunas, I never would.

So I slipped my fingers into the front pockets of his jeans, pulling him to me. His body pinned me up against the white porch railings, and the split-second our bodies touch, his dark stormy eyes went intent and hungry. I shivered, because it was exactly the same for me.

The static in the air surrounding us was electrifying. At this rate, we were bound to create our own lightning storm.

He must have seen it in my eyes, what was on the edge of my lips. "Angel, don't do it," he growled. "Don't you say it."

Ooops. Too late.

The words were already pouring from my mouth. And too bad he didn't want to hear them. I was going to tell him how I felt whether he wanted it or not. There was no way I could keep these emotions suppressed and bottled up anymore. They were eating me up inside, bursting to break free. So I did. I went for it, heart first.

"I love you," I blurted out before I even realized what I was saying. Did I really just say those three huge, monstrous, relationship changing words? *Oh God. Oh God. Oh. My. God.*

Now that it was out there, I was scared shitless, shaking in my black converses.

He squeezed his eyes shut, blocking his reaction from my gaze. Jaw clenched, the vein in his temple ticked, and I could feel his muscles constrict. "You don't know what you've done." His voice was strained like he had a bad toothache.

This was not the reaction I'd wanted. And when time elapsed and he didn't say anything else, I panicked.

Big time.

"I take it back. I take it all back. I despise you. I hate you. I loathe you," I ranted, shoving at his chest. I would have gone on and on, if he hadn't stopped me, but I think he got the point. Jerky, he wouldn't let me go, and I so desperately wanted to run.

Firm hands held me from escaping, keeping me close. The heat from his nearness infused my already flushed body. There was some emotion I couldn't identify that spread across his face. "You can't take it back. I won't let you."

Won't let me? He has lost his frickin' mind. *Let me?*

I ran a frustrated hand through my hair. "I can't stand you," I spat. This wasn't going as planned.

"Liar. You can't keep your hands off me."

And then he proved his point by sealing his lips over mine in a crushing kiss that rocked my sensory system into to orbit. Anger. Love. Need. A million emotions tangled inside me. My body went haywire, completely forgetting that I hated him.

Love.

Hate.

Really, there was such a fine line, and that line between Chase and I was more like a thread. I was drawn into him, swept away from reality. It was just him and me. And his lips.

His lips were a godsend.

My chest rose sharply as his fingers dug into my denim, holding me against him. I threaded my fingers into the soft hair at the nape of his neck. Balancing myself on my tiptoes, I gave him most of my weight and sunk into those delicious lips as he kissed me deeply. All I wanted was for this to never stop. Never end.

But of course all good things come to an end. If he hadn't pulled back when he had, we'd probably have done something wicked on my porch.

Softly he said, "You'll probably regret loving me. I don't deserve it, but…" His eyes interlaced with flecks of topaz, and I could feel his demon surface. "I'll never let anything bad happen to you. Never again."

I traced my fingers on his cheek and down alongside his jaw line, feeling his body tighten as he fought to stay in control. But that was just it. With me, I didn't want him to constantly battle with the demon inside. I wanted all of him. Every. Part. Including the demon. This was what I'd signed up for when I had told him I loved him.

"Chase," I whispered his name.

He closed his eyes, laying his forehead against mine. Around us the after winds of the storm blew.

My arms were still wrapped around his neck, and I absently played with the ends of his hair. "You don't have to rein it in with me. I trust you."

"That's just the thing, Angel Eyes. You shouldn't. You really shouldn't. But with you I can't help myself, and it scares me. I refuse to hurt you."

"You won't," I assured and nipped his lip.

"*I* don't trust myself."

"Let go," I murmured against his mouth. And before I had finished the words, he was kissing me like he never had before. I knew that it wasn't just him I was kissing, but also the demon that lived deep inside. He had finally let me in, and I ardently kissed him back with all the love I had swelling in my heart for them both.

It was a package deal.

Even with my love for him racing through me and the taste his lips on mine, I couldn't help but think he didn't return the three words my heart desired.

Chapter 20

The high of being in love didn't last long. Monday morning came and gave me a rude awakening in the form of none other than Emma.

Monday blows.

She was like a sliver under the skin that I couldn't quite get rid of—pesky and persistent. High school was swiftly becoming a place I dreaded, and it was entirely her fault. This was my last year. It was supposed to be filled with wonderful memories, life-long friends, prom, and epic parties, not wondering what underhanded objective a too slighted hunter was devising. Not feeling scared I might not make it to my next class. Not having to always look over my shoulder.

She seemed to be able to find ways to corner me alone like some sixth sense. In the girl's bathroom. At the main office. On the track field. It was maddening. She was everywhere.

Damned if she also wasn't inventive. And determined. I'll give her that. In the following weeks, I came to realize that for reasons I didn't yet understand, Emma was targeting me. To make matters worse, I was positive that Chase had come to the same conclusion.

Today was one of those December days where I just wasn't able to dodge Emma and her twisted games. She seemed to get off instilling the fear of God in me. If Emma hadn't been a hunter, I was certain her and Sierra would have been besties. They were both mean as snot and had it in for me. Lately however, Sierra was actually…I wouldn't say nice, that was going too far, but she'd been tolerable. I guess Emma had Sierra shaking in her 4-inch Dior boots.

My name whispered over my shoulder in the girl's gym locker room. Coach Jenssen had sent me to retrieve a cart of soccer balls from the storage room. A simple errand, yet that was never in my case. Again my name breezed through the stuffy room smelling of sweaty socks and hairspray. I spun around.

Nothing.

Then I heard the unmistakable voice of Emma Deen. "Hiya demon lover." Her breath was at the back of my neck and something pointy was jabbed into my side.

I froze.

Gosh, even in a mesh gym uniform she looked formidable. "Where are your bodyguards when you need them?"

I swallowed, afraid to breath. "If you are going to kill me, just do it already," I said, managing to sound bored and a lot braver than I felt.

She chuckled. Emma had a sweet voice, but she had way of

making it sound like vinegar—bitter and foul. "And make it easy for you? Where is the fun in that?"

For someone who was so scrawny, she packed the strength of a giant. "You tell me. I'm not the one with ideas of perverse fun."

She stabbed the object further into my side, and I winced. Okay. Wrong answer. "Do you think your half-demon will still like you if I cut out your tongue?"

"He'd probably thank you."

"Maybe you're right." There was enjoyment in her voice. She spun me around. Her emerald eyes shimmered with amusement and arrogance as we stood face-to-face. "It's just a pen silly." She held up a blue ink pen, twirling it in her fingers. "See you later." Then she walked off.

I fumed.

My temper skyrocketed. I was going to beat her into a bloody pulp. I took a step forward, toward her retreating back with visions of her blood on my hands. How dare she threaten me with something as stupid as a pen.

"She giving you shit too?" Sierra asked, suddenly beside me, and I further shamed myself by jumping.

I couldn't decide if I was more annoyed that she had stopped me from going Claude Van Damme on Emma's ass, or if it was because was her. "What are *you* doing here?" I shrieked. My heart couldn't take all this excitement.

"Coach sent me to see what was taking so long. Don't worry, I told her you had your monthly and probably had to change your tube." Her grin was downright conniving.

"Wonderful," I said sarcastically. Ugh, two in one day. It was more than I could handle. A person can only take so much. I could feel her smirking and I shrugged. "Emma's threats are nothing new. They are starting to grow on me."

She snickered. "Travis better do something soon. Chase isn't going to let this continue much longer."

I sighed and hugged my arms around myself. "I know." My voice was tinged with sadness. I got this feeling that felt like rocks in my belly. This wasn't going to end well, and I think I was more afraid that when it was all said and done, Travis and Chase might not ever be the same. It was an ominous mood that settled between Sierra and I, our thoughts both heading down the same road.

"What do you plan to do about it little Miss sassy pants?" Sierra goaded.

Like I had any control over the outcome or over Chase for that matter. And I wasn't sure how I felt about her insult. "I don't know yet?"

"Well, I'll tell you what I'd like to do to Emma."

I thought maybe I should cover my ears for the next part. It was probably going to be graphic and gruesome.

"I'd like to rearrange twinkle toes face and shove one of those arrows up her—"

"I got the point," I interrupted, not really needing anymore details.

"Do you?"

Yeah, she was as crazy as Emma. "We should get back to class."

~*~*~*~

After dumping my bag by the front door, I threw myself on our zebra print couch, staring crossed-eyed at the black and white stripes. I was mentally exhausted and had no plans to move from this spot for the rest of the night.

Of course plans change.

Twirling the charm bracelet twinkling at my wrist, I couldn't help but smile, regardless that today had been a craptastic day. Every time I looked at this bracelet, I thought back to the day I received it. It was one of those treasured memories that you never forget, one of those perfect days. This little silver piece of jewelry would forever symbolize that moment. It was what made it so special.

It was also the first gift Chase gave me.

Well unless you don't count the tattoo, which I didn't. That hadn't been quite what I thought of as a gift, more of a hindrance.

We had been sitting on the porch steps when he pulled

something out of his pocket. There was an unmistakable gleam shining in his eyes, playful and full of delight. "Here." He held out his hand with a tiny pink box in the center of his palm. I almost giggled at seeing such a frilly and girly color in Chase's masculine hand. The deep pink package was tied with a thin ribbon around.

"Did you buy me a gift?" I asked, my blue eyes narrowing in suspicion. What was he up to? I was almost too nervous to get excited in case this was some kind of sick joke. I wasn't naive enough to think just because I had professed my love for him that he would suddenly become the guy of my dreams. This was the real world, and I accepted Chase for exactly what he was, an arrogant, commanding, hot, bad boy with the temper of a demon.

How could a girl resist?

I plucked the square box from his palm.

He shrugged, stuffing his empty hands into his jean pockets. "It's no big deal. I saw it in the window and thought of you."

I tried my damnedest to not be touched, to not let my heart flop at the gesture.

No lie. It was hard.

Impossible really.

Unraveling the white ribbon, I tugged open the box. This little package was better than Christmas morning. Better than a fresh baked orange scone. Better than getting a new video game. Better than...I think I made my point. My insides fluttered like fragile hummingbird wings.

Wow, just wow.

Resting on a bed of that poofy, fabric stuff was the prettiest silver bracelet I'd ever laid eyes. I wasn't a blingy kind of gal, usually some earring studs and watch a completed my ensemble, but this was simple and beautiful.

With adept fingers he took the shimmering chain and clasped the charm bracelet around my wrist. The moon and stars chimed together as I spun it around, admiringly.

"It's beautiful," I whispered, afraid if I said anymore, my voice might give away too much, or there was the chance that I would choke on the intense feelings coursing through me.

He reached for my hand, sparks ignited on contact. You think by now I would be used to the whole cosmic tension that was always between us. "The two stars each have an engraving, see…" He spun the trinkets around so that I could read them, and my eyes ran over the etchings.

"AM and CW…" my voice broke off with a hitch. Our initials. Now he'd done it. For sure I was going to start bawling like a sappy twit, and I was definitely not a sappy anything.

Not a big deal? Who was he kidding? You don't get something personalized if it wasn't a big deal.

I came back from memory lane with a smile on my lips and suddenly heard the strangest sound. Don't get me wrong, my house made all kinds of weird sounds, but this didn't belong, sort of like a branch hitting the house. It started out as just a pesky scratch, but I couldn't pinpoint the source. Ignoring it didn't make it go away.

Drats.

Someday ignoring a problem was going to work.

Then those little scratches were accompanied by the teeniest cry. At first, I was sure that I imagined it. Yet, whatever it was, they were persistent, and those tiny cries became more of a desperate yawl.

We better not have mice.

Muting the TV, I tiptoed through the house trying to locate the source. It didn't help that every other floorboard groaned under my weight. As I approached the backdoor, it became apparent that the cries were actually more of meows. Cracking the door with caution, I wasn't too sure that the only thing behind this door was an innocent cat.

For once it was nice to be wrong. There pacing on the threshold was a tabby colored kitten. Cocoa colored stripes covered his fluffy coat. Where had this surprise come from? My guess, he was a wittle-bitty lost farm kitten. Poor fellow.

It was at least a mile to our nearest neighbor. I didn't even consider them neighbors, it was that far. I couldn't believe he traveled the distance by his lonesome. His sad green-yellow eyes looked up at me, and he gave another pitiful meow. I bent down to pick him up, and the scamp darted down the steps. What a little pooper.

Biting my lip, I debated going after him. In the end, I knew I couldn't leave him out in the cold. Evening was approaching right around the corner, and he would probably freeze to death if I didn't offer him shelter for the night. It was going to be one of those cold ass nights where you could see your own breath. Tomorrow I would take him into town and see if anyone was looking for him.

Now, I just had to catch the stinker.

I took a quick peek next door just to make sure I wasn't under lockdown. There was a driveway of cars parked next door. They were apparently having some kind of Divisa powwow, which I hadn't been invited too. Not that I wanted to be involved in their half-demon politics. Though I half expected someone to pop behind me and scold me for sneaking out past curfew.

Cutting across the slightly damp grass to the edge of the woods, I kept my eyes glued on the kitty. He turned his head up at my approach, eyes glinting off the half-moon that shone through the branches.

"Hey, little guy." I slowly crouched closer to his level. He watched me intently, looking ready to run. "Come here, kitty, kitty," I coaxed in baby talk and held out my hand.

We never had pets growing up, so I wasn't even sure if this kind of thing was effective. I inched forward and he dashed just inside the one place I wasn't very keen about entering.

"Seriously," I muttered in aggravation and regretted not grabbing a hoodie. The last thing I wanted tonight was to be chasing a stray kitten through the woods.

I knew that I shouldn't follow the little rascal into the woods, but I couldn't help myself. He was lost and alone. He needed my help. A little farther into the forest wouldn't hurt. It was not like I was miles away. I could still see my house in the distance. Straightening my shoulders, I took a deep breath and crossed into the place of my nightmares.

A chilly gust of wind lifted my dark hair and sent a shower of brownish dead leaves shimmering around me. An eerie shiver shuddered through me, skirting down my spine. Just like my spooky old house, there was something dark and forbidden living in these woods. Not just the hounds from Hell that roamed at twilight, not just the lower demons sent to cleanup. Or maybe it was all of that and more. Blood had dripped on the forest floor of needles and crumbled leaves. Creatures and humans hunted in here. Maybe it was that these woods had seen more than I could wrap my mind around.

Letting out a nervous laugh, I realized how incredibly silly I was being, working myself into a tizzy. Moving forward, I spotted the nuisance not too far in front of me. It was time for a new approach. Cautious be damned. I marched right up to the rascal, grabbed him by the scruff of the neck and—

The snapping of a twig sent my heart in a downward spiral. My heels dug into the partial frozen dirt as I stood and spun in wild circles, searching. The furball forgotten and my own instinct for survival kicked in. Though I could see no one, I knew I was no longer alone in the trees. A ghostly silence hit the air, and the only sound was the quickened rise and fall of my chest.

I never saw it coming. Never new was lurking about, because at that moment a wet rag was pressed against my mouth and nose from behind me. I opened my mouth to scream, Chase's name on the tip of my tongue—a fatal mistake. No sound came out, and it was followed by the smell and taste of a pungent odor. Frantic, I fought but in seconds my limbs refused to obey my brain. Heavily, I felt myself sink into oblivion.

My eyes lost focus, blurring the forest into a muddle of colors. There were voices behind me, smothered from recognition.

Then everything went black.

Chapter 21

I woke up with the feel of cold steel pressed against my cheek. Goosebumps covered my arms, chilling me to the bone. Disoriented, I slowly lifted open my eyes, fluttering against blackness. A musky dampness filled the air, tickling my nose.

I blinked, which to my annoyance didn't really do much.

There was heaviness to my lids that made it difficult to keep them open. A fog snared inside my brain. When the cloudiness lifted and my vision finally cleared, I wished for blissful darkness again. Nothing made sense.

What happened to me?

Where was I?

Because I was pretty sure I wasn't in Kansas anymore. And if this was Oz, where were my ruby red slippers? Had I slipped down a rabbit hole and landed in Wonderland?

All fairytales start with a bump on the head and as I sat up, I was damn sure I had one of those. Cursing, a stinging pain shot through the back of my head and made me gasp. I rubbed the tender spot and got my first glimpse of my surroundings. It wasn't a palace.

Nothing in a million years would have prepared me for the sight at which greeted me. This was far from a Never-Never Land and there weren't going to be any dwarfs at my rescue. Not in a room this tiny.

I looked around the closet size room wildly, my blue eyes going wide. There was nothing but a metal bed bolted to the floor and a door with thick bands of bars. It was a cell. My stomach knotted unbearably. Stark fear rose in my throat like bile, coating it with pure panic.

Reality descended upon me all at once.

I was trapped.

Captured.

A prisoner.

This was the kind of thing that only happened on CSI—only happened to other people. Not me. I did not want to make the local news. I was not that girl on the side of the milk carton who'd been abducted, whose mom was frantically going out of her mind with worry.

Mom.

She was going to be beside herself. What would she do without me? I hated having to think about her mourning for me. What she would go through? How long would it take her to notice I was missing? Sometime days went by without us really seeing each other, just a text here and there to make sure I was alive. I knew Devin would take care of her, but it had always been just her and I. She needed me.

I needed her.

Desperately.

Right now I would have given my right arm to see her, just one more time before I left this life, because surely this was the end. I had no plan. No means of escape. No one probably even knew I was missing.

Not true.

Chase.

He would have known something was wrong. I had to believe that he would have felt something. At the very least, he would have sensed that I was no longer near. For the first time, this soulbond meant something more than just a nuisance. It might save me. At least it gave me hope.

I'd barely had time to bask in the glow of being in love with Chase and now…

Would we ever see each other again? I was glad now more than ever that I'd actually had the gumption to tell him how I felt. It had surprised not only him, but me. Picturing his face, his silvery eyes, that impossible smirk, his dark and deadly voice, I missed him miserably.

My chest began to pang from being separated, knowing I was moments away from extreme panic. Memories of the woods, of voices, and the little tabby kitty I'd wanted to save came crashing back like a bad train wreck. I thought back, racking my brain for an explanation. I remembered someone sneaking up behind me. I remembered fighting and thinking if I could just scream Chase's name, but I'd never gotten the chance.

I had been silenced. After that it was just blank, like a gaping wormhole. There were a few brief seconds where I remembered a nasty, rancid scent.

It must have been chloroform.

That explained the quick and sudden blackout. What kind of sick and crazy person would kidnap *me*?

Really only one name came to mind. Yet I was still having a difficult time believing that *this* was real. It was too much of a cowink-a-dink that I just so happened to know a girl who had been missing for year and out-of-the-blue returned. Now her one mission in life was to kill half-demons, moi included.

Deep down I really wanted to believe that the old Emma Travis loved, fought for, was still in there. However, under recent developments, I was going to have to think Chase might have been right all along.

Emma was gone.

And by gone, I meant in the sense that the person she used to be had taken a hike, checked out, gone over the deep end. She was a ticking bomb, a loose cannon, and utterly deranged. This was my professional diagnosis.

Slipping off the metal bed, I stood legs wobbly and shaky as they touched the concrete floor. I knew in the pit of my stomach that there was no feasible way out of this chamber of terror, but I had to try. Even for just that teeny, tiny sliver of a chance that maybe someone screwed up and I could escape.

Running my hands along the block walls for stability (I thought I might pass out again) and also to check for anything out of the ordinary. Like I knew what that would be. Who was I kidding? I wasn't Agent Hotchner or Houdini. This wasn't a video game. There was no restart. There was no do over. And I wasn't an escape artist.

As far as I was concerned, this place was Fort Knox.

I pressed my palm against the frigid bars of my cell dejected, hands shaking. The distance between Chase and I had never felt so vast or dire. The aching in my chest started, telling me we'd been apart too long. It would only increase in tenfold.

Gripping the bars with both hands, every muscle locked up. I felt claustrophobic and knew I had to get out of this room. I don't know what came over me. One minute I was shaking from head-to-toe, the next I was rattling the bars and screaming at the top of my lungs.

All for nothing, except my throat was on fire, scorched and dry. I swear I swallowed blood. There hadn't been a peep, not a single movement from anywhere in the vicinity. It made me wonder if I was in a padded room.

Just fan-freaking-tastic.

When it became obvious that no one was coming, I began to pace, which was quite difficult. There wasn't much space and I ended more or less shuffling in place. Finally, I retreated to the bed with nothing else to do. Staring at the white walls, I figured I would go insane in a day. The least they could have done was giving me an Xbox. Hell, I would have even taken a Gameboy at this rate. Anything,

Pulling the quilt around me like a cape, I prepared myself for what would no doubt be the longest night of my life. The stark darkness of the evening filled the tiny room, except for the sliver of light from under the door.

The smell of the woods still lingered on my skin and painfully made me think of Chase. My chest ached in brutal pain, heavy with sorrow, fear, and missing Chase. I wished I could have seen the moon, the stars, knowing that he was out there under the same sky, frantic with worry for me. In a small way, it would have given me comfort, but in a windowless room, I had nothing but memories.

Curled on the small bed, I couldn't hold the tears a bay any longer. The floodgates opened like the breaking of a dam. Fat tears spilled down my cheeks, soaking the pillow. But once I started, I couldn't stop. My shoulders shook in time with my loud blubbering. An unflattering sob snuck out from my mouth and I sniffled disgustingly. Not only were my cheeks streaked with red-hot tears, snot was dripping from my nose.

On and on it went until there wasn't an ounce of fluid let in me, just those clenching dry heaves that were doing a number on my tummy.

When the hiccupping sobs stopped, a deep ache settled into my belly and muscles. I clamped my mouth shut until my teeth throbbed, refusing to shed another tear for these assholes. Then out of the dark, I heard the unmistakable sound of keys.

Someone was unlocking my chamber.

Chapter 22

I watched in blunt fear as the lock on the heavy armored door turned and clicked. The unknown of whom or what was behind the door ate away my backbone. I had the urge to hide my head under the pillow, plug my ears, and hum a lullaby to myself. Anything to pretend this was all just a very bad and vivid dream.

Except this nightmare was the real deal.

A burst of light broke through the darkened room at the same time the metal door scraped over the concrete floor. Blinking several times, I hugged my knees to my chest, trying to make myself as small as possible in the corner of the bed.

It was pointless.

The bed took up most of the small space, and I was hard to ignore in my white long-sleeve shirt. It practically glowed in the dark for heaven's sake. As my eyes adjusted, a profile of a woman began to take shape.

I expected to see the nasty Emma but the face that became clear was similar to Emma's, older. There was a strong resemblance, different hair color. Hers was a pale blonde compared to Emma's. But the eyes, there were unmistakably

Emma's. As green as summer grass, but they lacked Emma's cynic nature. She looked so darn familiar, but I couldn't place her face with a name. The woman was thin and had a soft, gentle smile on her lips, so opposite of Emma's hardass persona. It felt false and out of place considering the circumstances. She carried a tray of food that made my stomach lurch.

Hello, I'm a prisoner, my mind screamed. This wasn't an extended vacation, and I hadn't ordered room service.

There was nothing to possibly smile about. I wanted this woman to cut the bullshit and not give me any pitied smiles. It hit me then, why she looked so familiar to me. I'd seen this woman once before, outside the tiny dance studio in town. She had been with a little girl and her husband.

She was Emma's mom.

It was a family biz after all, and yet I was stunned to learn that she was involved. I couldn't see her as being the mastermind behind the madness. That had to be all Emma's dad, who I yet to official meet.

No rush on my part. I would be just as content to never set eyes on the nutjob.

She walked just inside the doorway, blocking the exit. My eyes flickered to the opened door and all I could think was, *if I could just get through that door.* The only thing standing between me and my freedom was a woman at least twice my age and not bigger than a stick. She looked like a push-over, nothing I couldn't throw my weight into.

"You don't want to try that," Emma's mom warned in a quiet and calm voice, sad almost.

I stayed silent, just staring at her while my mind worked like a hamster wheel, spinning and spinning. Why shouldn't I try to get free? I could totally take her. How much worse could it be outside these four walls?

She must have seen the doubt in my eyes. "I'm not alone," she sighed. "There are men stationed outside this room. Do you think you can get past them all? Men trained, armed, and ruthless."

My stomach dropped miles. My shoulders sagged. My eyes brimmed with hopelessness. "You're Emma's mom," I said, surprised at how foreign my voice sounded.

Mrs. Deen's whole face lit up at them mention of Emma. It made me wonder if she ever got to spend quality time with her daughter or if husband monopolized it all with his grueling-demon-hate training exercises to kill.

"I am." She set the tray of food she'd been carrying on a tiny table right inside the door. Again, the sight of food made me what to vomit all over the pristine room. I averted my eyes before I emptied my stomach. "Here, I brought you something to eat. You'll need to keep up your strength."

"Strength?" I echoed, afraid of what she meant. They were

just going to kill me in the end anyway, what did I need strength for? I wasn't deluding myself to think that they weren't going to hurt me. Emma had made it plainly clear that she wanted us dead. I would rather starve to death then lead Chase, Travis, or Lexi here. But still… "For what?" I couldn't refrain from asking, my own rapidly progressing thoughts got the best of me.

Her green eyes got gloomy. "It's not for me to say."

I got pissed. "The hell it isn't."

Irrational anger was what it was all about.

My emotions were all over the place, turning fear into anger. Anger because she wouldn't help me. Anger that I found myself locked up and alone. Anger because Chase wasn't here…with me…for me. But at the same time I was eternally grateful that he wasn't locked up with me, knowing that I didn't have it in me to watch the guy I love lose his pride. His honor. And most importantly his life.

Chase would stop at nothing to protect me, even if that meant giving up his own. Possibly even giving up the lives of those he loved the most. He might not have said that he loved me, but I knew in the deeps of my soul the lengths he would go to protect me, and that had to mean something.

Now, as I found myself in a modern day dungeon, those three little words I longed to hear didn't seem as important as just being close to him, or keeping *him* safe for once.

Mrs. Deen's haunting green eyes captured mine. "It will be worse if you fight them—worse for you both."

Both.

I got dizzy and sunk back down on the bed with my head between my legs. *Both.* Echoed over and over again in my head, and the tribal mark on my hip went tingling.

Chase and I.

This wasn't just about me. *Duh.* I was just bait, the booby prize. What they really wanted was Chase.

And that wasn't something I was willing to give up, not to save my own neck, not even to spare my own mother from the pain of losing me. Chase had already done so much for me. I owed him this and so much more. My only regret was I wouldn't be able to see his face one last time, kiss those heavenly lips good-bye.

A single tear ran down my cheek. I didn't even have the energy to wipe it away. Why bother?

She left shortly after that, locking the metal door behind her and submerging me to darkness. As soon as I heard the click, I lost it, like going-out-of-my-mind-koo-koo. Throwing myself against the door, I beat my fist on the immoveable door, screaming for her to help me. For anyone to help me. Begging someone to help me. With a fiery, swollen throat and now cut and bleeding fists, I sank to the stony floor, weeping uncontrollably.

And to think I thought I'd already wasted all my tears, but

here they came again. I'd be dehydrated in no time. How much puffier and red could a person's eyes get? I probably looked like an over rip raspberry.

Wracking with sobs, I couldn't help wonder if she was as much a prisoner as I was? And honestly I sat there, bawling my eyes out speculating if her situation was direr than mine. She was living with the enemy, sleeping with the enemy, nurturing the enemy.

I on the other hand, had the bitchin-of-all-half-demons on my side. And you can't forget the little tidbit that we were soulbond. If anyone was going to come out of this predicament, it was going to be me.

Fact.

Now I just had to start believing it.

What worried me most was not if I would be rescued, but what could happen to Chase. The longer we were apart, the weaker we both became. So that meant my part demon better-half wouldn't be at full capacity either.

That plain out sucked some serious ass.

Somehow I ended up falling asleep. My body was fried worse than a blistering Malibu sunburn. I had no idea how long I was out, but I woke up instantly alarmed with a hair curdling feeling chasing over my skin. My body went rigid as I lain as still as possible, listening.

I definitely wasn't alone.

Gathering enough courage to open my eyes, I saw a glint of something shiny. Confusion clouded my brain as I slowly recalled this terrifying horrible dream I had. But when eyes focused on a face that looked an awful a lot like Emma's dad, my heart plummeted.

He was leaning against the wall peeling a red apple with a very sharp and dangerous looking knife. Dressed to the hilt in black cargo pants, black t-shirt, and black combat boots, he looked like he had just finished an operative mission. All that was missing was a smear of black war paint under the eyes. Something told me he probably had gallons of the stuff in his garage. If he was going for the whole intimidation route, it was totally working.

I was quaking in my fuzzy socks.

Closing my eyes, I tried to pull myself together before I fell apart, which was the exact last thing I wanted to do in front of *him*. I didn't want him to think that I was weak, or that I was going to break easy. I wanted to be brave, strong, and indifferent to his sick little games.

Now if I could only pull it off.

I had faced demons, hellhounds, and the school bully, one round with Emma's dad should be a piece of cake. If there was one thing I knew about myself, it was that fear often made my tongue only that much sharper. I was counting on it.

"I was wondering how long you were going to feign sleep." His voice gave me the heebie jeebies. Big time.

I blinked. "Geez, Mr. Deen, I was wondering how long you were going to hold me against my will. It's a felony you know, kidnapping and whatnot. A pretty serious crime." Emma's dad scared the ever-loving-crap out of me. I was proud that I'd been able to control my voice, keep the shaky feeling from surfacing, because inside I was shivering in my sparkling converses.

His green eyes sharpened. I don't think he expected me to call it for what it was. Super duber illegal. "Let's skip the formalities shall we? Considering you and I are going to be spending quite a lot of time getting to know one another. Call me Eric"

"I think I'll just call you like I see it. You're nothing but a filthy criminal. A bastard."

"Emma warned me you had a tongue as sharp as a razor. Doesn't surprise me since the kind of company you prefer. It's no wonder you are rotten inside. They've poisoned you." He cut a huge hunk of the apple with his hunting knife. "Poisoned your humanity," he said, pinning me with his hateful gaze.

It was ten times as potent as Emma's. I dug my nails into my palms to keep from shuddering under his spiteful scrutiny. This guy was off his friggin' rocker. *My humanity?* I couldn't be held accountable for what I said or did next. "What are you, a cult leader?"

The jagged blade moved to his lips with a slice of apple at the end. He ate the piece of fruit right from the tip of the knife. "What I am, Angel…" his voice got scary low, and his eyes looked wild and crazed. "…is a savior." He tossed the rest of the uneaten apple across the tiny room. It hit the solid wall with a juicy crack.

I jumped, sitting up at the end of the bed. He was only feet in front of me, leaning on the concrete blocks. Yikes. Someone had anger issues. His levels of weirdness just went beyond acceptable. "Why am I here?" I demanded, skipping the formalities. We were way past that now.

He gave an uncanny short chuckle. "You are going to get me what I've been pursuing for years."

His mood swings were giving me whiplash. Yep, I was right. He was a total goner, a raving lunatic. Emma so needed to have a daddy dearest committed. ASAP. "What makes you think I would ever help you?" I didn't even attempt to hide my disgust of him.

"You and I both know that you will help me." His eyes darted to the four walls of my cell, smirking. "Really, what choice do you have?" The cockiness in his voice had me wanted to bitch slap him. It wouldn't be the first time that I slapped a monster.

Or probably the last.

My hand trembled.

"There is nothing you can do or say that would make me give up my friends. I'd rather die," I vowed.

He moved so fast, I didn't notice the danger until it was pressed against my throat. The blade in his fingers dug into my exposed neck at the same time he spun me around in some kind of head lock. I felt the tip pierce my exposed flesh, nicking it. Droplets of blood began to trickle down my throat. "Well, that can be arranged."

My upper lip broke out into a cold sweat as I fought to stay conscious. Plain sliced through me. It might have only been a tiny gash, but in my present state of fear, it felt like he had cut a major artery.

This was it. My life flashed before my eyes, which was like déjà vu. Snapshots of all the faces I loved played through my head. Mom. Lexi. Travis. Chase.

I half-laughed, half-choked. "I wouldn't hold your breath."

He backed away, a hint of surprise in his evil green eyes. "I'll give you some time to think it over."

"When Chase finds me, he is going to tear you to shreds," I spat, fueled by anger and fear.

A glint of anticipation lit in his green eyes. "I look forward to it."

I snorted. "Go to hell."

He tsked his tongue "You first." And then the door slammed in my face with the force of a typhoon.

His departure left me itchy and antsy. This place was getting under my skin, and my face-to-face with Dr. Evil left an acidic taste in my mouth. I needed a release for all this emotion turning inside. I was going to explode.

For all the good it did me, I screamed bloody murder, releasing a buildup of frustration, anger, distress, and hopelessness. It was just a brutal reminder that my voice was hoarse, and my throat felt like I'd had a run in with a weed whacker. Discouraged beyond belief, tears stung the back of my eyes, and I raged with hatred for that man.

He was going to pay.

Maybe not today or tomorrow, but someday he was going to get what was coming to him. Karma was supposed to be a bitch after all.

With nothing else to do, I laid back down on the cold metal bed. Curled in a ball with watery eyes, my muscles screamed in agony. I listened to the silence, dead air buzzing in my head. Letting myself relax after being wound so tight, everything, everywhere hurt. But it wasn't just the physical aches, I hurt inside as well.

Fiddling with my bracelet around my wrist, I thought of Chase. His voice filtered through my thoughts, and I pictured his blazing silver eyes. His lopsided stupid grin. His annoying pierced brow.

Minutes turned to hours. Hours into days.

And *he* never returned. But his wife did, delivering food.

Honestly, I didn't know if I'd been holed up in this prison for a day or for a month. I spent most of the time flip-flopping between being angry that Chase hadn't come for me yet and being relieved that he hadn't found me.

I also was getting weaker by the hour. The giant hole in my chest grew and grew. Just thinking of him made the pain tighten. Knowing Chase, he was probably ridden with guilt. His anger levels would be extremely dangerous, and he would soon be uncontrollable.

As much as I was worried about my own situation, I was even more concerned about him. I thought about home and how right now I longed for a hot shower. My own bed.

Those were my last thoughts as I dozed off into some form of unconsciousness.

Half-asleep, half-zombie I heard the sounds of scraping of metal on concrete but in my present state, it took longer to register that someone had opened the door. My name whispered through the darkness in a voice that turned my stomach.

Emma dared show her face.

I pried my eyes open, rubbing the sleepy goop from them, praying that I was having a nightmare within a nightmare. It was hard to tell at first whether my eyes were open or not, distinguishing between the darkness of the room and sleep became increasingly difficult.

"Angel!" the pesky voice called again more forceful.

"Go away," I groaned.

"Damn it, Angel, we don't have time for this," she snapped impatiently.

Damn. That was very real. Very Emma.

And what the heck was her deal? All I had was time. "What are you doing here?" I mumbled somewhat inaudible, sounding like I was drunk. I figured she was here to gloat. Searching the black room, I found her bright green eyes flashing at me in annoyance.

And I thought *here it comes*. A tiny smirk lifted at the corner of her peachy lips. "What does it look like? I'm saving your sorry ass."

Chapter 23

Excuse me. What?

I bolted from the bed to my feet so fast my head swirled in circles. Probably not the best move when I was feeling like utter crapola. "Why?" I asked genuinely confused. She had done nothing but try to kill me since she'd set foot back into town.

"Do I need a reason?" she countered, sounding annoyed. "Now get your hybrid butt moving, unless you like it here?"

I ignored her sharp tongue and the need to lash back. "I don't understand." Why the hell was I arguing? Just go with it, a part of me said. The other part didn't trust Emma. She was more likely to stab me in the back than rescue me.

She huffed. "Look mutant. I don't have time for this. We only have one shot here, and we are losing precious time arguing. Later we can play the fifty questions game, after we get out of here. Capiche?"

I nodded, tongue-tied and in shock.

I was afraid to believe this was real and not another trick. "You better not be shitting me," I warned, finding my tongue. It never left me for long.

She had her head out the door peering down the hallway. Looking over her shoulder at me, she placed a finger on her lips, signally that I should shut my trap.

Done.

With my breath held, I wiped my sweaty palms on my dingy jeans and waited for her next move, not knowing what it would be. I half expected her dad to coming charging into the room and yell *gotcha*. So when she stepped outside the door and motioned for me to go, I was swarmed with relief.

"Move your ass!" Emma demanded, with no lost love, or sympathy for that matter. I got the message loud and clear. It just wasn't my butt on the line. It was hers as well. She was after all going behind her wacked-out-of-his-mind father's back and helping me escape this hellhole.

I screwed up my face at her. "You are the worst rescuer ever," I muttered. I tried to keep reminding myself that she was sticking her neck out, risking being beheaded, but her attitude was making it difficult.

Though really, I shouldn't talk.

My boldness was quickly replaced with fear. I was so scared, I thought I would hurl. It didn't help that I was weak, malnourished and running on pure adrenaline. I was surviving on a thin thread of hope and seeing Chase's striking face one more time. He was gorgeous in a way that made girl's do stupid things. After that I didn't care what happened, actually I was pretty sure I would crumble at his feet and hit the ground like a dead horse.

Letting Emma take the led, I ran behind her. We barreled through a set of double doors at the end of one hallway only to open up to another endless corridor. Racing for my freedom never looked so far away. I ran like I was running for the last copy of Black Ops III.

She often glanced over her shoulder to make sure I was still there. My heart pounded in my ears, and my breathing was ragged with excursion. This was the most exercised I'd had in days and my body wasn't up to par, but I pushed on. There was no other choice, yet that didn't mean I did so gracefully.

Stumbling, my knees hit the concrete as I face planted the floor.

Shit. Shit. Shit.

The pain radiated through my entire body, stinging my eyes. It knocked the wind out of me for a few prolonged seconds, making it hard to inhale and exhale. A pair of strong, sturdy arms lifted me to my feet. Emma kept an arm under me, supporting most of my weight. I leaned heavily on her. "Thanks," I said winded.

Her eyes caught mine. "You can thank me after I get us out of here. You okay?"

I nodded, feeling our window of opportunity swiftly closing behind us.

Without wasting any more time, we took off together down the maze of never ending hallways. Since this was the first time I'd really been out of my room, I noticed how huge this place was. Some kind of headquarters was my guess. There were what looked to be offices and more closed doors that I was afraid to ask what was behind them.

When we reached yet another set of doors, Emma punched in a code and kicked it opened. I didn't really want to admit it, but Emma was sort of kickass.

Blinded by sunlight, I squinted, trying to clear my vision unsuccessfully. Somehow I'd expected it to be after midnight, not in the middle of the day. A brisk wind tore through the air as I took my first steps outside. Shaking inside and out, the breeze rushed over my cheeks and the clean air burned my nose, in a good way. My eyes strained against such brightness and white orbs shined behind my eyes.

I didn't get to enjoy my first seconds of freedom long. Emma was right there nagging me relentlessly in her pushy voice. "Hurry. We need to bust ass. We aren't home free yet princess."

It was unbelievable how she had the ability to rile me even as she was helping me—an uncanny talent. Wobbling as fast as possible across the parking lot, I winced with each step, my bruised and battered knees screaming at me. I sighed in sweet relief when a few short feet later we turned the corner of the white brick building and stopped.

I stared our getaway, the same midnight blue SUV that had tried to run Lexi and me off the road. I gave a short laugh. Of course. What irony.

"I don't know what you find so hilarious, but I swear if you are losing your mind now, I'll smack you," Emma growled.

I chewed my bottom lip, biting back a retort. She had to be just as tired as I. She had done most of the work after all.

Whipping open the passenger door, she helped me in. I say help, but it was really more like boosted. Scrambling around the car, she hopped into the driver seat and roared the car to life. "Buckle up. We're in for a bumpy ride."

I hoped she wasn't being literal, because that escape had wiped me out. I was dying for some caffeine. Starbucks. Hmm. My mouth watered.

I must have made a noise or something, because Emma barked, "Get your head out of the clouds. We still need to make it through the gate before we do a victory dance."

I didn't know about her, but I was most definitely not in the mood to dance. However, I was worried about the massive chain gate we were headed full throttle for. "Do you have a plan for that?" I asked, shifting restlessly in my seat.

"Yeah." She punched the gas pedal in her SUV. "You're wearing your seatbelt right?"

"Uh-huh."

She never took her gaze off the road. "Good, because it is about to get...rough."

I guess it had been literal. Emma's plan was going to kill us. Wasn't that a laugh? I was going to die not in captivity, but during the rescue. Gripping the *oh shit* handles in the SUV, I braced myself for what I knew was coming.

Emma steered the SUV straight for the locked chained gate at full speed. I was afraid to look at the speedometer, better I not know what insane speeds she was driving. The impact was nothing you could prepare for, and I've been in my fair share of car accidents, mind you they have all been since I moved to Spring Valley.

It threw me forward, the seatbelt stretched against my chest painful, and then I was tossed jarringly back against the seat. I felt my head snap back and the sound was deafening, but the SUV barreled through like a tank.

I could have kissed Emma, I was that overjoyed to still be alive and in one piece.

We drove down a private road, crowded with towering oak trees, never slowing our speed. My stomach churned, cycling with a mixture of disbelief, anxiety, fear, and hope. We were smack dab in the middle of no-man's-zone and I could taste the finish line.

At the end of the paved road, we hooked a right heading for

the interstate.

Heading for home.

I took a few silent moments to savor my exhilaration. And then I looked at Emma's profile, still in complete shock by what we had done. What she had done. Her strawberry-blonde hair was pulled back into a tight-no-fuss ponytail. It made her eyes look like two big emeralds. Much like her dad's had been. She was dressed in all black.

"Spill," I ordered, laying my head against the seat. "I don't get it. Not that I am not eternally grateful, but why would you help me?"

She shrugged, keeping her eyes glued to the highway as we cruised along. "My plans differ from my father's," she said like it wasn't a big deal, but I knew better. Then she added, "And your boyfriend is really freaking scary."

Technically he wasn't my boyfriend, but I didn't correct her. It sounded too nice. "Chase," I supplied just to be clear.

She snorted. "Obviously. Unless you are dating more than one half-breed?"

A small smile broke on my lips. "I don't think Chase would let him live."

She handled the SUV like a pro. "That we can agree on. He is a force to be reckoned with and he knows it." Subtlety wasn't exactly in Chase's vocab. "When he figured out where you where stashed, he—"

"Chase found me?" I cut her off.

She glanced at me and grinned. "You bet your ass. That man is like a machine. He has been looking non-stop since you disappeared five days ago. And by non-stop, I mean all day, every day. I don't think he has slept."

"It's only been five days?" To me it had seemed so much longer. More like five months.

She nodded and for the first time I saw something else besides judgment in her green eyes. I saw understanding. "Once he narrowed your location last night, he went ballistic—ape shit crazy. He wanted to storm the building and go all demon nuts. Basically get us all killed, including you. It took Travis, Sierra, Craig, and Hayden to hold him back. I didn't think they were going to be able to do it. If he hadn't been playing with all of our lives, I would have been impressed. Never have I seen anyone with so much…power. It was frightening. Thank God I brought a tranq."

"Wait. What?" I had to have heard her wrong. "You tranquilized him?" I gave her a *have you lost your freaking mind* stare.

Oh boy was he going to be pissed.

She got the message. "You don't have to tell me. I know he is going to chop me to pieces the first chance he gets. It's why I'm hoping that breaking you out will earn me some brownie points, or at least save my hide."

I wasn't so sure about that. "Why did you? Help me, besides to save your own neck?"

She didn't answer right away, and it made me wonder if I'd hit a nerve or pushed her too far. Emma was as unpredictable as the half-demons. To my surprise she did. "Because I know what it is like to be locked up against your will. Let's just say I've been in your shoes, and I wouldn't wish it on my worst enemy, not even a mutant like you."

It was on the tip of my tongue to tell her to jump off a bridge. If she insulted me or called me one more ugly name, I might forget that she saved me and push her from the car.

Before I had the chance to do or say something I would regret, she surprised me yet again. "I also know what it is like to be separated from someone you love. It sucks."

You could say that again.

She continued feeling in sharing mood, "Seeing Chase so distraught struck a chord in me that I've buried deep, deep inside. So Travis and I—"

"Travis and you?" I interrupted.

She gave me a glare. "So I was saying, Travis and I devised our own plan, and we knew it had to be done in secret because there was no way Chase's was going to agree. That would involve trusting me, which would only happen if Hell froze over."

I couldn't argue with that.

"We knew we had to get to you first. Chase might be a badass, but he is no shape to fight. Being away from you has taken a toll on him. We figured this was going to be our only chance while the drugs were still in effect. I have no idea how long they last on someone like him, so here we are."

She left out some important details, like how Travis and she were conspiring together. When did that happen? Probably while I was busy falling in love. I fiddled with the silver bracelet at my wrist and my thoughts shifted to Chase. For someone who always had something to say, I found myself unsure how to show my gratitude to the most unlikely of person. "Thanks Emma." Sometimes the simplest words were all that were needed.

She glanced at me. "See that wasn't so hard. The earth is still standing." We grinned at each other. Dare I say this might be the start of a friendship? A twisted friendship, but stranger things have happened.

The rest the ride home was like having my head in puffy marshmallow clouds. Eyes closed, I might have drifted off but not for long, because the closer we got to Spring Valley my body began to react to my bond to Chase.

"We're almost home," I said, breaking the comfortable silence.

"Can you feel him?" she asked, sensing that something was going on.

I nodded my head. "Yeah, but maybe not in the way you might think. The pressure in my chest is closing, and it is easier to breath. My lungs don't feel like they are going to collapse anymore." I left out that as we got closer and closer, the mark on my hip began to tingle. Each mile that brought me closer to home, the mark that was Chase's grew in intensity.

She eyed me warily. "Which means if you can sense your pending arrival so will Chase."

It made me think that she was uneasy about my connection to Chase, and I could get that. Some days I still couldn't believe what had gone down that night he brought me back from the other side. A bright smile crossed my lips. "That's a given."

"Great," she said drily. "Maybe I should drop you off down the road and get a head start running."

I rolled my eyes. "Don't worry. I won't let him kill you."

Her hands tightened on the steering wheel. "The funny thing is…I'm counting on it. You just might be the only person who could stop him."

Chapter 24

I wasn't sure what I expected to happen or feel when I saw Chase. The only thing I knew was that it was going to be monumental. Err, at least for me. The feeling inside built to a point that I was glad to be buckled in, because I wanted to leap from the car. I never felt such an overwhelming and desperate need to see someone. Not even for my mom when I came back from that month long stint at summer camp. And that had been brutal for a ten year old. I never went to camp again.

This was a thousand times more potent.

This was insane.

There was most definitely going to be tears.

And I was pretty sure he would never let me out of his sight again.

"Here goes nothing," I thought I heard Emma mumble, but it was hard to hear anything over the pounding of my heart.

It thundered in my chest as I spotted my house. The blood in my veins raced, and the tattoo radiated with a tingling energy. I had to force myself to wait until the car came to a complete stop, when what I wanted to do was jump out of the moving vehicle and run home. But that didn't stop anyone else from doing something reckless and irrational.

I mean irrational was *his* middle name, so it was of no surprise that he reached me before I even had my fingers on the handle. I sensed him before I saw. Actually, I don't think I ever saw him. One minute I was in the passenger seat and the next I was in his arms. The car door swung open with such speed, I heard Emma gasp beside me, and I wouldn't have been shocked to see that Chase had literally ripped the door right off the hinges to get to me.

I was crushed against him.

Burying my face into his neck, I inhaled the scent of him like it was my first breath of fresh air I'd had in years. His heart was racing in time with mine, mimicking each other in harmony. Bands of iron were secured around me, and I was so unbelievably happy that I didn't care that he was squashing me to death.

"God, please tell me you're real. That this is real." The sound of his voice broke me into a gazillion pieces. He sounded shattered, nothing like the arrogant asshole I loved.

"Do I need to pinch you," I whispered against his neck.

I felt him chuckle, winding his fingers through my hair. "Damn it, Angel," he rumbled.

I sighed contented. That was much better. Behind me Emma swore, Lexi squealed, and Travis laughed. They were all sounds that gave me comfort, sounds that warmed my heart. Holy mackerel, it was fabulous to be home. I wrapped my arms around Chase and squeezed for dear life. "Don't let go," I whimpered.

"Never," he vowed, brushing his lips over my hair.

And just like that I was swept off my feet, moving in impossible speeds. I closed my eyes until the dizziness left. The commotion outside was gone, leaving only the dark and seductive scent of him everywhere. I didn't need to see to know where he'd whisked me away.

His bedroom.

Hearing the tiny click of a lock brought a small smile to my lips. His hands framed my face, and I finally looked into his eyes, soaking up the sight of him. Radiating a beautiful blend of silver and gold, he stared at me like he hadn't seen me in years. The sheer intense color of them knocked me off my feet. I could have gazed at him for hours. He leaned back against the closed door never taking his eyes from mine and ran unsteady hands through his black hair.

I groaned at the loss of his touch, my body protesting that it was too soon. I still wanted to be in the his protective confines, but I could see that what he had on his mind was important, so I was going to try to be patient before I threw myself at him. I prayed it wouldn't take long because I missed him terribly already.

"I never got to tell before—" his voice broke, filled with such emotion, it tugged at my heart. "There is so much I want to say, that I've been longing to say, but I just couldn't find the words. I never expected you." He tucked a strand of loose hair behind my ear and my heart leaped. "Never thought I deserved you and maybe I don't. But it doesn't really matter now, because the day you showed up outside my house looking like something from heaven, you were mine. Meeting you was the greatest thing that has ever happened to me." He smiled, a quirk of his lips. "You gave me hope when I had none. Somehow you tame the demon inside me, when I thought that was impossible. There is no one else in the world for me, but you."

I was getting choked up, emotions clogging my throat.

He gave me a one-sided smile that made me want to slide back into his arms. "Not another girl can compare to you. When I walk into a room, I only see you. I don't feel at ease until I see your sapphire eyes." He leaned in, close enough that I could see my reflection in his silvery gaze. "And when we are apart, you aren't the only one who feels the pangs in your chest. These feelings didn't just appear because I saved you from Death, they have been there since the day you walked across my yard. The sooner you get that, the better. Because Angel Eyes, I'm never letting go, I can't lose you. Never again."

I couldn't swallow.

I couldn't breathe.

I couldn't function.

My throat had closed up with raw, pure emotion. His striking eyes searched mine, waiting for a response.

Holy guacamole.

Tears of happiness streamed down my face and he kissed them away one by one. "I'm so sorry. So very sorry," he kept repeating.

It was just like Chase to blame himself. I placed a hand on either side of his face, making him look at me. "This wasn't your fault."

"How can you say that? If it wasn't for me, they never would have given you a second glance. This is my fault, Angel, you and I both know. Now that you are tied to me, this kind of shit will happen all the time." The self-condemnation in his tone was gut-retching. It was like a knife in the belly. "I should have stopped them. I should have protected you better."

I wanted to argue, to make him see reason, but I knew a losing battle when I saw one. Nothing I could do or say would change or lessen his guilt. So the only way I knew how was to show him. Standing on my tiptoes, I wrapped my arms around his neck holding on like a monkey.

"I love you, Angel," he whispered against my wet cheek.

Wide-eyed, his declaration of love caused the air to puncture from my lungs. I'd expected to feel something when he finally got around to saying those three huge words, but it wasn't this. The moment the words tumbled from his lips, the ground slipped out from under me. Thank God I was already in his embrace. He pulled me tighter against him, and the world spun around me in dizzy circles that left me weak. A rush of ...

There were no words.

"Angel?"

I heard him say my name but it was drowned out by this painful pleasure that began to burn at my hip. Gasping, I looked to Chase who wasn't the least bit surprised about my sudden reaction. Instinctually my hand covered the spot where I'd been marked, and my head dropped to his chest.

"Angel?" he called again filled with concern. His hands stroked up and down my arms as I leaned on him for support. "It will pass it a minute. Just breathe," he whispered softly in my ear.

And it had, slowly and surely. "What the hell was that?" I asked when I was able to speak.

He looked into my shining eyes, dawned with understanding. "That...was my heart."

Confusion clouded my expression. "I-I don't understand."

He took my hand and pulled me farther into his room, sitting me on the end of his bed. "Do you remember what Ives said about our connection, about other connections?"

I nodded my head. "He said that our souls were bound

because of the deal you made for my life. He said that there are others who were linked like us but in different ways."

Chase nodded. "It's a binding triforce. You and I...we've just sealed two points of the triforce. Soul. Heart."

I searched his face, looking doubtful. "How?"

"By admitting what we felt, what was in our hearts. There is power in words."

I couldn't help but think he wasn't entirely happy about this. "Did you feel it when I told you...when I told you I loved you?" The words came out like a heady whisper.

The truth swam in his eyes, and it was all the confirmation I needed, but he spoke what I already knew. "Yeah, I tried to warn you."

Wasn't that just gnarly? I guess there really was power in words, at least in this case. I fiddled with the bracelet at my wrist. "What does it mean?"

He gave me a panty-dropping smile. "It means that our connection is a whole lot stronger, deeper. We've just kicked it up a notch. And I've potentially put you in whole shit-ton more danger. The usual."

"Soulbond and heartbond," I said out loud, testing how they sounded. "What is the third?" I asked.

"Bodybond." His eyes clashed with mine, and I flushed as I realized what that meant.

If we did the deed, if we made love, we would fulfill the binding triforce.

The ideal of completing the triangle should have worried me, not excited me. I shouldn't want to be tied to Chase any more than we already were, but truthfully the last one thrilled me to my core. I was more eager than I wanted to admit. Being with him in the most intimate way possible was something that teased my dreams almost nightly. Now knowing what it could mean, only heighten its hotness.

Just as my head filled with steamy images of us wrapped together, he pulled up his shirt. It was like he read my thoughts.

I gulped. *Sweet baby Jesus.* My mouth watered at the sight of his tan rippled chest. "Are you trying to tell me something?" I stood up and took a step toward him. My fingers were itching to touch.

He backed up, holding out a hand. "Just stay there a moment. I wanted to show you this." He looked down, bringing my gaze to his demon mark.

On sharp intake of air, I ignored his warning, reaching him in two quick strides, startled by the discovery that his demon art had an addition. I ran my fingers over the new markings. "Is this because I told you that I loved you?"

"You got it toots."

I was captured under his gaze. "Should I assume mine has also expanded?"

He gave me a devilish grin. "What happens to me happens to you."

"Lovely," I said dryly.

"You like it."

That was just it. I did.

A wicked glint filled his silver flint eyes. His finger traced my lower lip, and I suddenly realized I was still touching his bare skin. My hands roamed on their own over the solid planes of his chest, and I felt him shiver under my fingertips. "I could make you mine," he said. "I know it now. I didn't want to admit before, didn't want to believe it, but it is useless to deny. It would only take once, and there would be no going back. I'm afraid to touch you. I won't take away your freedom, the choice from you."

I didn't see another choice. I was already his.

Taking a step forward, I ran my hands up around his neck, diving into his hair as I brought his lips down on mine. I kissed him with everything I had so he wouldn't doubt my choice. There wasn't a moment of hesitation, not for me. My lips were on his, and I felt him shudder, but he was holding back.

If I was going to sink, so was he.

Sucking on his bottom lip, he made a sound in the back of his throat, half moan, half growl and final took the plunge with me. This was what I wanted, what I'd been waiting for, dreaming for. Deepening the kiss, I parted my lips, tumbling headfirst with the rush of sensations crawling across my body. Shivers of pleasure shot through as I pressed up against him.

Everything inside me sparked to life.

It wasn't a sweet kiss. It wasn't a gentle exploration. Oh God no. That's not what I'd wanted, not what I needed. It was raw, deliciously possessive like he was branding me with his essence, staking his claim. The energy I'd been lacking all day jumped to life, I was bursting in it.

With an unearthly precision, he backed us into his room, keeping my mouth extremely busy with the feel of his lips pressing down on mine. When we reached the edge of the bed, I found myself flat on his sheets and his hard body covering mine. I melted under his touch. He burned away the ugly memories and replaced my head with nothing but thoughts of him. There was no one, nothing, but him. My world became Chase.

In a single fluid motion my shirt went over my head and flew across the room. His was quick to join. I stared, drooling at his perfect abs and the cut form of his hips. Tiny dark hairs dusted his lower belly and then vanished into his black cotton boxers that were playing peek-a-boo with his jeans. His kisses zapped my brain cells, but his body rocked my socks.

At this rate, my socks were going to be the only thing left on me. And you can bet his fine ass I was going to love every second of it. His hands and mouth were enchanting. And right now that enchanting mouth was smirking smugly. I dug my fingers into his hair, sealing that smug mouth to mine.

"Angel," he murmured my name. He said something more, but it was lost to me. When he was touching me, kissing me, I couldn't think, let alone hold a conversation. That was just asking too much.

"Hm." That was the only articulate word I could form.

His breath whispered at the nape of my neck. "Are you sure you want this? Do you want me to stop?"

Stop touching me—no. Stop holding me—no. Stop kissing me—hell no.

I shook my head, my chest rising and falling raggedly.

He paused and stared down into my face. "Angel, are you even listening to me?"

"What?" I asked the haze was just beginning to lift. Why wasn't he kissing me? I ran my wandering hands up his chest impatiently.

Hovering above me, I watched his eyes, luminously topaz in the dark, shimmering. "I'm a selfish asshole. I won't let you go. Ever. You're mine," he vowed, going all caveman.

Holy hot demon babies.

Pleasure speared through me. I love it when he went all Neanderthal. "That's a two-way street baby."

He arched a brow, raising that silver hoop. "But we aren't

doing this right now, no matter how much I desperately, desperately want too."

"*What!*" There seemed to be an echo in the room. Me.

"I've had all binding to you I can handle today. If we do *this*," his palm cupped my cheek. "There will be no going back. We'd complete the third. I know it. You know it. Right now I just want to relish in having you here. Home."

Okay. If he put it like that...

I sighed heavily, and rested my head on his shoulder.

So instead, we fell asleep entangled in each other, afraid to let go. Life was precious and I think we both realized we didn't want to waste another moment without the other. Each time I awoke in the middle of the night terrified, Chase's arm would tighten around me and he would whisper in my ear, "You're safe. You're home with me."

And that was all I needed to hear to fall back asleep. It wasn't really the words that gave me comfort, just his voice. In the end, my first night home was perfect except for not yet seeing Mom, but it gave me something to look forward to in the morning.

~*~*~*~

A sleepy smile pulled from my lips as I opened my eyes. Rolling on my side, I looked at that impossibly glorious guy next to me. Dark strands of hair fell haphazardly over his sharp features. Unfeasible long lashes fanned his closed eyes. Sleeping, he lost some of his hardness. His face was softer, relaxed. I could feel his peace, his happiness exuded inside me, like a piece of him was planted in my heart.

Soul. Heart…Body.

We've knocked two of the three out of the park. Both of us knew it was only a matter of time before we were bound wholly, the complete triforce. And after last night, I don't think either of us were going to last very long. I wanted him – there was no doubt about that. But Chase and his sudden sense of morals was standing in the way. Since when had he grown an honorable conscious?

Since when I had I become such a hoochie?

Ives had been right about us. Now that I had given Chase my soul and heart, it made me stupidly happy—a testament that I had truly lost all common sense.

And I desperately needed a hot shower. I smelled homeless.

Sneakily as possible, I tried to wiggle out of his arms.

"Where are you going?" he mumbled in a deeply sexy voice still half asleep. He burrowed his head against the back of my neck, clenching his hold on me. His lips grazed a sensitive spot and I shivered.

Where had I been going? With his lips on my exposed skin I lost brain power. Thinking wasn't possible. Oh right. "Shower," I uttered.

"Do you need my help?"

I elbowed him in the gut and he released me. "I think I got this one covered Casanova." He was being so damn contradictory.

Edging out of bed, I headed for the bathroom. I could feel his eyes watching my every movement. Closing the door behind me, I was engulfed with the essence of Chase. His bathroom oozed him. Bottles of every shape and color lined the counter. Lord, he was worse than a girl. Curiously, I picked up one of the green bottles, popping the top and sniffed.

I screwed up my nose and put it back with the others. What could he possibly do with all this crap? On second thought, I didn't want to know. Then I got a glance of myself in the mirror. I was rockin' the messiest ponytail known to man. "Oh dear God." I ran my hand down my neck expecting to see a nasty cut, forgetting that I had this inhuman ability to heal. My neck was smooth and ivory. A good thing, I was thinking. If Chase had seen it...

I shuddered. Let's just say, I thought his anger would have rivaled Satan himself.

Immediately I started the shower.

Resurfacing from my long overdue cleansing of pure bliss, I found Chase exactly where I'd left. Sprawled on his bed with the corners of his lips tipped up and there was a distinct gleam of amusement in his eyes. "Do you know that you snore like a banshee in your sleep?"

"I do not," I denied. Jesus, I hoped I didn't.

He beamed at me, patting the empty sheets next to him. "Come back to bed. I missed you."

My heart tripped, and I gladly got back under the covers.

Pulling me into his warm embrace, he whispered my new favorite words. "I love you."

I clamped my eyes shut, savoring the moment. Never would I get tired of hearing him say those words in his dark, magnetic voice. It enthralled me. His arms tightened around me. "I love you too," I said, snuggling deeper against him.

"You better," he half growled, half moaned.

A smile tugged at my lips. "Oh yeah, just remember who said it first."

But as usual the joke was on me.

I felt his hand skim down my tummy and wasted no time making its way up my tank top. No longer was I smiling. My heart stopped at the first touch of his hand against my flushed skin. It was breathtaking. I gasped as he skirted the top of my shorts. Deviating just a little, his fingers began to trace the still slightly tender mark at my hip. It tingled wildly under the feel of his light touch.

"I'll never forget," he promised, kissing my neck.

Damn he was good.

Chapter 25

"I need to see my mom," I declared.

Chase's eyes softened with understanding. "I'll go with you," he volunteered but left no room for argument. I could feel his reluctance to let me go. And I had a feeling it was going to be a very long time before Chase would leave my side.

"She doesn't know what happened, right?" I asked again just to clarify. When he told me that he had compelled her, my feelings had been conflicted. On one hand, I was so freaking relieved that she hadn't spent the last five days worried sick about me. On the other hand, I hated that he had played around in her head. And from what I gathered, Devin wasn't thrilled either. At least we agreed on something, my mom's wellbeing.

His damn cocky grin spread. "Not even a hint of what happened." A fragment of ruthlessness popped into his eyes. "Which reminds me, Angel, we still need to talk about what *did* happen."

I didn't like the darkness that was hidden behind his calm exterior. He was playing it cool for me, but it was senseless. Now more than ever his feelings and emotions were powerful inside me.

I found it hard to distinguish between his emotions and mine. I was going to have to work on that. "Not yet," I answered softly, knowing the moment I told him, he was going to totally do something rash and idiotic. It was just Chase's way.

Waking side-by-side down the stairs an unusual sound floated from the family room. Youthful giggles. It wasn't so much the giggle that sounded out of place, but the voice that belonged to the girlish laugh. *Emma?* I didn't think the merciless hunter had a gigglish bone in her body. Something was definitely amidst.

Sneaking a glance at Chase, it was clear he thought the same. His dark brows were buried together, and I felt his body stiffen. Alarm speared through me. He was in the ask questions later kind of mood. An instant before he descended the rest of the stairs in warped speed, I placed a hand on his arm and shook my head. Knowing him, he would strike at Emma just because.

Together we entered the family room flooded with a vibrant cheer and were more than a little surprised at the scene that unfolded in front of us. When had things changed? How had I not seen it?

Emma was curled up beside Travis on the couch looking like a cat caught licking the milk bowl. Never had I seen her so delighted, so happy. Even her silly grin was catching. I found my lips twitching and thinking that when Emma truly smiled, it transformed her hard exterior into something beautiful.

I was finally able to see the girl he'd fallen in love with.

Travis was grinning like a total shithead. "Bow-chicka-bow-wow," he said in what I guessed was his sexy voice.

I rolled my eyes. "You did not just really say that. It was worse than a catcall from a construction zone."

Chase bit back a laugh.

Travis's blonde hair was in disarray like he spent the night on the sofa with someone in particular and very pleased with himself. "So was it magical?" Travis asked.

"Was what?" I played dumb.

"Knocking boots with—" he replied only to be cut off by Emma socking him in the gut.

A laugh bubbled up in my throat. "You are a total biscuit."

Travis's dimples winked deeply on both sides of his cheek. "I've been called worse."

"Go fly a kite. Better yet, wait until its storming," Chase added edgily.

I pulled Chase through the front door, leaving the two lovebirds before Chase and Travis started going for each other's throats. It was only a matter of time before things escalated for those two.

Weaving his fingers with mine, we crossed the yard. The autumn sun was beaming down on us, but it wouldn't have mattered if it had been pouring cats and dogs. Nothing could contain my happiness.

Walking into the kitchen, Mom was hacking away at the cutting board. For a moment, all I could do was stare, latching onto the sight of her. She had one of those dumb aprons wrapped around her waist. Her honey colored hair was pulled away from her face and thrown into a sloppy bun. It wouldn't have mattered how she looked or what she wore, to me, she was just my mom. And I had missed her dreadfully.

"Mom!" I yelled excitedly, letting go of Chase's hand and ran into her arms.

She was taken aback in surprise, and then her arms wrapped around me. "Angel, what's gotten into you?"

My eyes washed with tears. "Nothing. I just missed you."

Her hands combed down my long dark hair. "I missed you too baby. You're just in time for breakfast." Keeping her arm around my waist, she looked at Chase standing in the kitchen arch. "Chase, won't you stay and join us? That is if Angel is okay with it…"

Like he was going to turn down a free meal.

I wiped my eyes with the back of my sleeve, letting a short laugh. "I'd like that."

Spending the day with my two favorite peeps in the entire world was the best medicine any doctor could prescribe. The three of us hung out, watched old movies, laughed, and ate my mom's cooking all day.

It was divine.

Some internal mom instinct knew that when I'd walked through the door, I needed my mommy. Yet I was far from ready to let go of my boyfriend.

I think it was safe to call him that after everything.

Again that night I spent another mind-blowing evening sleeping in his arms. Mom none the wiser. The same couldn't necessarily be said about Devin, but I wasn't asking and Chase wasn't saying.

All the same to me, as long as he didn't budge from my bed.

~*~*~*~

"Angel, we have to do this," Chase stated.

The clan had congregated at the Winters house. Packed into their living room was the whole gang: Lexi, Travis, Emma, Hayden, Craig, Sierra, Chase, and I. Everyone wanted in on the action.

We were divided in our usual groups. Chase had me pulled in his lap, arms wrapped around me and had his chin rested on my shoulder. I think it was more of a technical move than him trying some funny business. He was probably afraid I would attempt to body-slam someone.

Emma and Travis were on the couch looking like the wanted to be anywhere but in a room full of people. They were so cute together. It was gagging.

Lexi was stretched on the lounge admiring her painted pink toenails with Hayden perched on the arm. I wasn't really sure what was going on between them. She hardly ever talked about him as more than just a friend, yet they went out to dinner, movies and other things that would constitute as dating. I should probably get the lo-down on what my best friend was doing with Hayden.

Craig and Sierra sat across from Chase and I. Sierra glared at me with hateful, piercing daggers. She looked ready to tear me to teeny tiny pieces. Thank God there was a coffee table between us.

A week had come and gone since I'd returned from my abduction. Things slowly returned to normal, a feeling of security just started to make itself a home in my heart again. Emma had yet to face her father's wrath. She had been *camping out* at Travis's. Wink. Wink. Every day he drove her to and from school. If Travis had it his way, she wouldn't have gone at all.

Emma was entirely different person. One I actually liked. One I could actually call a friend. Since we both had overbearing, overprotective badass half-demons as boyfriends, it brought us closer.

I was blown away by her transformation though. It was hard for me to imagine what she went through at the hands of her dad. There was softness to her round face. Her body was still disciplined and totally banging (that I was completely jealous of), not from dancing but a brutal workout regimen. That was one thing that had stuck. She had offered to train me, and I had regretfully declined. Then Chase had piped in and how he thought that it was a bad idea, which in turn so made me want to say yes.

Some habits die hard, even for me and I hadn't been brainwashed for a year.

During this meeting, everyone talked at once; they talked over each other until Chase took charge. Through some unknown method to me, they had gotten wind that the hunters were going to be storming the Winters house. Soon. And by hunters, that included Emma's dad as the leader. I doubted my escape sat well with totally-lost-my-marbles Mr. Deen. That and his daughter was missing.

"Angel, we have to do this," his words came back to me.

I understood that he had to do something—some form of retaliation or it would just be the same shit different day. Or different hostage. "I know. I just wish it could be different."

"Look princess," Sierra sneered. She was back to being my #1 hater. "Why don't you stop wishing and let us handle the dirty work. Actually, why are you here?" She leaned back and propped her spiked heels on the coffee table straight at me.

I totally took that as a threat. She was ready to stake me with her Louie Vuitton's. What I would give to be able to ripe the redheaded locks from her head.

"She is coming with us," Chase stated before I could slash her with a witty rebuttal. His hand feathered out on my stomach, causing my muscles to jump under his touch.

"You're joking. Please tell me you are joking. She will just get in the way. I am not getting shot with arrows because of her," Sierra went again, flapping her yap.

I had the overwhelming urge to sew her black cherry mouth shut. The idea made the corner of my lift.

Chase's fingers flexed on my belly. "She goes. Or you go without me. I am not leaving her behind, and I am sure as heck not going to let her out of my sight. Not for one second. End. Of. Story." There was absolutely no room for argument in his statement.

"You're pathetic," Sierra hissed outraged. Her eyes deepened, beginning to loose their hazel color.

"But at least he's consistent," Craig added, opening his big trap beside Sierra.

That last thing we needed was division. It was no secret how the rest of the group felt about me, but it didn't sting any less. Their refusal to let me be a part of this was putting a major dent into my becoming a badass…uh, something. Hey, a girl could dream.

"Before her, you actually had balls," Sierra taunted.

Chase stiffened behind to me. I could feel the muscles in his legs tighten. "Save it for the field big guy," I whispered for his ears only.

Lexi, always the voice of reason in an otherwise heated group. "You guy knock it off. It makes no sense to argue amongst ourselves. We need a plan to stop them now, before it's too late."

Finally. Someone who got the seriousness of our current predicament.

And then things got…interesting.

Tactical maneuvers where tossed around like hotcakes. Papers were strewn around the room with stick figures, chicken scratch, and the worse drawings in history. It looked like a football playbook, and I didn't understand a word of it. Through most of the bantering I just sat back and absorbed in wonder at the inner workings of this odd group. We were all brought together with a common goal, to survive and get rid of the hunters.

Yet that didn't mean there wasn't strife in the room. Trust me, there was plenty.

"We kill them. What else is there to discuss." This was Craig's big idea. With muscles the size of pythons, he was more brute strength than brains.

Emma who had been twirling one of her many large hunting knives, stabbed into down into the coffee table. "Let's get one thing straight or I blow your plans straight out to the water. No one harms my dad."

I might not exactly get why after everything Emma's dad put her through, she was still protecting him. Maybe it was because he was her father and she was harboring some kind of hope that he could change. I was realist. The man I saw was not going to be swayed easily from his beliefs. I didn't know how he could be saved.

"What do you expect us to do? Just let him walk away?" Sierra provoked, not the least intimidated by Emma's little display.

"We could compel them," Hayden suggested. Lexi smiled up at him, clearly thinking she liked his idea.

Emma shook her head. "It won't work. At least not with my dad, and probably not with the others either. There are injections he takes to counteract compulsion. A cocktail of Mother Earth's finest, except I don't have a clue what is really in them."

Sierra flipped her bold red hair, leaning forward on the edge of her seat. "How can we believe her? I surely don't trust her. She could be leading us all into a trap for all we know."

I wasn't the only who wasn't a welcomed addition to the group. Sierra wasn't capable of making new friends.

Emma stared directly into Sierra's disdainful glare, challenging. *Catfight.* "I was forced the injections for a year. It works. Ask Chase. He knows."

All eyes were on Chase. He nodded. "I can't compel her. She is telling the truth."

There might have been a few gasps. Chase admitting he couldn't do something was pretty gigantic. It was like saying the grass wasn't green.

"Then we are back to killing them," Craig said, leering in a creepy way that made me think he just wanted to kill something. Anything would do.

I shivered and Chase wrapped an arm around my shoulder.

"No!" Emma stated forcefully. "Travis and I have been talking and we think…"

Chase did not like where this was going. His body went ridged beside me and his heart rate accelerated. I could feel his distress coming in loud and clear. It was overwhelming.

"…that Angel could take care of him."

Sierra laughed.

Chase growled.

I was like, "Me?"

"No!" Chase bellowed at the same time. "Absolutely. Freaking. Not."

"Wait. I'm confused. Why would Angel be able to help?" Hayden asked.

I tried not to be offended that they all thought I was so useless and pathetic, but even I wanted to know the answer to that question. Why me?

"Travis, not another word. Do you hear me?" Chase

threatened.

"Chase, it's the only way."

In a flash, he was up in Travis's face, and I felt my butt hit the couch. "It's out of the questioned. We'll find another solution."

"Will someone please tell me what the hell we are even arguing about for the love of everything that is holy," Sierra yelled.

Chase jerked his head toward her, eyes ablaze. "Nothing that concerns you."

"Think about it Chase. She is probably the only one who could compel him. She can try it out on Emma," Travis rushed, trying to reason before he lost his head.

Chase closed his eyes and dropped his head into his hands. I swear I could hear him counting under his breath.

My ability to compel those who can't be compelled seemed to be what got Chase's boxers in a wadded bunch. Travis and Emma wanted me to compel her dad.

"Why the hell would you think Miss. Sassypants could compel anyone?" Sierra demanded loudly.

"She can't," Chase countered, lifting his head.

"Chase," Travis pleaded. "It is the only way to keep her safe. Keep us all safe."

He slammed his fist down on the table, standing to his full six-foot two-inch formidable height. "It is out of the question. I'm done discussing it." Then he promptly stormed out, slamming the front door behind. The house rattled under impact.

Chapter 26

I sat in a room full of half-demons and one hunter. All of them were staring at me. Shifting under their curious and puzzling gazes, I stood up without a word and went after shitbrick. I'd rather deal with him than all their questions.

I found him with his hands in his midnight hair, pacing up and down the driveway. Messy and windblown, he looked fabulous. Lines of strain creased the corner of his cloudy eyes.

He was troubled.

And if I had to guess, he was torn in half.

His hand clamped and unclamped right before one of those fists slammed down onto the hood of Emma's car. Chase was on the verge of going twenty-one flavors of crazy.

"God damn it, Chase. Can't you use something else as a punching bag? Not my car?" Emma spat from behind me on the porch. I hadn't heard her come out after me. Emma and I might be friendly, but Chase and her...not so much. They didn't trust each other. Truthfully, I think Chase harbored some resentment against Emma and the part she had in my kidnapping. It hadn't mattered that she was also the reason I escaped.

He turned his caramel eyes on her snarling, and she took a step back. "Jeesh. Fine," Emma relented, learning when not to push Chase's demon switch and hightailed back into the safety of the house.

Now I was the one on the receiving end of his rage.

Joy.

Jaw set, he said, "You are not doing it. You got that. I forbid it."

"You forbid it?"

After hearing the outrage in my voice, he realized that *forbid* might not have been the wisest choice of word. Not for me. "Okay, so that might have come out a little strong—"

"A little?" I crossed my arms over my chest. It was no secret I didn't like being told what I can and can't do.

"Fine. Whatever. The point is, I don't want you that close to him. Never again. We will find another way. I'm not yielding on this."

"Chase you are being unreasonable."

His brows slammed together and he bristled. "Am I?"

I nodded my head. "Yeah, you are. Trust me, I am in no hurry to be up-close-and-personal anytime soon with Mr. Wack-job, but if there is even the slimmest possibility that I can stop him, I have to try."

"And I disagree."

God, he had a fierce protective streak that was both enduring and maddening at the same time. "Err. Getting you to be sensible is like smashing my head against a brick wall."

He leaned against Emma's dented SUV. "No argument from me."

"Damn it, Chase. You could at least consider it. I might just do it with or without your *so called approval*. It's my choice."

He fixed me with an icy glare, closing the space between us. "Don't test me."

For the first time, I could feel the anger that was feeding him. It radiated inside me. Placing my palms on his chest, I tried again. "You really need some anger management classes. At least just let me try it out on Emma. If it doesn't work, no harm done."

"And if it does…"

"How about we cross that bridge when we get there, before going all he-ho about it."

He went rigid. "This is a very bad idea. I can feel it."

"So you are no longer forbidding it?" I steeled myself for his refusal.

He shook his head. "N-no. Like I ever could."

I think that was the first time I'd ever heard Chase falter his words. "D—did you just agree?" I asked.

He pulled me against him, squeezing in me in an epic hug, his mood veering sharply to despairing. "Angel," he murmured my name through my hair. "If I could tuck you away and keep you safe, I would. I'll never be able to give you the fairytale ending you deserve." His fingers stroked my cheeks.

I blew out a slow breath, stirring the long strands of dark hair that escaped my messy ponytail. "Thank you."

"Don't thank me yet, Angel Eyes."

~*~*~*~

"Are you even trying?" Emma asked. Her toned legs were stretched out in front of her.

I gave her dry glare. "Look, I never said I knew what I was doing. It only happened once and I didn't do it on purpose."

She sighed heavily. "I'm starting to think Travis made the whole thing up."

Every time I looked at Emma with the intention of full concentration she was making some stupid face at me, crossing her eyes, or sticking her tongue out at me. "I swear. If you do that again, I am going to rip your tongue right from your mouth."

Emma laughed. "Do you think you are going to have time to center yourself out in the field?"

"No drill sergeant," I replied, giving her a poorly executed salute.

She only laughed harder. "You would make a sorry excuse for a solider."

"And you are a crappy test subject."

She bunch up her nose. "I am not all that keen about you screwing with my head."

I rolled my eyes. "I'm not going to make you do anything crazy like jump in front of a train."

"Geez, that's comforting." As far as verbal sparring went, Emma and I were perfectly matched. "I can't believe your menacing shadow left you alone with me. Even for just an hour."

I shrugged, happy for a break. This compelling thing was taxing my brain. "Trust me. He is not far, probably lurking around a corner."

Emma's eyes shifted around the family room. "Uh, that's not creepy."

A small smile snuck over my lips. It might have made Emma nervous, for me, knowing Chase was never far was comforting. "Did you honestly think either of them would leave us alone? You've been out of the game too long."

"Yada Yada. Are you we going to do this or what?"

"Do I really have a choice?" I said, sounding reluctant, which I totally was. I didn't really want to do this anymore than she did.

"Nope. And no more funny business."

I rolled my eyes again. Yet this time there weren't any antics from Emma. Facing each other on the sofa, I sat on one of my legs and made my mind go blank. She and I were both on our best behavior…

Because I compelled her.

I couldn't explain how I'd done it.

Emma's eyes went from lively and teasing to wide and spacey. Her iris got big, the deep green in her them almost disappearing. Staring at her, I got freaked out. I had her under my spell so to speak and now…now I didn't know what to do. Did I have her do cartwheels around the room? Jump on the couch and squawk like a monkey? The possibilities were endless and payback was at my fingertips, except none of that was appealing.

Emma had put her trust in me, just as I had put my trust in her when she saved me as hard as that had been. I wasn't about to break this friendship we just had started to form. Angling me head, I briefly wondered how much control I had over this compulsion. I really didn't have a clue what I was doing or how it worked.

How the hell was I going to get her dad under my enthrall?

This had to be the absolutely worse plan in the universe.

Finally, I just decided to make Emma my cook. All this mind control stuff had made me hungry. My stomach rumbled. "Emma," I said in the calmest voice I could manage. "I want you to make me a turkey sandwich."

Like a robot, she mechanically stood up from the couch and started rummaging in the fridge pulling out food. I turned in my seat, resting my chin on the back of the couch and watched her. "Can you bring me a Dr. Pepper too? I'm dying of thirst."

She immediately brought a can and even popped the tab from me. *Oh man, this was great.*

Emma made a mean sandwich. "This is really good," I said with a mouth full.

I wiped a smidge of mustard from the side of my mouth, and then just like that, while I was chomping away, Emma snapped out of my hold. I didn't have any idea how I had dropped the veil. I sucked at being anything but human, and even then I had a hard time staying alive.

She shook her strawberry blonde head like she was trying to clear any remnants of me poking around in her brain and shot me a glare. "Did you just make me your bitch?"

I choked on my Dr. Pepper, spraying it all over us both and laughed. "I highly doubt you making me a sandwich constitutes as you being my bitch."

She shuddered beside me. "Whatever. Don't try that crap on me again. I don't like it."

"That's something we can both agree on." I didn't like it either, honestly. It felt too godly to control someone with my mind. "Can I just say that you are much more agreeable when you are compelled?"

She whacked me on the side of my head with one of the decorative pillows, and I had to bite back another laugh before I snorted burning pop through my nose. I shoved the last bite of my sandwich in my mouth and went looking for Chase before Emma could find something else to smack me with.

I found him in his bedroom, lounging on his bed with his laptop. A chunk of hair flopped over his forehead. He propped his arms behind his head as I walked into his room. "So I'm guessing from that silly grin on your face that you can compel her?"

It was more of a dazed grin, and I couldn't seem to control it. "Did you doubt that I could?"

"Doubt? No. Hoped you couldn't? Absolutely."

My smile slipped.

He set aside his laptop and edged to the end of the bed. "Look Angel, I am not trying to discredit the sense of accomplishment you are feeling. I just…I just wish it wasn't you."

"I know. Me too," I admitted, sitting next to him on the bed.

He wrapped me in his arms, and I hung on for dear life. "This isn't going to end well," he whispered.

~*~*~*~

I figured we would have time to prepare. More time to practice me messing with people's heads. More time to come up with a solid plan. But time wasn't on our side. What I hoped was going to be a week or more turned out to be hours.

Something was going down, and no one was telling me a damn thing. Travis was jazzed. Emma was back to being snappy and brooding. And Chase was just too keyed up. But I'd come to my own conclusions.

Shit was about to get real. It was go time.

"Let's rock," Travis said, grinning with a deep dimple on either side of his cheeks.

Chapter 27

I wish I could say that I shared his enthusiasm. There was a nervous flutter in the pit of my stomach and an excitement that hummed in my veins. My emotions and Chase's swirling together. I knew this day was going to come, but nothing could have actually prepared me for the real thing. I was quaking in my converses.

Before I could even wrap my head around what was happening, what we were about to do, the group had arrived looking ready to kickass. Sierra of course looked more like she was going to the club then on a hunting trip. I could tell it was on the tip of her tongue to complain about my presence, yet again. Chase silenced her with a demon glare.

Chase pulled a black hoodie over my head, and I obediently slipped my arms through the sleeves. It smelled like him, sinful and yummy. With my head still reeling, I was swept away in the group as we moved into the dark, damp, dingy woods—the place of many nightmares.

"You sure you are ready for this, Angel Eyes?" he asked, studying my face.

"I don't think I could ever really be ready."

He nodded his head, just a shadow moving among the darkness with bright yellow eyes.

Not knowing what precisely waited for us among the massive oak and soaring pine trees played into my fears. There were so many unknown factors. How many numbers did the hunters have? Were we walking into a trap of our own? Had they been tipped off somehow? Did they know we were coming to greet them with a battle plan of our own?

None of those questions mattered now, because there wasn't time to second guess what was already in motion. My companions moved like ghosts in the woods, soundless and incredibly fast.

Me. I moved like Bigfoot.

Chase stayed with me while the others took off ahead. I knew it must be killing him to not be in the thick of the action. But as much as I hated that he was antsy, I would have hated it more if we weren't together. As irrational as it might be, we both needed to know the other was safe. He squeezed my hand, eyes twinkling with anticipation. "Game on."

I shook my head and gave him a nervous grin. I loved it when he did video game references. It was just uber cute.

Everything always seemed to happen in the forest. I listened to the winds howling like a wolf on the hunt as blades of grass rustle around me. Deeper we traveled into the woods, relying on their sixth senses to give us the edge. The hunters might have technology, but we had supernatural gifts.

Tangled undergrowth covered the forest floor. We kept off the paths, traipsing through bushes, briars, and God knew what else. I tried not to think about the things I might step on or the traps I might walk in. I tried not to think at all.

A prickle of unease skirted over my skin, followed by Chase's entire body going on alert. I dared not move muscle or even breathe. The others had fanned out into pairs, but they were all within hearing distance of each other. Um, half-demon hearing distance.

With a yelp, Chase flattened us against a tree trunk as an arrow slashed through the air, straining to reach us. It hit the bark with splitting force. And one by one, a half a dozen tipped spears followed, sticking out of the tree, outlining us. Hugging the tree, I took a moment to pick my heart off the ground where it had fallen while I was being plummeted with arrows.

Chase's rage bellowed through the forest.

Snares and curses erupted in the air as bodies began to take shape through the twilight. This was it, the final moment.

Their numbers were more than ours, but I'd expected that. It wouldn't have been much of a fight otherwise. By the looks of it, this was going to be an epic standoff.

In horror I watched as hunters, like Jedi knights, swarmed

toward us, weapons raised and armed. I felt like I was about to be eaten alive. The hunters surged forward and Chase took a step back, shielding me with his body.

Anarchy was about to explode.

From the corner of my eye, I saw Emma and Travis circle in from our right. I sighed in relief, knowing that they were still alive, unhurt.

Then the unthinkable happened. Emma threw the dagger she had clutched in her hand through the air, directly into Chase's shoulder—one quick fluid motion. I stood shocked. He hadn't even moved, or attempted to evade. I knew him. He was too fast, too smart to just let Emma hit him. He had just stood there and took the impact of a knife into the shoulder.

I was flabbergasted.

And why the hell had Emma stabbed him for crying out loud?

"You stabbed him," I said astonished.

"It won't kill him, trust me. This has to look real, Angel," Emma said low with clenched teeth, her lips barely moving. "They have to believe that I am with them."

Her words barely penetrated through the thick haze of red now swarming in front of my eyes. "You stabbed him!" I growled right before I launched myself at Emma. It seemed to be my thing with her.

"Damn it!" a deep voice exploded, grabbing me in midflight.

"When we get out of here, I swear to God I am going to ring your neck," he graveled in my ear, and then set me on my feet. "We have bigger problems, and I don't have time to babysit you right now."

A part of me knew I should have been afraid of his temper, but I just could muster up the emotions, not when I was in the midst of my own rage. He had already removed the knife from his shoulder, but I could see the sticky substance of his blood staining the dark shirt he wore. I felt my head began to spin. There was so many things going on around me, and I felt myself losing touch on reality.

Suddenly he was there, steady hands on my arms. "Don't even think about it, Angel Eyes. I'm fine. It is just a scratch. Stay with me."

I heard Emma snort behind me. "Wuss." She was deliberately trying to get under my skin.

The dizziness passed just in time, thanks to Emma boiling my blood. He flashed her a quick look of annoyance before something else claimed his full attention. The hunters were moving in, surrounding us. Chase's eyes did the freaking-glowy-thing, fiercely, and his demon took possession fast. I watched him transform in front of my eyes to something lethal and deadly. There was no mercy in his taunt stance.

Then the sounds of chaos erupted through the thick trees.

Hayden and Lexi joined the crowd followed closely by Sierra and Craig. Now that the whole gang was here, the fun stuff was about to begin. I wanted to close my eyes and hide under a pillow. This was not my kind of fun. Fun was playing Skyrim. Fun was hanging out with friends. Fun was eating a chocolate fudge sundae.

I had a feeling that Eric found this fun.

He was a sick bastard.

A body dropped beside me, and I couldn't stifle the yelp that squeaked from me. I was too afraid to see if they were still breathing, knowing that if I took my eyes off the battle for even a fraction of a second, I could be killed.

They weren't messy around.

This wasn't a video game. There was no re-spawning.

This was life or death. Survival of the fittest.

There was a shuffle of feet behind me. Whipping around... I shuddered.

Chase's voice echoed through the woodsy clearing. "Touch her and I promise to make your death a slow painful experience," he threatened violently.

My knees began to buckle. Everything that I had gone through during my capture came flooding back. I wasn't in the woods anymore, but back in that four wall prison with Emma's dad pressing a knife to my throat. I shook in fear, frozen in place. How had I actually thought I was going to be able to face him?

Compel him? I could hardly look at him without cowering in terror.

"Touchy, touchy," Eric said, giving a dark, humorless chuckle.

At the sound of his voice I felt myself drowning in panic, losing my grip on the plan. He stepped closer to me and Chase growled deep in his chest. In my head I knew what I was supposed to do, but my brain wasn't cooperating. It was rendered useless at the sight of Eric.

He pulled out a long jagged wicked looking knife, if you could call it that. Damn thing looked more like a sword and he had a bow with a sheath of arrows strapped to his back. "I see you've brought my daughter home."

Chase's response was a guttural sneer.

I instinctual backed up. "Chase?" My voice was shaky as I pleaded for what I didn't know.

Strength.

Courage.

Help.

Regardless, the sound of my frightened voice unleashed an animal. Golden eyes filled with wildness. With one smooth motion Chase engaged Eric like he was born to fight. In the background I could hear Sierra sparring with one of the hunters, taunting him with her natural annoyance, but I couldn't take my eyes off the fight right in front of me.

Chase moved at ungodly speeds, so fast that all I see was the occasional glimmer of gold. He avoided the down swoop of Eric's blade many times, keeping Eric busy. Chase flickered in and out around him, making Eric's focus on only him. I screamed as Eric's blade sliced across Chase's stomach.

Of course Eric couldn't resist the chance to taunt me. Hearing the panic in my scream, Eric laughed. "Don't worry I'll take good care of him. Piece by piece."

Enough with the games, Chase blinked behind Eric. Lickety-split. I watched wide-eyed as Chase took Emma's dad by surprise in a moment of distraction, wrapping his demon-strength hands around his neck.

Our eyes clashed over Eric's shoulder and I knew in those suspended seconds of time what he was going to do. What he was begging me to understand. His feelings merged with mine. I closed my eyes, trying to block out the screaming, the fighting, and the mixture of every emotion possible. When I opened them again I took a deep breath and held Eric's gaze in mine. He wasn't smirking anymore. I gave Chase a short nod, letting him know that I understood.

I got his reasoning, but I was worried at what price.

At what price would either of us pay for what he was about to do. All along, whether I wanted to admit it or not, I knew it was going to end this way, with blood on our hands.

Eric's dark green eyes went large and detached. In a twist of fate, Eric became my prisoner. Unblinking I kept my vision locked with Eric's, compelling him not to move. One miscalculation and either of us could end up a bloody smear on the ground. The others were dealt with behind us, the least of our concern.

Chase didn't hesitate after that. *Sianara*. So fast I hardly saw the movement, Chase twisted Eric's neck like it was nothing. There was an unmistaken snapping of bone marrow that made my stomach churn in waves. I thought for sure I was going to vomit on my converse shoes. Then the life in Emma's dads green eyes flickered out, dead to this world.

Emma let a bloody curdling screamed, crying for her dad. She crumbled to the ground, mudding her jeans beside his lifeless body. I didn't move, unsure what I could possible do or say to ease her pain. Truthfully, I doubted she would even want my shoulder to cry on.

We had deviated from the plan—big time. We had killed her father. If I thought Emma and I were making any progress toward being friends, this just severed our chance. I seriously doubted that she was going to okay with what just went down.

Hunter or not, Eric had still been her dad.

This what Chase had been keeping from me. All along he wasn't planning on letting Eric walk out of these woods alive. I rubbed my arms trying to chase the chill that had settled over me.

Travis knelt down beside a weeping and distraught Emma, whispering her name. Reaching out, he tried to pull her into his arms.

"Don't touch me!" Emma yelled, shoving Travis away with a stream of tears running down her cheeks. "Don't. Ever. Touch me again." Her shining emerald eyes burned with betrayal and acute pain.

Travis staggered back, sitting on the cold ground looking like Emma had just slapped him smartly across the cheek with the force of a grizzly.

My heart lurched in my chest.

This decision we'd made was not only going to affect Emma, but Travis as well. Emma was going to hold Travis just as responsible for her dad's death as she was going to pin the blame on Chase and I. Just when Travis had finally gotten back the girl he loved, he lost her again in a bat of an eye.

Glaring with emerald eyes swimming with fresh pain and hatred, Emma got to her feet. In her hands she had grabbed her dad's bow and now aimed it at the center of Travis's heart. Her hands shook violently and I gasped.

Travis didn't try to defend himself. He kneeled, staring up at the only girl he ever loved. That loved shimmered in his turquoise eyes.

Time stood suspended before she lowered the weapon, her

body still shaking with gut-retching sobs and ran.

"Emma!" Travis called out after her. "Emma, wait!"

Chase put a hand on Travis shoulder before he could take off after her. "Don't," Chase said softly. "Let her be, Travis."

Travis spun on his heels, eyes searing his cousin with gold daggers. He shook his hand off him and pushed Chase in the chest. "How could you? How could you, Chase?" His voice was filled with hurt, anger, and treachery.

"It was the only way, Travis. You might be pissed at me now, but you know that it was the right thing." Regret tinged his words.

"The right thing? How the hell can you say that? You killed a man."

Chase's eyes never wavered, hard granites of steel. "And I would do it again in a heartbeat. I'm not apologizing. Not when it saved the people I love."

"You mean as long as it protected Angel," Travis said sharply.

Ouch that stung. I winced.

Travis didn't stop there. "But what about Emma? Were you protecting her?"

Chase's voice was low and taunt with frustration. "Does it matter?"

I stared at him in disbelief.

Travis shook his head. "That is low. Even for you." He turned on his heels and zoomed off after Emma.

Cautiously, I approached Chase, wanting to offer him comfort, solace, something to take away the sting his cousin's words had left behind. My body was still numb and in shock as I touched a hand to his shoulder. The eyes that I loved so much were brimming with morn, solemn. I almost preferred the glowing gold to the sadden silver. Seeing the weight he carried on his shoulders felt heavy in my heart.

"You did what you had to," I assured with the best sureness I could muster.

"Did I?"

Chase questioning himself wasn't a good thing. It worried me. Really worried me. He oozed cockiness. His surety was like armor—strong and unbreakable. I didn't know what route to take. Did I try compassion or did I sock with something smart in hopes of knocking him out of this stupor?

Instead I said nothing. I just walked into his arms and wrapped mine around him.

Chapter 28

Chase had killed someone to protect me. Protect his family.

There was a different ambiance that lingered in the Winters home now. Travis shut himself off from those who cared. He was unrecognizable to me. Every time I saw him, I prayed for just a glimpse of that boyish charm I loved. Just a hint at one of those dimples that made his smile so addicting. I missed my video game partner.

Mostly, I missed my friend.

But I didn't know how to bridge the giant gap that separated us.

Without Chase and Lexi, I don't think I would have been able to move forward. I knew that I was the lucky one. I still had the person I loved more than anyone. It was a bittersweet revelation. Yet still I couldn't help but feel sorrow even after what Eric put me through, or what his plans for me and the rest of us might have been. It still didn't make what happened any easier to digest.

The days following the death of Eric were hard on everyone in their own way. Emma was MIA, which was expected to Travis's dismal. It didn't matter how much he blew her phone up, she had once again fallen off the map. Travis mopped around. He went through the motions of day-to-day life, but he wasn't really living. He didn't eat. He didn't sleep. And more than not, his eyes sparked yellow. The demon inside was breaking to the surface more and more.

That scared me.

Chase might not have said it out loud, but he was worried about Travis. Seriously worried. They all were. Devin, especially.

Me... Er, I was doing my best to pretend it never happened. Yeah, I was totally going through a denial faze. That and I was biting my nails in nervousness, waiting for the police to rap on my door and accuse me of murder. Chase assured me that everything had been taken care of, but it was hard to believe that we would get away with killing a man.

Mom picked up on my odd behavior—on everyone's. Devin knew what had really gone down, but Mom thought it was a tragic hunting accident. Ironic. Hunting had definitely been involved except the target hadn't been Bambi, and I wouldn't have called it an accident either.

Oh, well. It was better this way for her. Better that she didn't know the real horrors that roamed the earth, better off left in the dark. The less she knew the safer she was.

As much as I tried to resume my life as normal, forget what we'd been a part of, or the hand I played in a man's death, my mom could see right through me. She knew something was weighing on my mind, that my smiles were fake. Regardless, it didn't stop me from trying to keep on pretending.

"Are you sure you don't want me to stay home tonight?" Mom asked for like the gazillionth time. She was concerned about me, probably with good reason. Today was one of my off days. I just couldn't shake this ominous feeling.

I gave her one of those false smiles that didn't reach my eyes. "Chase is coming over. Go. Have fun with Devin. You deserve it." I knew she would feel better knowing I wasn't going to be alone.

She slipped on a pair of heels and smoothed a hand over her caramel hair. "Behave yourselves." Her blue eyes twinkled behind the concern.

From the couch, I snorted. "I think maybe I should be saying that to you. Trust me. There won't me be much going on around here."

Her heels clicked on the floor as she strolled across the room. "I'm just saying...I know how hard it is to resist a magnificent butt."

"Mom," I groaned. Some things never change. Like mom always saying inappropriate stuff. Little did she know that it actually made me feel a tad better. It was the small things that could make a world of difference.

She opened the front door just as Chase was about to knock.

He gave my mom a dazzling grin. "Hey, Ms. Morgan."

"Chloe, call me Chloe. Anything else makes me feel old." Turning in the doorway, she winked at me. "Behave."

I rolled my eyes and watched her shut the door.

My mom was impossible, and the absolute best. I couldn't imagine life without her in it. Thinking about Emma, I knew that she and her dad didn't have the normal father-daughter relationship, yet he still had been important to her. She still loved him even though she realized how messed in the head he was.

Chase raised a brow. "What was that all about?" There was still a shadow of guilt lurking behind his silver eyes. It saddened my heart to see it lingering.

"My mom has it in her head that I need to get laid or something," I explained, scooting my legs up to make space for him on the couch.

"Your mom is seriously amazing," he replied, the corner of his turned up.

Chase's deep voice wove itself into my chest and my stomached squirmed. I smacked him on the chest as he sat down beside me on the zebra print couch. "I didn't have the heart to tell her that my boyfriend is a tease."

Stretching out my legs across his lap, he gave me a Cheshire grin. "Can I help it if I am irresistible and you just can't keep your hands off me?"

I tried to suppress my grin. "How the hell did I get saddled with such a prude?"

He propped his hands behind his and relaxed into the cushions. "Prude…hardly. If your mom knew the things I wanted to do with her daughter, she would bar the front door. Hell she would have to move you across the country, and even then you wouldn't be safe from me." The corner of his lips tipped up and he shrugged. "Besides, who said we can't be inventive."

I never saw it coming. Like most things with Chase, he moved at speeds that my eyes just weren't able to follow, but the stupid grin on his face should have tipped me off. When was I ever going to learn? Hopefully never…this was the kind of game that I actually liked to play.

I felt his hands slid up and fasten around my leg. All I could think was how warm and intense his touch felt, even though my jeans. And then he yanked. My breath hitched as he pulled me into his lap in one smooth motion. His arms slipped around me and he drew me close, kissing the side of my neck. I shivered.

He smelled so good, a mix of fresh fallen rain and earthy. Lifting my head, I placed a kiss right below his jawline, he drew in a quiet breath and his hands curled into fists at the small of my back. I felt his heartbeat quicken and my whole body tingled, senses buzzing. So many emotions, mine and his mixing together so that I couldn't distinguish which ones were mine and which ones were his.

I shifted to place another kiss on his ever tempting jaw, he ducked his head and our lips met. Just like that, and he was kissing me like I was going to meld into him. My hands slipped under his shirt, tracing the hard lines of his chest and stomach. Muscles jump under my nails. I captured him in my mouth and he nipped my bottom lip.

We should have known that being *so called inventive* would backfire. Like striking a match, we went up in flames. His hands squeezed at my hips while mine busily wandered over every inch I could get my fingers on.

I wanted to be devoured.

I wanted to devour him.

I wanted him to make me forget it all…at least for a little while.

I wanted to make him forget.

With his lips moving over mine, I felt the same from him. He wanted to lose the guilt that was munching away at his insides. Seeing his cousin suffering and bitterly angry was darkening his soul. It wasn't because he had killed a man, but that it had caused this strife between him and Travis.

I could sense the turmoil inside and the darkness that was swimming within. Chase was fighting his own personal demons, and I was going to do whatever I could to keep him from going over to the demon side. There was this unmistakable part of him that would always be deadly and dangerous. Today...it was rapturous.

A sane person would be wary, frightened even. Not me. I was attracted to it. That line he traveled between demon and human was exciting, thrilling. He tried to keep that part of himself shielded from me, the only problem was...now were we connected on multiple levels. It was impossible to keep that piece of him hidden anymore. Truthfully, I never would have wanted him too.

I wanted all of him.

The good, the cocky, and the demon.

The ornate mark at my hip tingled as his lips locked on mine, searing me his. Bunching my hands at the end of his shirt, I tugged up. The cotton tee was in my way, and I wanted no barriers between us. Yet somehow Chase and I weren't on the same wavelength.

With lightning speed, he pulled back, keeping me at arm's length. I leaned forward wanting, needing the closeness of him, but his arms didn't budge. "You have to follow the rules if you want to play."

"Rules?" I echoed confused. When did we have rules?

"You got it toots. The clothes stay on."

Annoyance flickered in my midnight blue eyes. I honestly couldn't believe that came out of his mouth. "This is your idea of being *inventive?*" I asked panting.

Eyes like liquid fire eyed me intently. "Not exactly. With you things always seem to get out of hand." His voice was gravelly and sexy.

Love and passion for each other swirled in the air around us. I never felt so close to anyone as I did to Chase at this moment, and never wanted anyone more. It was more than the connections we shared, it was deeper.

Tipping my chin up, I looked into his smoky eyes. "Angel Eyes," he murmured, his voice trailing off.

I ran my hand through his dark silky hair and for a moment I forget to breath. "Hmmm," I muttered, staring at his lips. I really wanted to kiss him again.

"Your eyes are doing that freaky thing again."

I shot him a look of exasperation. "No thanks to you."

He chuckled. "It's hot. Really hot."

I wrinkled my nose. "Only you would think so."

He placed a kiss on the tip of my nose. "I think about you more than I should."

That was one way to get a girl's heart pumping. "Good. Now can we get back to business?"

"Sorry, Angel Eyes. You're cut off."

Biting the inside of my cheek, I shifted on his lap.

He closed his eyes and moaned. "You are evil."

I laughed as his hands on my hips lifted me like a bag of sugar and tossed me to the other side of the couch. Served him right. Grinning, I stared into his smoldering gaze. "I play dirty."

His eyes darkened to a smoldering honey. "I'm in so much trouble," he groaned.

I only laughed harder. He had no idea.

Angel and Chase's story continues in...

CHASING ANGEL

Coming soon a Novella about Emma and Travis...

BREAKING EMMA

~*~*~*~

Connect with me online:

(I'm serious. I would love to hear from you.)

My Blog: http://jlweil.blogspot.com/
Twitter: https://twitter.com/#!/JLWeil
Facebook: http://www.facebook.com/#!/jenniferlweil
Goodreads: http://www.goodreads.com/author/show/5831854.J_L_Weil

Acknowledgements

First I have to thank Elena Boteva for taking time away from her busy day to comb this book with a fine eye that I just lack. Also Amber Bungo, you are a reading ninja. You are guys are A-ma-zing. Thank you so much. Between these two guys I might actually have a book without all the usual pesky typos. I want to give a GIGANTIC THANKS to the readers and book bloggers. I heart every one of you! It still amazes me that anyone reads my books. Kisses.

Bonus

Straight from the mouth of Chase Winters

(Unedited – read at your own risk.)

~*~*~*~

She was leaning against the porch banister watching me intently with eyes the color of wild blueberries, sweet and tart. I tried my damnest to ignore the fluttering in my stomach. With Angel, it was utterly pointless. She was part of me now.

And damn if that didn't excite me. It made my blood run wild, but I would never admit that to anyone in a million years, least of all Angel.

Travis walked across her yard toward me, looking like he had seen better days. My cousin's heart had been through the wringer the last year. Just another reason for me to avoid the plunge. Falling for a girl had not been on my list of things to accomplish before college. Being bonded to a girl hadn't even crossed my mind. And yet here I was…

I gave a short lift of my head in a guy-kind-of greeting as we met me halfway between our yard and Angel's.

"You better treat her good or I'll wipe the floor with your demon ass," Travis said in what I took as sort a brotherly warning. The kind we normally used with Lexi.

I arched a brow at my cousin, wondering where that had come from. Sure he was going through a tough time, and I hated the shadows that lingered behind his eyes. But I didn't have time to dwell on what was going on with Travis because my eyes caught hers again and my breath slammed into my chest.

Something was up.

I could feel it charged in the air. I could feel it coming from inside her, it was written all over those expressive eyes. The fact that they now changed hues with her moods helped. It wasn't hard to read what kind of mood she was in currently. Troubled. Sad. Confused. She chewed on her lip, and I knew she was working through something in that head of hers.

Lord help me.

But it didn't stop her from looking at me like she wanted to gobble me right there on her porch. It was all just part of my irresistible charm. However, if she kept eyeballing me like that, I wasn't going to be held accountable for my actions. So instead I shoved my hands into the pocket of my jeans and looked her over. I needed to make sure she was okay after last night and more so because I wanted to. "Hey," I greeted. "You look better," I added, my gaze finally landing on her face.

She shuffled her feet in a cute nervous gesture, and the corner of my mouth twitched. The fact that I found all her little habits cute was alarming. Very alarming. What was it about *this* girl that got to me? Never before had someone gotten so completely under my skin as Angel did. Why her?

The question plagued me night and day. Don't get me wrong, it had more to do with than just her being stunningly beautiful, or maybe that was just the way I saw her. I'd been attracted to other pretty girls before but this…this was way different. This was on an entirely different level, even before the soulbond thing, I'd felt it. Really, if I was being totally honest with myself, I'd known the second I caught her on my porch that first day looking lost and unsure of herself. Well, that was before she got her panties in a wad, which hadn't taken much effort.

"Better than what?" she countered.

I looked forward to this. No one bantered like Angel and I did. "Do you always have to argue with everything I say?"

Her eyes flashed. "Maybe."

I leaned a hip against the railing needing a little breathing room. I could smell her shampoo and the subtle sweet scent of her skin mixed with perfume. It was intoxicating to say the least. The last thing this little minx needed was to know how much she affected me, how much power she had over my actions. What I needed to do was get to the point. I hadn't come over to be seduced by her or seduce her, but suddenly the idea had merit.

Focus.

Pulling my gaze from her lips, I got to the point. "I didn't get a chance to mention it last night, but I think it would be best if you didn't let it get out...what you can do. Not everyone will like the idea that you can get inside their head."

Understanding dawned in her cornflower eyes. "They'll think I'm a threat." I could see the wheels turning in that brain of hers, putting together all kinds of scenarios. Her chin lifted just a fraction. "I don't plan on broadcasting it over the six o'clock news." She shuffled her feet again over the wood planks of the porch.

She had gumption, loads of it and I couldn't help but grin. Something was definitely on her mind, other than being able to play with people's minds. One way or the other I was going to pull it out of her. "Okay, with that settled, you can stop the nervous shuffle and just spit it out."

Her lips turned down in a delectable frown. "Why would you

think I have anything to say to you?"

My brow shot up.

She looked down at her hands, and I wanted to reach out, pull her into my arms. Whatever it was, it was making her very nervous. Sighing heavily, she relented. "Fine." Then she crossed her arms and leaned back into the railings. "I don't understand what is going on between us. One minute you are all over me and the next you can't get far enough away. What gives?"

What gives? If she only knew. Too much was the problem, there was too much going on between us and for the first time, I felt my control slipping, no tumbling away from me. Sure, I've struggled with control my whole life, being part demon was no walk in the park, but this thing going on between Angel Eyes and I made my demon seem miniscule. "Nothing gives, except your bad taste in company." I couldn't resist the jab at my cousin and the opportunity to change the subject.

"Did you and Travis have some kind of falling out I don't know about?" she asked.

I shrugged. "We just have different ideas of what's right. This Emma thing hasn't got him thinking straight."

Her lips were set in a thin line. "Let me guess, your way is the right way."

I gave her my signature grin. "Of course."

She didn't look convinced. "That still doesn't explain why you are acting all weird. I feel it remember?"

Yeah, I didn't need a reminder. She wasn't the only one who was dealing with this connection. I wasn't used to having these extra emotions, the extra worry about another person, and don't get me started about the persistent and annoying separation anxiety. This bond could be darn inconvenient at times.

Like now.

"Ever since we got back from seeing Ives you've been acting strange. What could he have possibly said to make you bug out?" Her voice was filled with frustration.

I glanced over my shoulder staring into the woods behind her house. I didn't want to lie to her, but she made me feel so exposed. Vulnerable. I didn't like the feeling. Not. One. Bit. But I owed her honesty.

Here went nothing. "I'm not bugging out. And it's not so much what he said, but our situation."

"Situation?" she echoed, puzzled. "You're talking about being strapped to me for all eternity?"

Immediately I got defensive, the demon in me roared to life. "It's not like that and you know it." Never for me. I didn't let myself think about the future, or what *our* future would be. If I did then I would hope and hope wasn't something I trusted. Hope in my book equaled pain.

Like always with me, she answered in anger. That I could

count on. Her sarcasm usually cloaked hurt. "What is it like Chase? Because I'm not getting it. If you are having second thoughts—"

My eyes slammed into hers. If there was one thing I didn't want to cause her, it was pain. "I don't regret the outcome of what happened that night I saved you. I would do it again in a heartbeat." There I'd said it. It felt like an enormous weight had been lifted from my chest. So I kept on going. Hell why not. I'd come this far. "I just wish that I had been able to save your soul. Knowing that it's been darkened by Hell kills me." I pushed off the banister, standing in front of her. "Then there are all these feelings that I don't know what to do about. When I'm not near you, it feels like there is a gapping whole in my heart. The further and longer I'm gone, the bigger it gets. Suddenly, I find myself unable to get a grip on my control. It gets more difficult every day I see you."

How was that for honesty?

Seconds ticked by turning into minutes and she hadn't said a thing, just stared at me like she hardly recognized me. Wasn't exactly the reaction I'd been expecting, but then again I wasn't really sure what I had expected. Surely not her looking so...thunderstruck.

"Angel...say something," I said, breaking the silence.

Nothing but more silence. It was driving me crazy. And then I was distracted by her eyes. They were the darkest blue almost black and such a contrast to a few minutes ago when she had been nervous. "Your eyes are doing that weird voodoo thing again," I commented, trying to fill the lack of response.

Her mouth dropped open, and the look of surprise on her face made me wish I had told her sooner. "You've always been in control around me," she rationed.

That couldn't have been farther from the truth. With Angel, I wanted more than anything to lose myself into that part I buried. The demon surfaced more and more where she was concerned. I was getting tired of fighting it. But I couldn't trust that part of myself around her. She could get hurt, and I would die before I hurt her.

Taking a step closer, I boxed her in. "Then I put on a good front. The truth is I've never felt more out of control than when I am with you."

Let's see how she handled that. I assumed that I would shock her or frighten her. I should have known that Angel Eyes would never fail to knock *me* off my feet.

She slipped her fingers into the front pocket of my jeans and tugged. Our bodies slammed together and this time I was the one left speechless. But not for long. Pressed against her, instinct took over. The darkness inside me rose like wildfire, swift and hot.

She shivered in my arms.

The static electricity surged through the air around us as

things started to heat up between our bodies. I couldn't tear my gaze away from hers. There was something brewing behind those stormy eyes, and I was afraid I knew what it was. Part excitement and part disbelief that she could feel for me what I felt for her overwhelmed me.

"Angel, don't do it," I growled. "Don't you say it."

But it was too late. There was determination in her eyes and her chin was set. The words were already at the tip of her tongue and tumbling from her berry colored lips. "I love you," she blurted.

And just like that, the universe threw me a curve ball I wasn't prepared for. My hands fisted on the banister behind her, and I clamped my eyes shut not wanting her to see the reaction that tore through my whole body from head-to-toe. Clenching my teeth against a sensation that wasn't quite painful, but not entirely pleasurable, I waited for what felt indefinitely for the new link between us to seal itself to my heart, seal her deeper to me. The mark at my hip tingled vigorously. She didn't have the foggiest clue what she had just done.

"You don't know what you've done," I said when I was finally able to. My voice was still strained with the emotional onslaught I couldn't yet get a handle on. Her love for me engulfed me in waves after waves.

Okay. That might not have been the smartest thing to say.

Eyes the color of twilight shot daggers in my direction. "I take it back. I take it all back. I despise you. I hate you. I loathe you." She shoved at my chest, oblivious as to what had just happened, and I wasn't in any condition to enlighten her. I needed time to process what had happened.

She jerked in my arms, attempting to take off. I held onto her unable to let go. Not yet. I wanted, needed more time with her. The new bond she had just forged demanded it. I demanded it. I stare into her eyes that were deep blue pools of hurt and rejection. "You can't take it back. I won't let you."

Her eyes quickly blazed with anger and she ran an unsteady hand through her hair. "I can't stand you," she spat, lashing out and I didn't blame her.

I was more than not an insensitive pig, but I needed to make her understand. I needed to put things back the way they were between us until I could figure this out. "Liar. You can't keep your hands off me."

And then because I wanted it more than anything, I kissed her. I poured all those feelings that she had just given me into this one mind-blowing, crushing kiss. And she responded, clinging to me as if her life depended on it. Right now, it felt like that both our lives depended on it.

Tenderly I pulled away and said, "You'll probably regret loving me. I don't deserve it, but…" I searched her eyes, begging her to understand why I couldn't give her the words she wanted in return. "I'll never let anything bad happen to you. Never again."

She lifted her hand and outlined my cheek with her fingers, running her nails alongside my jaw. *God.* She was driving me mad, crazy with the need for her. Couldn't she see, feel what she was doing to me. My whole body tightened as I fought to control the beast that was hammering to be set free. He wanted Angel as much as I did. Sometimes I think he wanted her more.

And that was some serious scary shit.

"Chase," she murmured my name.

I loved hearing my name whispered for her lips. My name. Only my name. Whether I wanted to think about *us* as a future, I knew then that I would only love her. I might not be ready to seal this heartbond completely, but she already had my love. There would never be another soul for me. I would never love another as I loved Angel.

I was scared shitless.

Closing my eyes, I laid my forehead against hers, praying that I had the enough strength left as it was quickly evaporating. The air stirred around us, picking up pieces of her hair.

Her fingers teased the ends of my hair at the nape of my neck. "You don't have to rein it in with me. I trust you."

"That's just the thing Angel Eyes. You shouldn't. You really shouldn't. But with you I can't help myself, and it scares me. I refuse to hurt you."

"You won't," she assured, and then proceeded once again to surprise me. She nipped my lip, grazing them with her teeth.

If only I could share her confidence. *"I don't trust myself."*

"Let go," she murmured against my lips.

Sweet Jesus. What was she trying to do to me? It didn't matter at this point, because I was kissing her before she had finished the words. Then I did what I'd never done before. I let go. Our lips met in a fiery and hot—explosive kiss. The demon I tried to keep banked purred inside me. I could feel its need for more—one shattering kiss would never be enough. And it wasn't long before I reached a point where just kissing wouldn't be enough for any of us.

When we finally broke apart, she looked up at me like I was the moon, the sun, and the stars. I didn't deserve that kind of devotion, or that much love, but I wasn't fool enough to turn away from it. I knew that she wanted me to give her the words, but I couldn't. Not yet.